TWISTED TRYSTS

A SPICY MONSTER HORROR ANTHOLOGY

DEAD FOX PUBLISHING

TWISTED TRYSTS © 2026 Dead Fox Publishing
Published by Dead Fox Publishing deadfoxpub.com

Curation: Kelley York
Editing: Kelley York, Kala Godin, Syd Tomac
Proofing: Syd Tomac
Cover Illustration & Design: Sleepy Fox Studio
Interior Formatting: Sleepy Fox Studio

Digital 978-1-960322-25-8
Paperback 978-1-960322-27-2
Hardcover (Website Exclusive) 978-1-960322-28-9

DEAD FOX
PUBLISHING

Copyright & Reprint Information

TABLE OF CONTENTS

CONTENT NOTES

Standard horror tropes apply. This includes but is not limited to:
violence, blood, gore, death, and body horror.

For a full list of content notes organized by story
please visit our website.

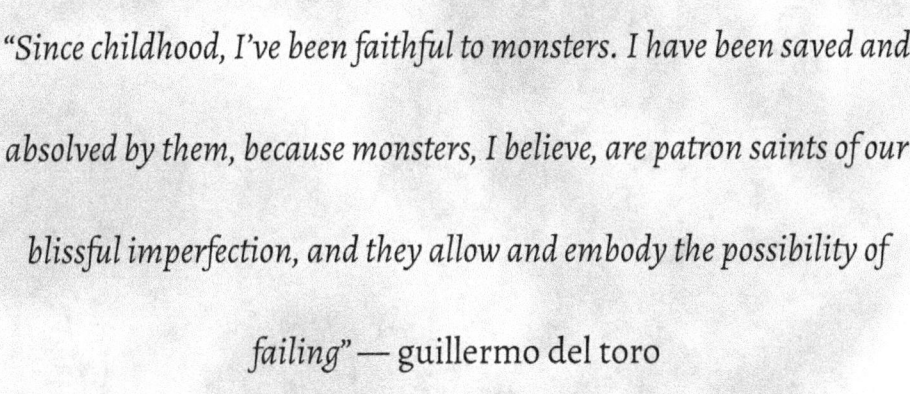

"*Since childhood, I've been faithful to monsters. I have been saved and absolved by them, because monsters, I believe, are patron saints of our blissful imperfection, and they allow and embody the possibility of failing*" — guillermo del toro

FISHER OF MEN
HANNAH BIRSS

The music rattled Lukas' bones, the vibration pulsing through him in time with his own heartbeat. He threw his head back in bliss, the flashing black of the Midnight Zone filling his sight with visual snow that drifted down to colour the dance floor. Hot, swirling bodies pressed in around him, painted with various glow-in-the-dark patterns, limbs distorting as the fake bioluminescence slowly liquefied down the exposed skin under the onslaught of sweat. Lukas was tossed and turned, thrown about in the waves of eager and inebriated flesh. The beat dropped with his stomach, and as he danced, he felt part of something much bigger than himself.

The song ended abruptly, blurring into another wave of sound that washed over him, and Lukas became painfully aware of his dry and fuzzy tongue. The tablet that had melted on it earlier had furred it, making him desperate for a drink of water. When the edges of his sight had softened, he turned and forced his way through the black, brushing against soft and exposed pale bellies as he headed toward the bar that occupied the entire front wall of the dance club.

It was surprisingly empty. Lukas slid onto a vacant stool and signaled the bartender. He flashed his credit card against the bar's machine and took the dripping bottle the bartender handed him from a large tub of half-melted ice, its wet wrapper quickly flaking off in his hands. Lukas threw back his head as he chugged the water, his Adam's apple bobbing as it flooded him. At that moment, all his senses focused on the cold; it was everything he'd ever wanted, reviving him in a way he hadn't known he needed. The wispy edges of his vision began to solidify, and when he crushed the empty bottle in his hand, gasping for air, he finally noticed the woman sitting at the bar next to him.

Her feet were perched on the rungs of her stool. She was tall—easily as tall as his own six feet—and instead of the exposed flesh that was normal for a Saturday night at the club, she was draped in a ton of sheer, creamy fabric that obscured any curves she might have had. Her outfit reminded him of cotton candy: a fluffy cloud so sweet he could sink his teeth into it.

Unlike everyone else, her skin was clear of the black-light paint. He had only meant to glance at her, but her large, dark eyes caught his and promptly drew him into their depths. Those eyes—a striking combination paired with her pale complexion and milky garments—regarded him from underneath a curtain of hair so black it seemed to absorb the light around her. The eye contact extended a moment too long past politeness, but instead of turning away from him, she only smiled.

"Hi," she said, her voice a deep murmur. It was almost masculine in its timbre, but he enjoyed it. It suited her—it was as extraordinary as the rest of her. "I'm Angela."

"Hi," he said back. "Lukas."

She gestured at the seething mass of people still lost in the music. "Enjoying your night?" She spoke softly. He moved closer, leaning in to better hear her over the noise. She smelled... different. A good different.

"I am. How about you, Angela? Have you been dancing a lot?"

She shook her head. The black of her hair shimmered. "Not a dancer. Not really my scene."

"Not a dancer?" he said, surprised. "Interesting choice to come here if you aren't a dancer. What are you here for?"

"Can I kiss you?" Angela asked with an inquisitive tip as she looked him straight on; her answer to his question was clear.

Was she on something? Her eyes were so large, so wide, so bright, so *strange* that he couldn't imagine that she was totally sober. Then again, neither was he.

A lump formed in his throat, followed by a rush of desire so strong he couldn't do more than nod. He wasn't usually the hook-up type—he had not come here looking to get some action, only to sweat out some stress—but a thrill went through him at her request. Nothing like this had ever happened to him before; he was caught up in a bizarre and unfamiliar flow, and it seemed stupid not to go along with it.

She leaned over, and her lips brushed his. Lukas deepened the kiss almost immediately, leaning over so far he nearly fell off his seat, but that didn't stop him from devouring her mouth.

She tasted like sea salt—like the taffy his mother would buy him when they visited family on the East Coast. He had a sudden and visceral memory of unwrapping the white wax paper of individual candies to reveal the brightly coloured snack within, the way his jaw ached as he chewed, taffy sticking to his teeth and sliding down his throat in small lumps as he had walked along the creaking piers. She reminded him of that childhood delight, and he chased that feeling.

Lukas wrapped her hair like a ribbon around his hand, giving it an experimental tug. He had never been an exhibitionist, but he was considering it. Angela responded enthusiastically, moaning into his mouth, and it was only when teetering on the very edge of losing control that he finally drew back.

Angela stared intently at him now, eyes clouded with lust, her swollen lips still parted to afford him a glance at her neat white teeth and pink little tongue as she breathed hard. A shudder ran through her body, and he grinned at her wolfishly.

"You're... entrancing," he said, and he meant it. For the first time in his life, he felt bewitched.

"Come with me," she said to him huskily. "I like you."

He grinned wolfishly at her. "I like you too. Where are we going?"

She winked and looked him up and down languidly. He was so hard it hurt; he would follow her anywhere if it meant he got release.

"I know a place," she said. "A storeroom. No one ever goes in it." Her hand slipped into his and gave it a small and encouraging tug.

"Do you work here?" he asked curiously.

The corner of her mouth quirked upwards. "Sort of."

He paused to give her a moment to elaborate, but she didn't. Instead, she stepped down off the stool, her long pale legs unfolding like flower petals. Her dress further unfurled, fabric and tulle floating about her body like clouds, giving him tantalizing glimpses of creamy skin. *She must be a fashion or art student*, he thought, but the strangeness of her attire did not deter him; he would unwrap her like a present, drawing out the process instead of tearing into her as if it were Christmas morning.

Angela tugged his hand again and led him into the seething, sloshing crowd. Lukas obediently followed. Her lips moved as she drew him along in her wake, but he couldn't hear her. Her palm was smooth and cold. Nobody noticed them, the revelers' eyes glazed with drugs, their limbs flailing to the beat. It was as if Lukas and Angela were ghosts—they passed unknown and unseen.

They traversed deeper and deeper into the crowded dark until eventually they came out on the other side of the club. She pulled him down the wall to an even darker corner, where a long hallway waited for them, lit only by a single red light. The music faded as she led him down it, and at the second door on the right, she took her hand out of his, her fingers trailing down his palm in a promise.

She lifted her index finger to her lip and winked as she jiggled the doorknob with the other hand. After a moment, something clicked and the door opened a crack. She cast a flirtatious smile over her shoulder as she disappeared into the room beyond.

Lukas barely hesitated, glancing once back down the hall from where they had come. The music itself couldn't be heard now, but the thrum of the bass came through the walls and the floor until his entire body hummed.

The room inside was clearly a storage room. A single hazy bulb from a wall-mounted fixture in the corner threw the shelves of supplies into strange and twisting shadows that seemed to sway and ripple. She waited for him there, her bright eyes shimmering with anticipation.

"Come here often?" he joked, his words flailing like a drowning swimmer.

Angela said nothing, didn't even chuckle, only cocked an eyebrow at him in a question, a smile playing on her lips as her eyes narrowed. He swallowed and waded through the dim towards her. As he put his arms around her, he noticed that the painted swirls on his bare chest were already transferring to the creamy fabric. It glowed faintly in the light of the storage room.

"Oh, shit, your dress."

"Don't worry about it," she whispered. "Just cover me."

He obliged, pressing her roughly up against the wall. Her dress enfolded him like a dream, and he slid his hand up her thighs underneath her voluminous wrapping. Angela's legs parted eagerly for him, and he hardened painfully, his erection straining against his shorts.

Her teeth caught his lower lip, scraping against it and bringing blood to the surface. He shuddered under it. He drew away, his fingers skimming up her ribs to wrap themselves in her hair, drawing her head back so that he could look down at her.

"Who's in charge here?" he murmured. "You or me?"

She looked up at him, limpid eyes shimmering, and he found himself staring deeply into them. Her smile, however, held a proud and predatory edge. "Whoever you want to be."

He buried his mouth against her neck, tongue darting out to taste her. She tasted like salt, something deep and primal, harder than the saltwater taffy of her tongue. His hands dug into the flesh of her wide hips. He hadn't seen her dance, but he knew without a doubt that she would be an amazing dancer. He pictured her hypnotic hips swaying, drawing in partners who waited in a line for their turn with her, and he groaned.

His hand crept up higher underneath the layers that wrapped her. To his surprise, nothing but bare skin, silky smooth, greeted him. He trailed his finger up her folds, and she shifted, allowing him better access, head thrown back, her lips slightly open in anticipation. His fingertips grazed against her clit, and he gave it an experimental twitch as he stared at her face, entranced by what he saw there. She gasped, and the sound hooked him. He did it again and rubbed her harder.

Angela's breathing was fast now, little mewls escaping as she writhed against the wall. She was wet, coating his fingers and the inside of her thighs. She hadn't even touched him yet, and he was glad for it; if she had, he would have exploded right then and there. He had wanted to take his time exploring her, making her come over and over again before he took his own pleasure, but she had other ideas.

"Fuck me," she moaned. "Please, just fuck me." Her leg came up to wrap around his hip. She made quick work of the button on his shorts, and he sprang free. She grabbed for him, her fingers grasping his aching cock and drawing him closer, and he slid inside of her, the walls of her contracting around him hungrily as her warmth enfolded him.

He found himself filled with a hunger that he had never experienced before; within seconds, his careful plan to tease her and bring her to the brink was abandoned, and his hand drew away from her clit so that he could reach further up to grip her hips. His fingers dug into the flesh there, but she welcomed the bruises. She lifted herself up so that he could better angle his cock to go deeper, his hands reaching back to cup her ass as he rammed inside of her fully, hilting himself as she stretched around him.

His senses full of her and her full of him, he pumped into her as hard and as fast as he could, his rhythm skipping with his own heart. Nothing else existed—the dark of the room had wrapped them in a thick blanket, and as he drove himself into her, he imagined they were floating in a tank of black. There was only him, and her, and them; it was the best sex he'd ever had. She felt good, felt *so* good. His stomach churned with his desire, and he plunged into her again and again and again. He didn't think he could be satiated—he would always want more. Lukas wanted to devour her, never wanted this moment to end.

She welcomed his greed eagerly, bucking her hips up and wrapping her ankles around him as the two of them drew closer. Her mouth trailed kisses and bites along his shoulder and neck.

"Fuck, you feel so amazing," he groaned. Nothing had ever felt as good as she had. "I'm gonna cum. I have to pull out." He had never fucked a stranger raw before; caught up in the moment, he had forgotten about the emergency condom in the wallet in his shorts' pocket, but he remembered just as he hovered at the edge of ecstasy.

"Don't," she moaned. "Stay with me." Her breath was hot against his shoulder. "Cum with me. It'll be okay."

"Yes," he said, not needing much convincing, repeating the word once more. It echoed back at him from the dark, his voice layering over and over and over like a promise.

Angela grasped the back of his hair as he thrashed against her. He could feel his orgasm building faster, harder now, and he raced towards it as his thoughts evaporated. He needed to finish, needed to cum inside her, needed to do it again and again and again. His cock throbbed and something pulsed within him. The slight pain of her hands wrapped in his hair heightened his pleasure and his want, and his eyes rolled back in his skull.

She reached down between their sweat-slicked bodies to touch herself, her fingers going to work in a practiced manner. Her eyes stared into his, and she groaned, her pupils blowing to take over her pale irises. He could feel her tensing, and he fused his mouth to hers, wanting to swallow her orgasm whole, until she abruptly pulled away.

"Bite me," she begged, pulling the fabric of her dress aside so that one delicate shoulder was exposed. "Bite me, and cum for me. Cum for me, baby. Stay with me."

He did as she asked, his teeth latching into the bare flesh. He bit down hard, unable to hold himself back on either count. Angela screamed with pleasure and pain as he pushed himself as deep as he could, his legs trembling and his heels beating a tattoo against the floor as he came harder than he ever had.

His cock pulsed, pushing his seed deep into her and spilling it in her warm embrace. Her body drank it greedily as she locked him in place with her legs. "Every last drop," she whispered, and he obliged that request with a few final pumps as his body began to give out.

She let go of his hair, and she stroked the back of his neck. Her fingers were strangely cool and he welcomed them. They stood there for a minute, aftershocks tracing the way through both of their bodies, his teeth still buried in her shoulder, beginning to loosen their grip. He was empty and satiated, drowsy.

Lukas made to disengage, but found that he could not move. His mouth refused to unlatch from Angela's shoulder, and when he tried to open his jaw further, he couldn't do that, either.

His mouth had fused to Angela's body. He reached up with his right hand to feel at it, and from his cheek down to her skin was a smooth expanse of unbroken dermis, as if his body had become another one of her limbs.

Lukas tried to scream, but only muffled shouts came out. He disengaged, his now small and shriveled cock falling out of her. He shook his head violently in the hopes that he could tear free, but her strong arms wrapped around him. As they struggled, the pin holding up her clothes fell away, and the naked expanse of her was revealed to him entirely for the first time.

He scrabbled against her, and his fingers came across a protuberance tight against her body. Looking down her back from where he had become fused, he could see what he assumed to be a similar lump on her back, between her shoulder blades.

His frantic hands raced over Angela's body and found another lump, a third and then a fourth, fleshy sacs of skin not unlike his own testicles that hung against her. With dawning horror, he realized that the growth on her back had a small and deformed face, the details sunken and wrinkled in their distortion. It opened two little cloudy eyes, and in them he saw an intense pity.

Lukas grunted, a high-pitched squeal emerging from his nose as the two eyes blinked up at him in a regretful manner. He could move no further as Angela held him tightly, a snake devouring her prey. As he thrashed, he realized he was *shrinking*, his bones liquefying like hot fire as his arms and legs pulled up into his body, his skin collapsing around him.

Angela was stroking him now as he rapidly shrank. She cradled him like an infant in her arms, murmuring reassurances. "Don't worry, baby, it only hurts for a moment, and then we have forever. Forever," she said, "just like you promised."

His thoughts slowed, blurry between pain and panic. From the corner of his gaze, her face begin to change as she whispered her entreaties to him, the bones and flesh of her striking features rearranging themselves as he watched. Her eyes grew even larger, the edges reaching the sides of her face. In them, glittering stars danced. Her jaw jutted forward, a hundred needle teeth pushing out through her thin and stretched lips.

"Together, forever," she lisped through her dagger-mouth, reaching up to caress him lovingly. "You and me."

Lukas was small now, so small. His body finished collapsing in on itself until it was no larger than an apple, a soft and fleshy lump hanging off of her shoulder, his mouth still fused to her as he dangled. The veins inside him shifted like snakes, his digestive system wiggling up like worms through his mouth to connect to Angela, sneaking in under her skin as he became further attached. In what was left of his chest, his heart stuttered and then gave out into a hollow silence.

One second stretched into two stretched into three, and then his entire body, or what remained of it, shuddered as his veins pulsed with life again, the blood circulating from her body into his. Her heartbeat became thunder in his being, the echoes of her pleasure and satisfaction at the process moving through him.

She let go of him and bent over, and Lukas grew dizzy as he was suspended by the spot where his mouth used to be. Her face merged back into normality, the features becoming familiar but no less terrifying. She gathered up the mix of fabric and gauze and wrapped it around herself again. The fabric closed over him several times, securing him against Angela's body. There was a final movement of her arms as she affixed her pin, and then she patted him reassuringly, almost absently.

In the suffocating dark, Lucas felt her move; the music grew louder again as she returned to the pulsing horde of club-goers, back to the hunt to look for another mate to drag back into the dark with her and keep with her forever.

In his mind and in his mind only, Lukas continued to scream.

A Sigil to Bind the Night

Tonja K. Johnson

Men roam the eight corners of the world in search of power because they have none within themselves. So they siphon it from those they perceive to be weaker. They chart maps, sail seas, and navigate by stars to find the entrance to my secret domain just for a taste of it. Humans believe I am immortal. That I can grant them eternal life. So they waste their limited time in search of something I will never give. Some believe I am djinn; others, fae. Some think me the Wata orisha. But I am all and none of those things.

Centuries ago, those same men bound me to this cave because they feared the power I wield. Because they couldn't own it for themselves, they couldn't abide my reveling in a freedom they would never taste.

A vast lagoon sits at the heart of my cave; there, I lounge on a bed of lily pads. Beetle flowers bloom over the water's still surface. Their petals, the same iridescent shade as mayfly wings.

Its waters are a translucent cerulean. Pure. Clean. Untouched. My tentacles fold through it as I allow my legs and arms to float up around me like a fallen star. Glowing koi fish skirt the pool's perimeter, stealing little suctioned kisses as they glide past. Their trailing fins carve infinity patterns through the placid current that fade from a brilliant emerald to sapphire to citrine.

A SIGIL TO BIND THE NIGHT

The little light that pierces cracks in the limestone ceiling also slices through the water, down to the sediment below, and glitters over treasure hidden therein.

"I grow hungry," I wave a black taloned hand at my children, "bring me a feast." Impish dragons, petrified gnomes, and ten-legged spiders hobble off to do my bidding.

My children bring me small tributes. Small human femurs for my collection of bones. Fresh bore hearts as tasty morsels. But it's not enough. After all this time trapped in this godsforsaken cave, my hunger only grows. No matter what I eat, I can't be sated.

My goblin son, Nestar, diligently scrapes the algae and coral from my tentacle suckers with his stone tools. "We could go out and raze a village in your honor," he offers. "That always brings you joy."

He's so sensitive to my mood—always eager to please. "No. You did that three moon cycles ago."

Little chalky centipedes crawl along his winding horns. Every so often he flicks them off with his tail. "Oh, yes, Mother. I remember the screams very well." Nestar licks thin lips, scaly emerald skin turning pink at the cheeks with the happy memory. "You could call down the mountain for a tribute. Have the human women send all their firstborn babes."

"No. We did that last century. It took months to eat all the babies. You know they make me gag."

Nestar thinks, twisting his brow in narrowed concentration. "Ah! I have just the thing, Mother. Just the thing!" He sets down the cleaning devices, swims to the bank, and scurries into one of the back passageways.

After a moment he rushes back with a copper flute and a glass vial full of unicorn blood.

"What do you have in that tiny mind of yours?" I swim to the pool's edge, fanning out my many dark tentacles along the surface.

"We will bring you humans most enjoyable."

"Enjoyable?" My lips purse.

Nestar nods enthusiastically, bulbous opal eyes shining for my approval.

"You are a good child." I rub his balding head and scratch beneath his boney chin. "Now run along with your siblings."

My spider child scurries up my shoulder, dragging little molars. I kiss her stone carapace and accept the offering.

Impatient footsteps echo at the entrance of my cave. Silently, I plunge beneath the surface, allowing only my sable eyes and the long serpentine darkness of my locs to remain visible. A human wanders into the dank mist.

Male.

Wild-eyed. Ebon-skinned and lean. A gleaming blade fisted in both hands. Stinking of alchemy.

The mortal man takes in my domain. The stalactites that drip from the cave ceiling like gold tipped vampyre fangs. The human-shaped husk of my too-long-ago meal. The ruined carcass that rots near an overgrowth of bladderwort. Little indigo clovers sprout from its nostrils. The mortal's bulging eyes flit to the crimson rivulets trickling between cracks in the cave floor, to the slabs of skin stretched amid the stalagmites, and then to me.

He points the dagger in my direction with a sloppy, underhanded grip. "Give me my three questions."

Of course. All men are the same. All they ever do. Take. He doesn't even offer tribute.

"How did you find this place?" The passage is concealed from all but those who know what to look for.

"A little green monster piping a flute said if I drank his potion I would gain riches beyond my dreams."

Nestar. Such a good child. It has been so long since I had fun. "You have traveled so far. You must be parched. Come, have a drink from my waters."

He swallows thickly.

The steady *smack, smack* of water weeping from the ceiling to smooth stone below fills the cavern. Rising, I tuck my eight tentacles to my side and mount the few steps to the edge of the pool. Even with the level disadvantage, I still tower over him. He is small for the males of his species. His eyes immediately flit to my chest; the dagger lowers a fraction as if he has never seen pierced nipples.

Water slides over my bare breasts, down the curve of my waist, between my legs. He wets his lips.

Still not looking me in the eye. "So the myths are true?"

I ignore the question.

"You can't leave these waters. You're bound."

"Cursed is more like it." I cup his manhood. It too is small. With a groan, he hardens to an unimpressive length. I stroke him, brush my talons over the head of his shaft.

He whimpers, blade now forgotten. The useless metal splashes into the lagoon and my tentacles deftly flick it to the trenches below.

The male looks me in the eye now, babbling incoherently about his wishes, and how wants me to plunder his body in so many unnatural ways. The weak-minded find my gaze to be an enchantment impossible to resist. I could tell this male to suck himself off and he would happily fold into incredible positions, suffocating on his own semen.

With a smile, I lean in, brush my lips against the shell of his ear and whisper every terrible thing I plan to do with him. Before he can scream, my fangs pierce the throbbing vein in his neck, immobilizing him with my venom. I continue stroking as his heartbeat slowly fades from Nestar's potion.

The male shudders.

Twice.

Thrice.

Spends hot seed into my palm through his trousers. There was not even much of that. Disgusted, I wipe my hands on his woolen cloak, and he sinks to his knees right next to my last meal.

They are all the same. Selfish. Self-important. Over-sexed.

He thought himself the monster—that he could sate himself on me.

I drag him by the collar into the pool. He makes pathetic bubbling noises through his nose as his face submerges underwater. I throw him on the stone slab seated at the center of the lagoon where light filters through the brightest. He lays supine—a little gasping starfish.

He feels everything as I stab my fist into his stomach through the belly button. He stares in wide-eyed horror, unable to make a sound. Grinning, I plunge my tongue into his gaping orifice. A little bitter. Tastes like regret. Unmet dreams and disappointment.

He is still now.

The flesh peels away easily from tendons. I pick through his butchered abdomen with black claws, fingers slick with viscera. He breaks so readily for me akin to the split and gush of overripe fruit. However, his innards are sweet, intestines bloated and waterlogged.

The squelch of organ meat echoes through the cave system, drawing my children close. Dermestid beetles file neatly into the cavity. My darling ones have a healthy appetite. They don't discriminate between flesh, fur, feathers, or fibers. They leave only the calcium deposits behind. The bone fairies will have much to cart away to their graveyard villages.

"Hello?"

I lift my head at the unfamiliar voice. A woman's voice.

She steps around the bend, mist dissipating around her.

And she is a succulent morsel indeed.

Skin like the black prairie fire. Eyes dark voids. And her lips, sweet blood. Her textured hair is plaited in a mass of long braids that hang down her back. Little crystal jewels adorn the ends. On each one her knuckles is a bone ring talisman. Her crooked thumb is fitted with double rings.

My lips lift at the corners. She was wise enough to ward herself against evil.

"Have you come to slay me?" I push away the carcass of the small man. The pieces of him float away. "Was this your husband? Have you come for revenge?"

"I will take no husband in this life, but I will take vengeance."

A flicker of interest sparks in my lower belly. "Are you not afraid?" I wave a hand over the mess of the man who was so sure he could use me. "Do I not terrify you?"

"There are worse things than monsters."

Her words are spoken with the surety of a person who has seen such terrors. Lived within that hell. "What are you called, mortal?"

"I am the crowned princess of Nemwae, the land of your origin."

My jaw ticks. What does she know of my origins? I had destroyed the world twice over before her line was ever on the throne.

"But you may call me Ozil. And what is your name?"

This stops me short. My name? It has been so long since I was asked such a question. "I am mother to the creatures no one else claims. I am the one who speaks with the voice of the wind and screams with the shudder of the earth."

My name?

"I walk through the moon cycles and call forth the scourges. I..."

My memory turns hazy at the edges. The beginning of a migraine throbs at my temples.

I...

Her shoulders shake and then slump, Nestar's potions taking effect. I watch her knees go weak. Then I'm swimming to the edge of the pool, climbing up the steps. Reaching—

I stop.

I cannot pass that ring of smoldering sigils. The spice of alchemy chars the air with the burning of my flesh against the spell.

"Come, brave one. Rest in my waters a while."

She looks at me, unsure. Like I might devour her. The day is still young, I just may. But something deep—something entrenched within me—wants to know what kind of monsters she's seen to make her eyes so full of emptiness.

I've never invited a mortal into my sanctum—my prison. The previous man is now in pieces thanks to the hungry work of my children.

At first, she surveys wearily, eyes flitting over the carnage staining the water. Then, seeming to make her decision, she flattens her full lips into a determined line, tucks the knife into the leather belt at her waist and walks over. More stumbles, but her knees only buckle once, and she is close enough that I can stretch out my tentacles and catch her before she collapses.

Her weight is warm and solid. Lush curves and sturdy muscle. A potent mixture. One of her arms wraps around the back of my neck, pulling me close.

Her right hand never leaves the hilt of her dagger.

Wise. Stupid.

I could snap her neck. Smash her skull in until her brain is a fine pulp pouring over my hands.

"Do you actually grant wishes?" She studies my face for some unknowable answer. She must find it. "... I didn't think so."

She wraps strong legs around my waist as I retreat down the stone slabs.

"Then why did you come?" A dangerous spark flares, a hope that maybe she came not to take. But to give me something instead. Her delectable body would be quite the treat.

"To find you."

I push distance between us, coldness settling in my chest. Humans always want. And this vicious princess is no different. "What is it you covet? Riches?" My voice is the same hollow ice that slices between my ribs. "I have plenty." I swipe aside the mangled foot of a dead king and show her what glimmers in the trenches below.

She barely glances at the stunning collection of wealth before returning those serrated eyes back on me. Her words are just as sharp. "I did not come for coin."

"Magicks, then?" My mind races with the hundreds of demands I've received over the years. Eternal life. A path to the underworld. Unlimited power. A dragon.

She shakes her head. "I came for *you*."

"I don't understand."

"To set you free. There are old tales of a woman with immeasurable power. They say she was the first wife. A woman no man could resist. And that she brought terror unto any that crossed her path."

A buzzing trickles down my spine. "To free me?" My mind winds in impossible knots. "You lie."

"And why would I? If you're free, then I will eventually get what I owed."

"So it is death you seek?"

"It is a *certain* death I crave above all." Her dark eyes glimmer with hearth light and the spark of something else that makes even me tremble.

"I've been bound here for a thousand-thousand years. What makes you believe that you can break the chains the ancient alchemist created?"

She looks around at the severed body parts littering the surface of the lagoon. A split stomach sack with remnants of half digested food. An eyeball with mangled nerves trailing after it. Other organs partly submerged, some being nibbled on by glowing koi fish.

Ozil lifts her chin. Defiant. "I am descended from the one who locked you here."

I hiss, deep and guttural, clamping a hand around her slender throat. "I should kill you. Wipe clean the entire pestilence of your bloodline."

She wheezes in a breath. "You could do that," her words halt and trip as she struggles for air, "or you can be free and end all those who dared confine you here."

My hold loosens a fraction. Just enough so that she can draw breath. Ozil coughs but doesn't attempt to remove my hand. She grinds against me. A shock of want pulses from between my legs.

Her breasts heave over the restrictive pressure of her corset, spilling from her dress, exposing her. I could disembowel the man who created such stifling contraptions, but I can't help but bend down and flick my split tongue over one dark nipple. Just a taste. The little bud tightens under my caress as she sucks in a breath.

"How?"

"I'll need time to unravel the alchemy. I don't see any chains."

A deep, throaty laugh cleaves the air before I can bite it back. It echoes with bitterness. But I release her throat while my limbs make slow work of unfastening her stays. "They may be invisible to the mortal eye, but they are there all the same."

The corset comes free. Floats on the water with cadaver pieces. Her eyes soften, losing some of their edge. "Maybe the chains are tightest here." She places her blade against my temple; the cursed metal singes my skin, wafting a trail of smoke through the air between us. I lean into the pain she gives me. And she adjusts her hips so her heat sits low on my belly.

Her legs are smooth silk in the water. I slip a tentacle between her thighs, taunting her sensitive places with my suckers.

"And here." She glides the dagger between my breasts, points the tip at the place my heart used to beat, and presses into me.

At the same moment, I slowly thrust into her. She is wet and wanting. I curl until I reach that sensitive spot, teasing those upper ridges.

"How much time?" I tenderly work her.

Long, dark lashes flutter. A hitched breath. "I'm not sure?" she pants. "A month. Maybe more."

Her breasts bounce with each thrust. She already feels close, the way she is pulsing around me.

"Why so long?" I lean down, take her nipple between my teeth. I suck and lap as she cries out. Her sounds of pleasure, just as gratifying as the dying keen of men.

I pump faster and she sucks me in greedily.

She doesn't have to say it, but she would kill me if she could. Take what she needed from me to better her chances at whatever it is she was desperate enough to come here for.

Ozil pushes me against the wall. Knife at my throat. With sure fingers, she cups one of my breasts and runs the point of her tongue over my nipple. She circles the gold ring, sucking, flicking. Pleasure radiates through my core and I force back a growl. I don't want to scare her off just yet. Her other hand caresses between my legs, fingers edging to where I really want them. Each of the alchemy-infused bone rings on her fingers scalds when they make contact with my skin. But the need to have her near outweighs the pain.

She brushes light circles on my clit. A burst of white flashes like fireworks behind my lids with each circuit. It's not supposed to feel this good.

Hands holding her ass, I wade us out to the stone center. I lay her out completely naked on the sun-warmed limestone. She stretches out, arms above her head, and my eyes don't know which part of her to devour first.

A SIGIL TO BIND THE NIGHT

The pool is tainted with blood, half-eaten limbs, and broken organs around us. My children have disappeared through the cracks in the cave wall. Now all is silent except the gentle gush of the falls behind us.

Ozil wets her lips—pulls me in for a kiss. Our nipples brush and I groan as that insistent pulse in my core intensifies. Her tongue is unyielding. Eager. And I let her explore. She clamps down on my lower lip. The bitter taste of metal floods over our tongues, but she never once breaks the kiss. My control slips as I attempt caution. Mortals are so easily broken.

"Let me taste you." I try to make it sound like a question, but I need to have her on my tongue, cumming in my mouth, writhing beneath me.

Eyes half-lidded, she nods.

I bury my face in-between her legs, sucking her clit in a pulsing rhythm. Her pleasure echoes through the cavern, shaking the stalactites with the vibration. She tastes of berries and sweat and life.

She is nectar against my tongue. So wet. So very needy. She tries to drown me in her juices.

And then she is on top of me, running her mouth over all my tender places. Tracing each scar with delicate precision.

Our legs cross. She grinds her clit against mine, pulling my nipple ring to the brink of pain. Eyes locked, I slip a tentacle inside her, then into myself, curling and twisting. I can't hold back the scream that tears from me as I shatter. Again and again and again.

We hardly catch our breaths before we're reaching for each other again.

I don't know how long we stay in that state of ecstasy.

Days?

Weeks?

Stolen eons.

By the time Ozil finally climbs naked from the lagoon, her skin is ashen and pruned. She lies on that center slab where sun slants through the rocks in the ceiling to dry. Her dark skin glistens with pearls of water. She is perfection. The artists of old would have murdered to make her their muse.

Between bouts, she works on removing the sigils. She studies them by torch-light and little pieces of stars I pinched from the heavens before I was trapped here.

I forgot mortals can't survive on sex alone and send my children to gather her proper food and clothes. She eats like she is famished. Some of the lushness that I loved about her has turned gaunt. I have Nestar collect all her favorite delicacies.

Every day, Nestar delivers more men for me to feed on. With his flute and the unicorn blood, they all come wanting, willing. I teach Ozil how to carve a heart. How to rend a body. How to bleed an eye. And how to arrange the organs while still keeping your victim alive.

By day she tinkers with the alchemy that keeps me confined in the lagoon. It is long, tiring work, and she is often irritated with herself. She ties her braids at the nape of her neck and traces the sigils.

"Why is it taking so long?" I ask her one morning when the sun is full and hot. Rays that slice through the cave have turned mist to dank heat.

Ozil wipes sweat from her brow with the back of a hand. It has been long since she last wore clothes. Like she is becoming one of my wild creatures. How-ever, today she is buttoned up to her chin with complicated layers despite the heat. Curious about her work, I bask in the warm pool while Nestar plays war with the spiders.

"Because the male gods are all but gone. The seers say he swallowed down the other four, and so there is one. And he leads the men to destruction. To violence. To lust. And women are kept from learning the sacred arts," she snaps. "If I had been born a man, I would have learned all this outright. Not in stolen moments from texts I pilfered off priests."

"So the world has not changed."

"No, it's much worse." There is that glimmer of darkness again. Like a specter haunting her waking memories. "Woman are no better than broodmares, born to work and fuck and serve at a man's pleasure."

"And you, Ozil, princess of Nemwae, have you been treated as such?" Rage, ichorous and acrid, flares in my chest, burning, burning because I already know what she will say. It's the same wretched inheritance handed down to too many women. A tale older than recorded time.

Ozil nods. Breaks my once-beating heart with that one scant motion.

My jaw ticks. "How much are you willing to give to see this cycle of suffering end?" I ask even though the answer is carved in clear sigils across her face.

There is no hesitation. "Everything."

Ozil doesn't speak for many days. I watch her slowly fading, and there is nothing I can do to take her pain away. She ignores me, scratching symbols into loose soil. I swim closer to where she toils away with her rotten alchemy. Still, she remains silent.

Nestar hobbles forward and pats my hand. "Don't worry, Mother. Nestar will make the princess happy again. Nestar will do it. She only needs a distraction. A nice distraction."

Tension melts from my shoulders as I embrace him. "You are my most beloved." But I fear that this is something that can't be fixed with simple games.

Nestar beams before slinking away.

That evening, the cave is well anointed with the perfume of venomous oils and fresh flower petals. The leprechauns play golden-throated flutes. Candles blaze poised atop the stalagmites and float amid the lagoon.

My children toiled long to make this an evening that will be sung through the histories. They have crafted twin thrones of ivy and prismatic beetle skeletons for Ozil and me. A grand banquet table stretches before our watery thrones, filled with all Ozil's favorite meals. The hearth burns bright at my back. It limns her in crimson light.

The silkworms spun her a dress that flows over the water's surface. It's dyed a radiant cerulean with minotaur tears and phoenix ashes.

My locs are twisted in tight coils with poison ivy. My nails are freshly sharpened and capped with gold. My lips are blushed with newly squeezed hydra venom.

I asked for a feast and they delivered me a festival. My heart swells with pride. I will need to reward my children for their trouble. Even amidst all this splendor, Ozil remains reserved. It is only when I take her hands and dance with her amid the falling constellations that she finally looks at me and smiles. And that simple expression holds the weight of my world.

"You don't have to break the sigils. If freedom means losing you, I don't want it."

Ozil cups my cheek tenderly, tears like crystals glittering in her eyes. "What is your name? I asked you that first day and you never told me." My princess speaks with a honeyed tongue.

She is nothing more than a collection of bones in my arms tonight.

"I want to know all of you as you know all of me."

An ache blooms in the hollow between my sternum and spine. "I am what I am." I thread my fingers carefully through her beaded braids, wanting to mold my tongue against every one of her crevices. The brittle strands break away with the stroke. Bald patches blot her scalp. She is breaking, and there is nothing I can do to put her back together again.

She pushes away, sucking her teeth. "You sound like the male gods."

I suppress a growl. "Do not speak of them."

Ozil turns to me in the water. She moves as if this place were made for her. The koi fish now pepper her with kisses, ignoring me. "Then tell me. Speak to me. You slate yourself with my body day and night, you open your legs to me, but what is here remains shuttered." She stabs an index finger between my breasts. I hold her hand captive before she pushes away again, drawing her close. She struggles at first, but she is visibly tired, that little bit of fight having taken everything from her, and she nestles into my breast, lips at my neck.

"Please," she whispers.

Tension unspools from my shoulders. If I tell her this thing, there is no retracing those steps. I have never spoken of what happened to me. Not even to my children. "It is a long story," I say.

"We still have some time." Ozil lays a kiss on my nipple as she traces lazy rivers up one of my arms.

I take a shuddering breath, and then I begin:

"I was once human. I dwelled among the mortals. Slept in their rancid villages. Sang praises to their male gods and tasted the bitter caress of a man as he writhed forcefully on top of me. When I beseeched the gods to give me retribution, tears streaming down my face, bruises blackening both my eyes, they laughed at the virgin blood staining my thighs. These same gods to whom I had paid tribute and worshiped all my life were no better than their mortal counterparts.

"They lifted me into the heavens and gave me more of what the men do best. When they had finished with their games, they hurled me back to the human realm, through the burning stars, past glittering nebulas. I plummeted back to Gaia like a meteor. The ground cratered from my impact.

"But I did not die.

"My broken bones fused back together. Skin stitching over torn muscle. Though I begged for death's release, the little reaping gremlins did not come. They passed me over for safer conquests, for the male gods had seeded inside me. Within my womb grew a bastard for each of the five that took their twisted pleasure on my flesh.

"Each day, strength slowly leeched back into me. The roots of the earth stretched into my mouth and dripped nourishing water down my dry throat, the way the mighty oak nurses from soil.

"'Kill me,' I pleaded with whoever was left to hear. What remained of life? The villagers didn't even leave flowers at my grave. Over the long walls of my crater, I could still hear them chanting praise to the gods who did this to me.

"Begrudgingly, I lived.

"Tiny forest creatures and pixies with iridescent wings fed me with poison berries and bitter sap. By day the larks sang, teaching me the forgotten histories and secrets of this world. By night, the babadooks and the basilisks hissed the stolen magicks, showing me the ways of darkness.

"Since death would not come. I lived for spite. I seeded it in my heart—allowed it to eat. Fester. Mutate. Until all that remained was a molten core of rage.

"The gestation period lasted two decades. All that while I remained, roots of Gaia satiating, making me strong. By the time the foul pregnancy ended, I'd learned what it meant to taste the moon and hear the river's scream.

"When the five babes ripped from me, suffused in golden light, I devoured them. Crunched their too soft bones. Lapped their tender flesh. My spawn did not wail as I swallowed them down, down, down.

"Then, their light radiated from me. Shining and bright.

"That was millennia ago. So long that I nearly forget I was ever fragile. Now, I dwell on the crest of the highest mountain, nestled between lichen-riddled boulders and trapped in this eternal prison. I am the one who never stops hunting."

Ozil slides her palm against my cheek. I don't know tears have slipped down my face until her trembling thumb brushes away the offending liquid.

With a raw throat, I unearth for her the one treasure I buried leagues within myself. "And my name is Tisiphone."

Eyes rimmed red, Ozil whispers in the forgotten tongue, "*Vengeance.*"

We each hold one another through the day, hoping if we squeeze tight enough we can force our splintered pieces back together. From the first moment I saw her, I knew we were mirrors. Cracked reflections of the same whole.

Then Ozil channels the remaining fragments of ancient sigils into herself. She sucks in a sharp breath, holds me tighter.

"The alchemy is broken, Tisiphone."

She kisses me tenderly, so soft I can almost believe this wholeness isn't breaking. I want to continue pretending she's not dying—that destroying these sigils hasn't drained something vital. But she is wasted away—fragile bones between my hands.

It was always going to end in blood for us.

"I need to go back." Her eyes peer beyond me—to the death she asks me to help her wield.

Ozil trails those kisses down my throat. Nibbles the abused skin there then slides her tongue over the hurt as if to seal in her mark. I will never be the same. Just like when the male gods threw me back to earth, body broken and burning. I came out of those ashes a different being. Ozil, too, has transmuted something inside me—her own special alchemy. And when she is gone, I—

I don't allow myself to finish the thought. I push away helplessness and call on what I know best. Blood.

The first step beyond the glowing sigils feels like finally breathing again. Like the first bite of flesh. I relish the freedom for a moment. Let that wandering heat spread through my veins. I am the night and the horrors and now I am unleashed again. Ozil stares at me from the pool, morbid smile lighting her eyes.

"You are *magnificent*."

I gather my children. My impish dragons, the warbling beetles, the blood-biting shrews. They come to the hum of my stolen song. They flock around us, a dark nimbus, teeth rotted and shining. Hoofs scraping limestone, igniting sparks. Hornes sharpened for the gutting. They have come for a war.

"It is time," I tell them. They don't need a speech to ignite their lust. They were born hungry for flesh. They howl at the starless night. Their screaming echoes into the mountain pass, a warning call to all that vengeance will arrive on swift wings.

Ozil trembles as I dress her down with the shed exoskeleton of a colossal scorpion. She glitters like stardust. Her life, a nova. Short and blindingly bright.

Then we ride.

The night shivers as we mount. A stampede of winged unicorns takes us to battle—a gaggle of gnashing children at my back. They screech and sing a bastardized version of that mortal song. They chant with teeth and venom and bloodlust.

We descend upon the castle Nemwae. A hive. A legion of everything that was ever outcast from the world. The gates fall under our barrage. Their high protective walls crumble to dust. They have my blessing to ravish it all.

The people penned outside the gilded walls scream as the fires consume them. Their mouths open in horror as they set to the pyre they had built for my Ozil.

She hisses and jeers as we swoop low. Her magick protected fingers scoop up embers, ashes, and plume, and she throws them, smiling, into the night sky like glimmering fireworks.

My children unleash for feeding. My botflies swarm the faces of men who kneel amid the flames. They howl for their gods to help, but none comes. I am their judgment—their god; I find them all guilty.

Before me, a man's skin chars, fire mounting higher lick by foul lick. His tongue is last to go. His mournful bleating is a symphony until the chorus fades to a gurgle of choked blood.

Soldiers pour like tempest waves into the burning courtyard, swords aloft, chanting war songs into the night. Their armor is shined to a high gloss. They march in lockstep. Well-practiced battle formations splinter around me.

I murder them all. Tear them to pieces with talons and tentacles and teeth. They come apart so easily. They try to swipe at me with their blades. Once they collect their wits, they come at me in pairs. Groups. Armies. But their weapons are brittle glass against my skin, their blows like puffs of scattered wind.

It is a slaughter. A cacophony of screams. They carol through the eventide. The bone fairies will have much to collect before the night is done.

And then there is only her. She stands blood-anointed, hair plastered to her skull with viscera. With a dagger in her hand.

"You are beautiful," I tell her, brushing a fleck of flesh from her cheek.

Together, Ozil and I slip into the king's lower chambers where he cowers from battle like a spineless toad. Ozil does not need me to hold her up as she creeps toward his hiding place. There are no guards left to stop this reckoning. I sliced them all to pieces before they could touch her.

The king quakes against the far wall, hands up in surrender, unaware of the death that has stalked him across the stars. Young women, likely girls, are propped on stakes like human shields before him. My stomach turns sour at their mangled bodies. Only hell knows what he has used them for. Ozil's eyes glimmer with unshed tears as she holds her cursed dagger aloft.

She knows.

There is something heavier than darkness in this place, deeper than black. Older than the night. I untie the girls quietly. Allow them to flee this place if they can.

"Daughter, you have come to save me." He knows that is a lie, likely hoping if he speaks it, it will be so. The sun has set on his power, and now it rises with Ozil.

"No, Father. I have come to spare the world from men like you." She rams the blade home into his fat stomach. His eyes flare, blood frothing from the corner of his mouth. Ruby spittle splatters Ozil's face, but she doesn't blink, doesn't flinch. She stabs down again.

Again.

Again.

Like her soul is on fire and the only way to put out the blaze is with his blood. She is coated with him. Ozil doesn't stop until I snatch both her hands in mine on the next upward arc.

"It's done," I say, gasping. "It's done."

Her eyes are wild—pupils blown wide with the rush that comes with a violent kill. She shakes her head, sinking into my arms as if all energy is finally spent now that her father is gone from the world. "It's not over until this whole wretched empire burns."

"And it will, my love."

The ground trembles. Earth-splitting, world-ending tremors. I clutch Ozil in my arm, bracing against the onslaught.

Then all is still. Breathless.

I know what's come even before peering out the window of the now crumbling castle. Dust falls like an ash plume from the buckling ceiling.

"Stay here." I lay Ozil on a bed of furs swiped from the dead king. "I'll be back."

Her smile is thin and watery. Too much of her fading too fast. I need to get this done quickly. She grabs my hand and presses her cursed dagger into my palm. I know what she wants without words.

"Bring it back to me," she whispers.

I kiss both her cheeks. Not saying goodbye because I'm not ready yet. Without looking back, I jump out of the window and into the fire.

The male god does not like what he sees. The collective calls of faithful worshippers has brought him down from the heavens in a cloud of inky smoke. He materializes amid the rubble and ruin of his once great city.

I swallow a bitter laugh. Without the prayers of his followers, he will be nothing.

He doesn't see me break from the treeline at a sprint. Gathering my magicks, I latch onto his neck with my fangs, wanting to tear his throat out in one bite. But his obsidian skin is impenetrable. I clamp down harder and my canines shatter.

He fists my throat in his hand, crushing down on my windpipe, and flings me through the debris of the tattered city. He shoots a burst of miasma after me. Before my battered body bursts through the broken stone, I am already out of magick. The darkness doesn't come to me as easily as it once did.

All around me, his ghouls rim my periphery. Their savage teeth rend through my skin like the first rays of day-cut twilight. One rips me to the ground. Others hold my legs. More pounce onto my tentacles, immobilizing me. Fetid breath rinses over my nostrils from their drooling mouths. The ghouls try to tear me open. They want to get back the shards that belong to their master.

I groan, trying and failing to move my limbs.

"Rise, Mother."

Nestar. He runs out onto the battlefield, staff swinging fiercely.

"No, be gone! Leave before they kill you, too!"

My child shouts for me to get up.

But I am smothered in darkness. My magick gone. I am weak once again. Trapped under the weight of those who wish to make me hurt.

"Rise!" Nestar hurls his limited magicks to banish the ghouls, but he is not strong enough. Neither of us are.

"I won't let him hurt you again, Mother! Nestar will protect you."

The male god jumps through the black mist engulfing us, spear in hand. I know where the blow aims. I twist in the ghouls' grasps. Their claws shred and shred but I don't care that they are shearing my innards open; I can finally move. Then I am sprinting—reaching for him.

A SIGIL TO BIND THE NIGHT

A spear splits Nestar through his little stomach from behind. Organ bile splatters my face. I open my mouth. Everything moves like time winding down. So slow. I see every flicker of pain on Nestar's face as the life winks out of him.

No. No no no no no.

I scream. Rage. If I could tear every mortal who gave the male god his power to pieces, it wouldn't be enough. Then I would tear myself to pieces for not being able to protect the child of my heart.

"I will kill you for this." The words rip from my throat. My eyes blur as tears flood, making crystals of my vision.

"No, you'll do what you were made for and bear me fearsome sons."

"Come and try it."

He grins, all teeth and promised pain. "It will be fun breaking you a second time."

A woman's worst fear is not death. It is the things a man wishes to do with her body before he grows tired. Death is easy. Death is final. But the lust of a man knows no barriers. No sacred limits.

For millennia, humans called me *monster*. They have made me the stuff of children's nightmares while they freely worshipped the true beast.

But not this time. I am not the same creature who came to him pleading. I am something much worse. And this is the last time he will ever take from me.

The male god stands over me, unsheathes his stunted dick to piss, but before he can release the first stream, I unleash a tentacle. Break free of his ghouls, grab hold of the only thing that makes him a man, and pull. My suction grippers don't let go even though he beats me over the head with his stone fists. With all my strength, I pull him close, lick my lips and bite down. The crunch of dick meat splitting is a symphony. Blood sprays my face, runs down my chin.

I spit the placid organ onto the searing pavement.

He falls to his knees, both hands cupping his missing root. But I am so familiar with him. It's not done yet. He would happily grind me under his boot. I housed his parasite for over two decades, and that sliver of power that was supposed to be passed down to his son like an inheritance now lives within me.

While he's dazed, I siphon every last drop of magick from him. It pours into me in wavelets. Streams. Rivers. I reclaim what was always mine. The power shivers inside me, rattling my marrow. I let it fill me with light until I am a beacon eating away at all his darkness.

The ghouls dissipate in a burst of luminescence. They extinguish like so many stars.

"Don't worry. You'll like it." I resend the words he delivered to me before he and his pantheon forced me on my stomach and took turns. I take the lance he plunged through my child and stab it through his mouth and out the back of his head.

Now it is done.

The sun drags ragged claws up the horizon. I cradle Nester's limp form in my arms and swallow down the wail raking my throat.

He was a good child.

Looking out into the fading darkness, I decide to bury him among the hemlock and the black dahlia near the entrance of the cave where we were happy for a time.

I once had a name, and it was men who took it from me. They have taken so much. And now that I am unleashed on this realm, they will learn justice.

Through my armor, I feel Gaia's trembling keen at the loss of life. I will have to face her when my time comes, and she will judge me harshly for the bodies I have returned to her too soon.

But before then, I will be what I have made myself: vengeance. I will wield my rage and cleave those who follow the male gods from this world. I will wipe every trace of them from the histories.

Boots crunch through rubble behind me.

Ozil treads unsteady steps into the first minutes of morning. I rush toward her, battle aches temporarily forgotten, and wrap her in my cloak to ward off the early chill. Little flakes of her face drift up into the air like dust motes.

"You should be resting." I'm afraid to touch her—that she might crumble to nothingness in my hands.

"Let's go home," she says, her voice no more than a croak. "I want to be with you in peace."

In the background, my children laugh and pick the little treasures from the bodies that didn't burn in the first wave of our assault. The sounds of their happiness fill me with a bittersweet pang.

Throat tight, I claim Ozil's hands, bringing her close. She is already disintegrating. Her hair is gone. The dark strands float up around her, carried by the wind. One of her eyes turns to glittering dust.

And then an arm.

Her legs.

"I will follow you soon." Even as my eyes burn with tears I refuse to shed, I hold my lips in an upward tilt until the last possible moment because I want the last thing she sees of this world to be my smiling face. To know she goes with all my love.

Her now empty battle armor slides to the ground with a hollow clank. The jeweled carapace glimmers in the rising light. She is pure brightness and heat as the last of her turns to ash. A light fleeting.

"You are beautiful," I say with the voice of the wind.

And I am not surprised when she answers in the song of the sun, "And you are fearsome, my Tisiphone."

WINCH CAVE
GAAST

The unofficial reunion afterparty is being held in a chamber of Winch Cave. Someone dragged a generator in here and strung up lights. It's an open cavern, so it doesn't feel crowded, but our voices echo so much it feels like there're many times more people here than there are.

I'm sitting on the floor, trying to collect my bearings. A low, thumping bass track is playing, and I'm wrapped up in it with my heartbeat, thoughts, and body all moving with the rhythm. Whatever's in this punch, it's *strong*.

Some of my former classmates are also taking a breather, but most of them are still mingling and dancing. A few, it seems, stuck together through college and are grinding against each other like nobody else is here. Most of the other dancers are just following their feet, going where the beat takes them. I wish I felt that kind of liberty. But most of these people won't be here after tomorrow. They'll go back to wherever their lives are. I'll still be here, one of the few who hasn't left.

But it's easy to push aside thoughts like those. The edible's wearing off, but the remaining high is keeping me steady. I should take another one. I'm not the one driving.

Kennedy sits next to me. "Doing okay, man?"

"Yeah. I'm having fun."

"Just sitting here?"

"You should try it."

"Not when I'm sober."

"Julia's over there. Why don't you hang out with her?"

He laughs, punches my shoulder. "That was years ago, dude. I'm over her now."

"So if she came up to you right now and begged to suck your cock?"

"Look, that's different. That's just a blowjob. It ain't love."

We laugh. I devolve into a fit of giggles. "Sure it's love. Being inside someone is love."

"Whatever, man. When do you wanna get outta here?"

"I don't wanna leave."

"You really have changed. You're the one who used to drag *me* away from parties."

"I've only gotten more pathetic. I never get to have anything like this anymore."

"Hey, you should visit me in Toledo sometime. It's not that bad, I swear."

Suddenly, I don't want to be having this conversation anymore. I fish a baggie out of my pocket and swallow one of the gummies within.

I should say something. Say I'll visit. Or change the subject. Lie, tell the truth, I don't know. Something would be better than nothing. I just have to open my mouth and speak. But carefully. I can't really let Kennedy know how I'm feeling. We've barely stayed in touch since high school. We used to talk about how we were inseparable, and now I had to learn he has a newborn when we ran into each other in the fucking VFW's bathroom. We graduated, we spent one last summer together, and we went off to college, and that was it. He was in Ohio and I was still in Rose County. I couldn't even keep up enough to get my associate's degree. And now Kennedy is a fucking CPA. I thought he was going into sports broadcasting. And he's a CPA.

What was I going to be? I can't even remember if I ever had an idea, or even a dream. I'm hoping I'll get to manage a McDonald's in another five years. That's my dream now.

"You okay?" he asks. Shit. I forgot to say something.

"Yeah. I just—let me go piss. Then we can get out of here."

"Uh, right here? Or you wanna get back to the woods?"

"I'll find a spot. Just, hold on."

I don't want to leave. I don't want to be alone again. Just a few more minutes.

I stand up. It's not an easy task. My head swims a little as my legs stumble. I wobble away, opposite the direction we came in. I sink into the darkness, wandering until I find a secluded chamber—and hear the distinct sounds of moaning. I find another chamber, not too much deeper. I'm about to just whip it out when I realize I should make sure I'm not about to piss on anything. Or anyone. I turn on my phone's flashlight, see I'm clear, put my phone back into my pocket, and start relieving myself.

Goddammit. I left the flashlight on.

Once I'm done, I get my phone back out, and, just as I'm about to turn off the light, it illuminates something. It's not much. Barely visible. Just a circular hole in the wall. I don't know why it catches my eye. Must be the alcohol. I stumble over to it. It's about hip-high, an inch or two across—I don't know. "Hey babe," I whisper, my words dredged up through an intoxicated haze. "Where've ya been all night?"

I can still hear the bass music faintly in the distance. I stroke the hole with my fingertip. I push my finger inside.

And I yank it back out. Immediately.

I compose myself, then stumble back to the afterparty. Kennedy is waiting. He smiles, putting on a kind face, but I can tell he's annoyed and confused and disappointed. We get no service in here. He probably wants to check on his daughter.

He walks me gently out of the cave and into his car. "Thanks," I say.

"Don't mention it."

"No. I know I'm, I'm..." I trail off and hiccup. "I know I'm pathetic and everything. I needed this. A lot more than you did. So thank you. I couldn't have done it without you."

"Dude, we're friends. This is what friends do."

"Yeah. Yeah."

He drives me home in silence. I wait outside the apartment complex until he turns a corner, then I drag myself a few blocks away to my parents' house.

It's only during the brief moments between my head hitting the pillow and falling asleep that I let myself think about the soft, warm insides of the hole.

It's a good thing I asked for today off. My head is pounding.

I barely manage to drag myself out of bed before noon. I'm still wearing what I wore last night and don't particularly care to change.

Kennedy sent me a few messages letting me know he was leaving. "It was great seeing you, really," he wrote. "Keep in touch, man."

Yeah. Keep in touch. Have a great summer. Too bad he can't send me the *cool S.* Then it'd really feel like a yearbook.

But who am I to complain? After five years I'm still living in the same bedroom, slumped in the same positions against the same walls, eyeing the same edibles and video games, struggling to decide between the same wastes of my time for the day. The only thing different is that tomorrow, Monday, I'm not going to school. I'm just going to the McDonald's three blocks from school, working a grill for six hours, sweating my ass off, and trying not to think about anything, just hoping someone will notice that I'm doing a good job and maybe, just maybe, give me a new responsibility.

But that's tomorrow. What do I do *today?*

I grab a gummy but just before I pop it in my mouth its texture reminds me of the soft stickiness of the hole I noticed last night. Why the hell am I thinking about a hole? Actually, no, isn't it normal to think about a hole that weird? It felt like, just beyond the rock wall, there was flesh inside, a creature. It was warm and, in my drunken state, inviting. I wonder if it would be as inviting to me now that I'm hungover, dirtier, and sadder than last time.

Before I realize it, I'm grabbing my keys. I tell Mom and Dad I'm heading out for some air, and suddenly, I'm on the road to Winch Cave, praying I'll be able to remember where exactly I found that thing last night.

Winch Cave isn't anything except a cave, and it never was anything, either. Not a mine, cavers' haunt, nothing. Just a lonely, untouched cave next to Red Rose, Pennsylvania, a place unrivaled for being Nowhere. I think the more adventurous kids liked to use it as a party spot, like last night, but I was never one of those. So it's always been a gap in the woods, named for the *potential* towings it could cause were a car to somehow drive into it. All it is, is blank.

Even still, it's easy to reach it. Evidence of the afterparty lingers outside, with tire tracks, empty bottles, and condom wrappers littering the area. Inside is more or less clean until the chamber where we spent last night. Whoever brought them took the lights and the generator, but everything else is still here, from cups to bottles to a few discarded articles of clothing. I barely register any of it as I search for the path I took through dark, winding chambers, ears hearing phantom music to accompany my otherwise silent investigation.

It doesn't take long. It's not like I went too deep. I find the chamber where I wasn't alone first, then quickly find the one where I was. The puddle's still there, and the smell with it. But that doesn't matter. What matters is the hole's there, right where I left it. For some reason, I now realize, I thought it might have vanished.

Now, with more time and more certainty that were I to kneel, I could get myself up again, I bend down to study the hole a bit more closely. I want to give it another name—maybe it's shallow enough to be a divot—but it's just a perfectly circular space of nothing dug into the wall. From the outside, that's all it seems to be. Perhaps that's strange enough on its own. I don't know caves. But it seems weird that such a perfect, pristine hole could be here, where no others are; it doesn't seem like a water flow was responsible, but then how would I know? And who would take a drill here and make a single hole and do nothing else? It's Winch Cave. This entire place is its own hole.

But, honestly, I don't care about any of that. What I care about is whether I was so crossfaded last night that my body made up sensations. I again stick my finger into the hole. And again, I feel warmth inside, and softness, and maybe even a little moisture.

So I was right. It really feels this way.

I push my finger as far inside as I can, but I don't press against an end. It's big enough, so I stick another in, hoping I can get some extra leverage, dig just a little deeper, and maybe find wherever it is the hole terminates. I find only more slickness, more warmth.

It doesn't feel like rock inside. Sure, the stone around it is smooth, but not like this. It has the soft, elastic quality of flesh. My fingers push it slightly, pressing against it, like textured folds line the inside. It's like... It feels like...

I look at my fingers. Slowly, I withdraw them. A thin, sticky slime is on them. I slide them back in, and I start fucking the cave with them.

I hardly know what I'm doing—it's not like the cave is giving me any signals—but I stroke around inside of it, luxuriating in the soft fleshiness of its strata. Slowly at first, and carefully, until I feel something quiver, be it my body or the cave's, and go harder, faster. I crook my fingers, I flatten them, I spin them; I try everything, get every angle, get *everywhere*, feel my cock harden, feel the cave moisten, feel the air inside grow hot, heavy, feel my body sink against the wall, start panting, sweating, craving the rock with more parts of me than just my fingers, and suddenly a low rumble shakes through the whole cave, and from deep within echoes a growl like rock grinding against rock, a sharp and painful sound, and it sends jitters through my body and sparks through my soul.

My fingers slide out, much more easily this time than last. I've never been so turned on, especially not from just—just *fingering*. Fuck. Do I want to fuck this cave?

Even if I do, the pressure in the room keeps me rooted to the spot, still trying to catch my breath. By the time it dissipates, the slick coolness is back, and I feel, somehow, that the cave wants me to leave. But only for now.

"I'll be back," I whisper. Maybe it can understand.

The way back out felt... straightforward. I didn't have to remember how to get back to my car. My feet just took me there. I didn't have to do any of the winding or doubling back that I thought I had to to get out. Maybe I've just built a better mental map now.

The *drive* back, though... That was depressing. It was fun, alone in the cave. That's pathetic enough, I guess, but to be driving back home, as always, to my parents. They had been excited to hear that my high school class was having a reunion. They even sought out some of the kids I used to hang out with. Apparently, they'd been keeping in touch with a couple of them.

"Hey, Mom. Hey, Dad," I say on my way inside.

They nod at me. They don't ask questions. They're watching *Jeopardy!*. I sit on the loveseat and watch with them. They call out answers they know, but I just sit there. I'm too busy thinking about what happened in the cave.

During commercials, they ask me about the reunion. How it was, if I had fun. That quickly segues into asking about people who I didn't even remember knowing. And when they ask me about people who I actually talked to, they can't comprehend why I didn't ask where they are now, what they're doing.

"It didn't occur to me."

"How could that not occur to you?"

We've had this same argument dozens of times.

The platen lowers and sizzles when it touches the patties. A tray with a fresh liner is waiting for them.

It's easy to tune out the unimportant things now. I'm experienced with it. It's just a matter of knowing how much noise there is. If there's more, I better keep making patties. If there's less, I can step back and help clean. The rest doesn't matter. They call to each other to distinguish between burgers, or to hurry the guy making the nuggets and fries. The most difficult sound to manage is whoever's taking the drive-thru orders. They're the only one having a different kind of conversation, so it cuts through the rest. Once you can do that, you barely need to think anymore.

That's probably why the manager is always at the prep table or the cash registers. You can't tune out on those jobs. And that's why I'll never get promoted—if that's even something you can be at a McDonald's in fucking Red Rose.

The dinner rush ends and the flow of incoming customers becomes a trickle. Everything's clean, or as clean as it can be before we close. There isn't anything to do. So Bernie comes over to me.

"What's weirder than a cave on the move?" she asks.

"What?"

"A happy-looking McDonald's employee," she laughs.

Bernie's the only person I know who lives here but isn't from here. She came right after graduation. We met after my first wasted semester at community college. We gravitated toward each other, both knowing life held nothing more than this for us. We dated for a bit after I gave up on school. It was fun. We didn't really end it for a reason. We just had more fun seeing each other at work and hanging out occasionally. That's how we work. Besides, she's more into girls, and whatever I am is not that.

"How was that reunion of yours?" she asks. "Have fun?"

"At the afterparty."

"Yeah? Get up to anything hot?"

"Nah. Just got wasted and had my friend drive me home. I heard other people getting some, though."

"Too wild," she says. Insincerely.

"What were you hoping to hear?"

She giggles, leaning against the freezer full of meat. "That you and an old acquaintance were finally able to realize your feelings and spent a night deep in the throes of passion."

"You know what's crazier than a whirlwind romance?"

"What?"

"A McDonald's employee in the throes of passion."

"Ha! Got me there!"

I pause. "Hey, what was that about a moving cave?"

"You didn't hear? The cave outside of town moved like a half-mile closer."

"What?"

Bernie shrugs. "You should see the news. They measured out the *canyon* it made."

"Huh," I say. It works. It's enough. She changes the subject. So naturally. Flawlessly. Why is she here? She should be somewhere. Anywhere. Why isn't the cave *there*? No. No, it's a joke, a prank. You'll see. Don't worry about it. Don't think about it. Just calm down. Why are you so terrified, anyway? It's not like it has anything to do with you. It has *nothing* to do with you. Maybe it's just angry because of the trash. That's it. It moved because of the trash, not because of you...

I retreat into the bathroom, sitting in a stall and shaking until my shift ends.

There's caution tape and surveyors' equipment around, but it's apparent even from a distance that the cave is no longer where it was. Those objects are the only signs of people at this hour, so I duck under the tape and approach the chasm that the cave's movement opened in the earth.

It really looks like the entire network of rock and chamber dragged itself wholesale through the ground, directly toward Red Rose. Winch Cave must be more expansive than I realized, because in the darkness I can see neither the bottom of the chasm nor the other side of it.

Why am I here?

Instead of heading home after work, I came right back to the cave. I feel like I would have done so anyway. I can't explain why. I wanted to go back to the hole. I wanted to—I *want* to—explore it further. But the reason *why* I want to, why I want to fuck *this* hole, when I have any number of things I can fuck at home, eludes me.

I walk a ways down the chasm and even in the darkness I can tell it's a long distance between here and wherever it ended up. I get back in my car and try to follow along its path, at least until I remember that it went straight for town. Then I just try to hew close to the treeline and keep a lookout for evidence that safety crews are working nearby.

And yet, for all the effort I put into driving, following along, keeping alert and observant, I roll up without noticing to a chain-link fence erected impetuously in the middle of the woods. I was driving, and there was nothing, and then I was here, the cave barely visible, a shadow in the distance.

Cautiously, I climb over the fence. Nobody's around. What more do they have to do? The cave moved. What's the investigatory protocol for that? Nobody comes to Winch. Put a fence up and call it good. Hell, this is the only news Red Rose has had in years and nobody except for me is here to see it.

Before I realize it, I'm in the cave. My feet carry me swiftly to the chamber. Again, it feels like the cave itself has been rearranged to make my trip easy, linear. I don't even use my light. My feet sink perfectly into place with each step, as though the ground itself has worn away specifically to guide my trek deeper inside. The cave pushes gently against each footfall, a pressure both spurring me on and responding simply to my presence, my touch. Like a lover's idle smile.

I don't know why, but I'm hard as shit. I'm panting, marching through the cave, a heat radiating from my bones. The space widens, opens up, and even in the pitch blackness I know the hole is there. My palms press against the wall above it, catching my momentum. I was running.

"You want me," I whisper, "that badly?"

My fingers are already inside of it, and the whole cave seems to tremble around them. The fleshy insides pulse and tighten, responding to my touch. I reward them, stroking ever more vigorously, fucking the hole like it's any other toy there for me to use.

But it's not enough. It's not enough for either of us. Without thinking, I trade my fingers for my tongue, licking around the hole, then the hole itself, tasting the cold, earthen notes of ancient rock. A tremor jolts through the entire cave, unsettling dust and dislodging stone. Encouraged, I push my tongue deeper, my nose pressed against where its clit would be, and delight in the sweet juiciness pouring from within. It's like sugared metal, iron and powder and age.

As its insides keep searching desperately for the pleasure of my tongue, I can't help but think of the other people I shared moments like these with, from girls I met at the only bar close enough to town to the guys I dated in senior year.

Their time in Red Rose was temporary, as was their time with me. They extracted all the joy they cared to from us, then left. I don't blame them. I don't want to be here either. Red Rose isn't much of a home.

But to think that I was never enough to help make one.

If I was just a stopgap for others, I'm delighted to be something more substantial for Winch Cave.

The oppressive heat and humidity flooding the chamber are too much to bear. I tear off my clothes and keep licking, exploring every fold with my mouth. Everything rumbles, and in the distance rock grinds against rock, deep moans billowing up and through and out the cave itself. There's something intoxicating about the sounds, something that fills me like smoke and presses against my edges. Every inch of me is charged, heated, melted; I'm soft and viscous and pressing gently against the rock and being left with a perfect impression of every crag in my skin.

My body moves automatically. When my cock enters it, the whole world seems to shake.

The hole fits perfectly around me, and it squeezes me gently as I thrust confidently into it. The rock wall caresses my desperate body, hundreds of fingers pressing against my skin, pulses of lust dancing in the minute spaces between us.

My hips pound against the stone, hard enough to scrape my skin. The folds, the heat, the wetness inside ensconce my dick, each bit of surface area devoted to it and only it. Pleasure builds inside of us, expressions of mutual desire. In perfect syncopation, I moan, and the cave trembles, seems to lurch, grinds against itself. I search deeper, trying to find the hole's furthest point, to reach the very depths of Winch Cave. The rough rock makes my balls bleed, my hips leak, my nipples sore with friction against the wall.

But the cave—the cave is about to come, I can feel it, its insides shudder, contract; the heat becomes unbearable as thick waves of stone jolt and twitch and grind. I have energy for nothing but my hips. I collapse against the wall and keep pounding, pounding, pounding, adrenaline rendering me oblivious to any pain I might be in.

Maybe the cave will swallow me whole. Maybe I'll merge with it. Maybe my dick will become part of it, and I'll just be a toy for it to use.

Maybe I'll sink so deeply into the cave that it can force its way into me and emerge from itself and walk out of the world, naked and bloody, a new shape.

I don't care what happens, though. I want the cave and the cave wants me. I don't have to leave, to grow, to change, to work, to live, to die. I can be what it asks of me. And that's plenty.

I can't hold back anymore. With shaking, unsteady thrusts, I come. However deep I shoot, I doubt I approach anywhere near its bottom.

When I'm too dehydrated to go again, I reluctantly exit the cave. By now, it's totally rearranged; only one chamber separates us from the exit.

It takes a while for my eyes to adjust to the light. Once they do, I see that Winch Cave stopped just under my parents' house. A swathe of destruction cuts through Red Rose in the direction where the cave used to be. That's all there is: destruction and empty houses.

Our neighbors across the street left their front door open in their haste to leave. Their sink still has running water. I drink deeply and eat whatever I can grab in their fridge.

Now that I'm in the light and can take a good look at myself, I'm impressed it took me this long to need to recuperate. Angry scabs line my midsection, with my scrotum in particular dealing with some nasty wounds and pus. They hurt, too, from slapping against rock so much.

I don't really care.

Once I've eaten and rested, I climb up the crags my parents' house is now perched upon. There's no sign of Mom or Dad. Everything has fallen over, and mostly everything has been shattered or destroyed. Something's blocking my bedroom door from the inside. I laugh dryly and leave the house.

I'm standing naked in the sunlight on my parents' porch. I'm covered in grime and dust. I'm bleeding. I am totally spent. To take another step would be to risk getting light-headed, wobble, and tumble to the ground, right at the mouth of the cave.

Of course I take another step. After all, I want to go home.

A Rotting Crown of Birch

Celia Winter

"Do not go near the water, Marichka."

"I'll be fine."

"It's freezing! The snow has only just melted! You will catch cold, you will grow sick and die."

But Marichka ignores her brother. Ivan likes to think he is a man when he is a boy less than half her age, always commanding her and then complaining when she does not obey. Spring has come at last, and the river, which has been frozen for months on end, is finally breaking free. She will dip her feet in and feel the sharp shock that only frigid water can bring, then she will put on her socks and shoes again and they will return to town as though she hasn't done anything at all.

If she doesn't do it today, she will miss it entirely. Spring will blossom from the ice, incense and Easter hymns will burn through her ears, and the water will warm—mild and soft and all-too-gentle against her toes.

"Father will be mad at you!" Ivan yells at her, clearly annoyed that she is not listening. His face is screwed up in frustration beneath his wheat-gold curls.

"Only if you tell him," Marichka calls.

She already knows what her father will say: "You should listen to your brother." The words will hurt more than the bruises her father leaves on her belly when he hits her. Ivan isn't yet big enough that he dares strike her when she doesn't do what he wants. He isn't old enough to be allowed to tell her what to do—not yet. Not ever. He doesn't understand the joy of the water. He can't even swim; he's too afraid he'll drown.

Marichka isn't afraid of drowning. She's not afraid to live, either.

"I'll tell! You know I will if you don't get back here!" Ivan shouts, and Marichka begins to hum the way she always does when she ignores him. She loves the way her chest vibrates under her clothes. Everyone has always told her she has a lovely voice, and when she sings the liturgy, others sometimes sing more quietly so they can hear her better.

She strips off her socks, the words about young lovers meeting in the birch grove joining the melody on her lips. She walks toward the river, cool mud squelching deliciously between her toes. She does not look over her shoulder to her brother as she clambers down to the water's edge, the rocks shining with fresh snowmelt.

"Marichka!" he shouts again, but she only lifts her voice as she balances at the water's edge for just a moment, her song echoing off the trees, off the bubbling water until—

Marichka gasps when she touches the surface—just her toes at first, and then her soles, then her ankles, the sharp chill sprawling over her skin under her skirts and vyshyvanka[1] so that even her sheepskin coat cannot keep her warm. Her whole back arches as the cold climbs her veins like a ladder, up her legs, through her belly to her throat. Her heart slams in her ribs, and she feels *alive*. It's only water that's ever made her feel like this—more than running through fields or sitting in pews and praying.

"Come back!" Ivan shouts while her blood courses through her body, a river of its own. "Come back or I'm telling father!" He is still afraid of the water. There will be bruises on her belly come tomorrow, she knows that, but better a bruised body than a bruised heart. Besides, she'll have been in the cold: she won't feel it.

While she is in the water, the only thing that matters is the thrum.

"You're supposed to listen to me!"

[1] **vyshyvanka:** a traditional Ukrainian (and Belarusian) embroidered shirt or blouse, made from natural fabrics like linen or cotton, featuring intricate, symbolic patterns that vary by region.

"You still don't have a beard on your chin!" Marichka retorts. The current makes her daring, the cold piercing her lungs and heart. "Little boys do not tell me what to do!"

"I'm not a little boy!" Ivan shouts again, his voice cracking like ice. It's been cracking a lot lately, which makes him think he's nearly a man.

"Little boy, little boy," Marichka croons just to annoy him, changing the words to a song about goats. "None of the young women like him. He thinks he's a man, but he's just a boy. Less than a boy. A baby!"

"Shut up!" Ivan howls again, voice thick like he is trying not to cry.

"Little boy, little baby, his sister makes him cry. What kind of man lets a girl make him cry? Not a boy, a baby."

The rock strikes the side of the head, sharp as the cold. Marichka tumbles forward onto the ice, which cracks under her weight. Then it is not just her feet that feel the piercing wet; her woolen skirt and coat pull her down, down, her lungs fill with it, every chasm in her body, her soul.

Somewhere above her, Ivan screams. He has always been so afraid of drowning.

They drag her corpse onto the bank. They give her a Christian burial in the softening spring earth. They do not ask her what she wants, so of course they do not leave her in the river.

When the night falls and the stars twinkle innocently overhead, Marichka does not sleep. She should be in the water, not the earth. She claws her way out of the pine box they put her in with a strength the icy water gave her, and worms her way through the unpacked dirt.

She runs back to the river—the river that preserved and protected her, the river that froze her soul so that it could continue in her mottling body. She leaps into its bubbling embrace and lets herself sink down to the very bottom.

She doesn't need to hold her breath. She doesn't need to breathe at all.

Marya is frigid all the time now, and how she *loves* it because she is free.

When the river's bubbling echoes off the poplar trees, she chooses to breathe so she can fill the woods with a descant. When the river cracks and melts, she gasps with joy. Her dark hair is a wet crown she weaves with rotting birch leaves.

Wool weighs her down, so she sheds it like a frog's skin and eats it.

The cold doesn't thrill her dead heart anymore. Now she longs for heat to warm her in the icy water.

Now she dreams of the hot shock of spring.

The forest is full of trees, and when men weave their way through, she sings to them. Now it is the men who pause, who turn, who listen to her.

What a heady power, to make something else obey.

The men she serenades all have wheat-gold hair and river-blue eyes, her brother's coloring if not his fear of the water. She always gives them a choice. Her icy heart doesn't care about them—oh no. Her rage froze with her corpse, and revenge is an instinct as natural as the tides. Marichka was a rebellious girl, but not a spiteful one. Marya would have to crack her bones to free the hunger for retribution from her marrow, and even then, she doesn't know if it would be gone. But for every man she sings to, she always wishes her choice had been acknowledged. Their obedience is sweeter because they choose it.

Sometimes, she lures them as far as the water's edge before they awaken from her trance, run from her screaming. Even a beautiful, willing girl, naked and dripping, isn't enough to hold them in her thrall when they notice how clammy her skin is, how blotched and deathly, and fear crashes through them like a bursting dam.

But so frequently, the men choose to claim her, as they were trained by their fathers. What man can resist a beautiful girl, pale from the cold, water making her bare nipples shine like the cresting sun? What man *would* resist such a thing, and still be called a man?

They would only care about her heat if she were still a living girl, so she does not care that she will take theirs until they are cool as stone, like her.

There are whispers in the woods, whispers that *something* drowns the men in springtime. A ghost, they say—a witch. A hag.

The men ignore the old women who name her correctly, who call her *rusalka*, for witches are real and rusalkas merely folk tales. She wonders if these flaxen youths admit they're wrong in those dying moments when warm gasps send sharp hot shocks into a dripping abyss.

"Do not go near the water, Dmytro!"

"You worry too much!"

She blinks her eyes open. Spring is coming, the river is cracking, and Marya longs to be warm. Slowly, she emerges from the gaps in the ice. Staying low to the ground, she crawls over the frozen river towards the bank, a lizard more than a snake.

Ah yes, gold hair like the sun, blue eyes like the sky. Dmytro has a handsome face and a well-kept beard.

"Don't you want to see the water?" she chants, her voice light and breathy as it mingles with the breeze.

He pauses mid-step, clear eyes flitting from poplar to poplar. He heard her.

"Who's there?" he calls.

"Don't go out on the ice!" his friend shouts. "It's dangerous when it's this close to melting."

"I didn't grow up under a hill. I know not to walk on thin ice," Dmytro snaps at his friend, his eyes still probing the woods.

Should she show herself? Usually she waits for sunset, for nightfall. A naked girl by night is more tantalizing than a decaying one exposed in the day.

"What are you doing?" the friend asks next.

"I thought I heard something," Dmytro says slowly, staring at the trees as though begging them to reveal a secret.

Marya steps out from the shadow behind a poplar, her hair crowned in fresh spring leaves, just long enough that Dmytro's eyes widen in surprise, in curiosity, in hunger. "Come to the river tonight," she harmonizes with the breeze.

Dmytro takes a step back, and for a moment she wonders if he will be one who bolts, one whose dread protects his life. Then he cocks his head, his lips part and he shows a wolf's sharp teeth.

So he fancies himself a hunter, then. "Come back to me, sweet Dmytro," she croons again, and even though he continues on with his friend, his step is sluggish, and she knows the song will whisper in his ear when he tries to sleep that night.

The sunlight trickles through the poplar branches as she hums to herself and waits.

He comes to her in the night, his wool coat belted tight about him. There are stars and moonlight in his eyes and she stands in the riverbed and serenades him. How beautiful he is, this Dmytro with his beard and sunrise hair. He is a man, not a boy.

"You called to me," he rumbles at her as he approaches, content and confident.

"You came to my river," she croons to him, keeping her voice light and high—a girl, not a monster. "Come to the water."

He begins to remove the coat. Hair dusts his body like spring grass pushing from soil. He stands tall and strong as a tree, hunger in his eyes as his feet squelch in the mud upon their approach. He gasps when he sinks into the icy water up to the ankle. Marya remembers the cold shock climbing her bones years ago, the way it made her feel alive and dead both at once. But that was another lifetime. She has lost count of the turning seasons.

"Don't you love the springtime?" she sings to him as she twines her arms around his neck, her lips ghosting over his. "Spring is a time for lovers among the poplars."

"Spring is a time for lovers among the poplars," he repeats with a growl. He pulls her body flush against his and it is her turn to gasp.

She'd forgotten what hot flesh felt like, for her own has been icy since the river froze. His skin sears across her, heat flooding her belly, making her veins pump fire.

If she is not careful, the water that trickles unendingly from her hair, down her skin, between her legs, will boil to steam. But it is a good warmth, a sharp warmth, and when he bends his head to kiss her, she drowns in the taste of his tongue.

"You are so beautiful," he murmurs into her lips.

"As beautiful as spring," she replies and reaches a hand down between them to cup him.

He gasps, recoils, and her grip tightens on his shoulder. "No," escapes her lips before she can stop it. She doesn't want to lose this one too. He doesn't seem to fear the river and the night the way others might. He hungers for her like he wants to tame her.

"Your hand is cold," he complains.

"Then warm it," she commands.

His hot fingers unwind hers from his member and he lifts them to his mouth, sucks them between his lips, grazes them with dull teeth while he drinks the clammy surface of her skin until it's nearly dry.

When he lowers her hand to his cock again, he gasps in confusion. "But you were warm," he tells her in surprise. "It's already so much cooler."

The wrong part of him was making her warm, and she caresses him, pulling him closer. Hot blood just beneath his surface—that will warm her hand better than a brief incursion into his mouth.

"Warm me," she murmurs as he pants, misting breath into her neck. "Make me warm for you."

His fingers slip into her, water and slick making her smooth as silk. There it is—heat and cold alike sending spasms into her gut, awakening her with every thrust of his hand.

"How are you this cold?" he asks, and this time there is a stretch when he adds another finger.

Death keeps me alive, she does not say. "I was waiting for you."

A groan rumbles so deep in his chest, she wonders if it is coming from the earth. His free hand, the one not breaking and remaking her, comes to grip her hip, to grind her into his fingers while her dead heart flashes life through her. And when the ice melts, when the river crashes, her song echoes through the trees, for she is warm again, warm at last, warm the way warm was supposed to make her feel, but which she only ever got from cold.

"Yes," he murmurs into her lips while she echoes through the woods, but it roars through her ears like the wind. "*Yes.*"

Down into the mud she pushes him next, her veins full of spring. Her knees sink into the wet earth all around him as her hot cunt, flush and ripe and wanting, pulls him in, drowns him in everything she is. She bends and arcs and rides him while he thrusts up into her, warm enough for him now. Her hair tangles between them like forest roots as she bends her head to his and claims his tongue with hers while he gasps and pants and moans.

He is so beautiful, her golden Dmytro.

She likes that he made her sing.

Water seeps from her skin, more dewy than slimy now from elation. The crown of dead birch leaves in her hair feels more like flowers as he pulls himself into her kiss. She does not weep as wet dribbles onto his face. No one wept for her, after all. Her father stood stony faced when they dragged her corpse to land, and Ivan wept for himself, not for the sister he killed.

"Yes," he moans into her lips as she fucks him into the earth. "More," he gasps as though he himself cannot stop. "Mine," he gargles as his mouth is full of dripping water, even though she is no longer kissing him.

He does not plead a fourth time as his body shudders and fills her with his last seed of spring and goes irrevocably still.

Marya rises from the mud and rolls his body to the river, past the rocks that will hold it still and mottled until morning. The water will carry him south, away from town, towards the sea.

Then she sinks back beneath the surface, warm enough that she brings spring to the cracking ice.

A Place of No Mercy

Jeannie Marschall

They say the Terrors will charge you skin for skin and blood for blood if you fight back. Every night, we can all hear their howls echo from the rough mountainsides and feel their claws scrape along the edges of our dreams. No one has ever stepped outside the city walls after dark and come back alive. No one, that is, but me. And for that, I have to thank the ones who, from the days of our youth, declared me their enemy, their victim, their toy.

"Lagertes?" I turned from the closed front door to glance at my master. She looked at my fidgeting form, the knapsack of undelivered wares hanging from my linen-clad shoulder, and back towards the door with a meaningful eyebrow lift. I'd always dreaded those eyebrows—bold black slashes across her forehead that never failed to let you know when you were being a useless git.

"What are you doing?"

Even muffled through glass and the thick boards of the front door, the noise of the street was loud behind my back: the rumbles of carts, clanging of tools, the shouts on the cold and dusty morning air, the laughter. Hells, that laughter...

"Lagertes!"

I jolted. "Sorry. I'm sorry."

"Those orders—"

"—will not grow feet and walk to their owners by themselves. I know; I'll be going." I adjusted my grip on the coarse sackcloth, feeling the tools inside shift with the movement. Metal clinked as my gaze flicked between Aneste's frown and the street that was, at that moment, a trap. I needed more time. They'd walk past if I gave it just a little more time.

Aneste knew, even though she evidently didn't understand. She finished tying her leather apron around her waist with irritated speed, strong arms straining as she reached behind her back. "One would think you're still a sprig of six instead of full-grown and a moon away from earning your anvil."

I closed my teeth over whatever I might have said to that and turned away, knowing that she'd have a dismissive retort for any answer. It didn't matter that there were four of them, or that hiding was the one thing that reliably averted agony, or that my hands too often forgot how to do anything useful at the sound of that laughter; and Aneste, hard of will and unafraid of pain, could simply not bend her mind around the most important part: I did not *want* to fight.

My forehead thudded against the thick wood of the door and I sighed, free hand coming to the door latch. "They've never liked my face."

Aneste snorted. "Nothing to do with your face."

Nothing to do but shrug at that. "It is what it is." I listened to the flows down the alleys, judged them too murky still. More waiting would mean that I'd have to end my day late again, but that was preferable to bruises.

"I guess appealing to the council remains out of the question."

I huffed. "Given which children they sired, I'd just end up in their bad books for tattling." Tale as old as blasted time. Pathetic.

"Got nothing to *do* with 'tattling'—they came at you with clubs last time!"

"Sticks. And never caught up to me." I sighed. "Sun willing, they'll grow bored of it someday soon." The laughs outside were only of children at play and neighbours jesting now. Time to go.

"For what it's worth," my master's voice came again, "I wonder less at you than at them. Bleating louts full of piss and steam, prancing around wanting us to say *town guards*." She spat the words, sweeping her walnut hair up into a work-ready tail. "These are Terror lands. Guard us from what, having a quiet time of it behind the walls? More'n twenty summers each they have, and barely two decent traits nor one useful trade between them. You can't be the only one they's plaguing either, that's for sure. Someone will teach them, mark my words." A tiny, tiny pause. "If you managed to snap, it might just be you."

I couldn't help but smirk at her unwieldy hammer of a hint. "Well," I said, lifting my head away from the door and pulling it open. "I don't know about snapping, but at least I've always been faster than them out in the open."

They cornered me on my way back to the smithy that evening. There are only so many routes to choose from in a town of barely two hundred souls, and I chose poorly. I squeezed my body and my bundle of late-afternoon groceries past the miller Freyer's horse and cart, waved at their retreating backs, and collided with a shove against my chest that sent me tumbling backwards onto the gravelled street.

"Evening, bellows brat."

I sat up, checked that my bundle hadn't spilled all over the alley, and tilted my head to look at the owner of that overly cheery voice. "Korr... do we *have* to keep doing this? It's becoming ridiculous, it really is."

His grin widened on his fine-boned face as his fellows—Semest and Hespin, his sister Rufah—fanned out around him, blocking the last of the light. "Well, you're still here."

"At the risk of repeating myself, that's because I live here."

"And it seems astonishingly hard for you to grasp that we don't *want* you to."

"*This town isn't large enough for the both of us?* Really?"

"It's not for the likes of you. People want you gone, we've made that clear so many times, but it just doesn't stick in your thick skull, does it?" Someone approached from around the corner, and all four shifted their stances, leaning against the wall or squatting down to play with a pebble—nothing to see here! They always took such care not to let people bear witness. I briefly contemplated talking up the newcomer with some question made of sweat and improvised memory, but let it go with a wince when I saw the man's face: a tailor, lived at the other end of town. I didn't even know his given name. Damn.

Korr sunk his hands into his soft woollen trousers' pockets, gave a nonchalant shrug as the man passed us. "It doesn't stick at all. So this continues."

I sighed after the tailor's fading footsteps and rose to my feet, finding myself eye to eye with—and uncomfortably close to—Korr. I wouldn't give him the satisfaction of shrinking back like some panicky rabbit and hitting the wall looming over me; I'd learned not to do that years ago. At least I did not have to look up at any of them these days. Rufah, with all her fierce blonde warrior airs, was the only one who stood taller than I, and by barely half an inch, if that. I had at least a stone of muscle on each of the four, wide shoulders and hands toughened by years at the forge—but none of that mattered, because I stood with my palms out, arms limp and placating by my sides, and my tormentors knew as well as I that I'd not put up a fight. Their chuckles at my open stance said enough.

"Come on, Korr, we're really getting too old for—"

The vicious slap that stung across my face ripped the words right from my lips. Disbelieving, I looked up at Korr as the other three watched with caustic glee. His sneer was a scar over his face and his dark eyes promised war.

"That was all the respect you'll get from now on. Proper punches are for people who fight back. You," he said, reaching down, and metal clinked. "You'll get the belt like the little bitch you are."

My eyes went wide and Semest laughed at the sight. "Told you Lagertes would hope for something else!"

"Don't be disgusting." Korr slid his belt free, and I took a single look at the expensive, shining leather before I grabbed Korr's now-loose trousers, yanked them down his legs and shoved him sideways into Semest and Rufah. I barrelled past a stunned Hespin, not stopping to admire the pile-up of limbs and caught ankles I'd created. The gloom in the alleyways would swallow me, but only if I ran fast enough and found a hiding place before they could recover and follow the telling crunch of gravel under my leather-soled boots.

No time to check for open doors, no time to loop back and slip into the smithy and lock the heavy door behind me. I'd have to wait them out. Veering left,

I dashed along a narrow street that ran right up to the town wall and positively flew up one of the narrow wooden stairwells. At the top, I swung myself over the chest-high balustrade and onto the ring of near-horizontal stones that protruded from the wall like a noble's ruff. Originally, they'd been set that way to stop anyone—or anything—from scaling the wall and ravaging the town, but beyond that, adventurous children had given their parents nightmares playing out here since time immemorial. It still made for a handy hiding spot for an adult if said adult was willing to squeeze themselves into the shadow of one of the three pot-bellied archers' towers that squatted over the main gate and near two smaller doorways.

Breathing hard, I pressed my back against the stones and let my head rest there for a minute, listening for the sounds of pursuit.

None came. I shifted my feet and settled in, cross-legged. It wasn't the most comfortable of nooks, and my ass would complain in a little while, but it was as safe as I could hope for. Childhood experience told me that no one could spot me from up on the walkway, not in this light, and the gates were shut and bolted by now, so no one would see me from below either. There was nothing to do but wait until it was late enough for them to have given up and lumbered to bed.

In the falling dark and setting silence, I contemplated the vague outlines of fields and wildflower-dappled meadows and steaming forests; the breeze carrying distant owl calls; the beauty of the mist obscuring the lake in the distance; the town behind me, motley and safe and snoring; the frank humiliation of being full-grown and still chased by bullies, still stuck on a stone ledge that was cold even in the middle of a summer night.

People want you gone.

That was bullshit, and we all knew it. If they'd been serious about driving me out, they'd have tried to turn the town against me—and Aneste—vendor by vendor and neighbour by neighbour until I left just to give my master back the peace and safety she deserved for looking after me in the first place. Sneers and rejection from a community this small weren't something one could live with for long. These people didn't keep you if you were wrong. It had happened before—eight years back, with the butcher's son, who'd beaten his wife into an early grave and their daughter near enough after her. The whole town had been clear about their feelings, up to and including a torch through his window. In the end, he'd vanished in the middle of the night—no one thought he'd made it across the plain and up the mountains before he ended up prey, and there was little remorse about that. This land of ours was uncompromising, and any land shaped the people in it. If the town wanted me gone—led on by the opinions of their chosen leaders or not—I'd know it.

No, that wasn't what kept the four coming after me. Stuck in this quaint town on this picturesque plateau, surrounded by a swarm of mountains and monsters, and with no prospects that suited who they thought they should be, they just plain *wanted* a whipping toy. I guess having one simply... passed the time. Somewhere down the march of the years, they had decided I was to be the one.

No, not *somewhere*. I knew exactly where.

It's not for the likes of you.

The "likes of me". The soft ones. I chuckled soundlessly. Served me right for handing Korr a flower when we were five. Didn't take long after that 'til I sported my first bruise. Took no time at all to lose whatever spark had made me pick that flower for him in the first place.

I collected a great many more bruises after that, dark blue and sickly green and bile yellow. I thought I'd got used to it. Now, for the first time, anger kindled in my chest. My head thunked against the wall again.

Sun grant them the wide world they dream of, and let it be more than they can handle. I didn't care, as long as they ended up far away from where I was perfectly fine doing everyday nothings with everyday people.

I sat, trying to empty my thoughts but instead picking at memories the way a brain is wont to do when a wound keeps breaking open.

Bastards. It wasn't like they were actually *trapped* here; not by anything more substantial and never-ending than familial expectations, surely. Daytime was perfectly safe, and the mountains not more than half a day off. You could make it there before nightfall just fine if you wanted. And even if not... Blazes, but would I really care if they wandered off into the lethal darkness—?

A sound from below me made my heart stumble in my chest for two aborted beats. Barely breathing, I came back to my body and noted how still the air felt, how little I wanted to move a muscle, how even the distant owl seemed to have dropped its voice to a softly cautious squeak. I didn't know for sure how much time I'd lost, but I knew what was below me even before I saw it. If I were wise, I'd sit as still as the rocks of the life-saving wall and hope for a sleepless night and a swift dawn... but I wasn't wise.

Boot-leather creaking, I tilted my upper body forward, forward, and looked down into the darkness pooling at the foot of the wall.

The Terror looked up at me with jewelled yellow-green eyes that cut easily through the gloom, arresting me entirely. Mesmerised, I could only just make out its huge, dappled body, four-legged and muscular, tilted forward and upward, broad nose testing the air under my perch. Its lashing, leathery tails and its halo of snare-limbs moved soundlessly, reminding me of the town's many very cute and distinctly harmless cats, and I felt without a doubt which one of us was the hunter here and which the mouse.

The Terror had one taloned paw-hand resting curiously against the smooth masonry, as if it were just then pondering the odds of a jump. My throat closed around my rising fear. None of them had ever scaled this wall, but this one was large, lithe, perfect, and to feel that jump land against the stone, to feel that power rip along the mortar and through my body...

It crooned then, right there below me, holding me fast with its verdant, birch-leaf gaze. I had known that these were no mere beasts—it was what made them as dangerous as human raiders and more difficult to deter—but at that moment, I truly understood the depth of their selves. It blinked, and I blinked back in wonder, and I had to smile when it gave a little, deep, gurgling chirp, frustrated in the way of thwarted pouncers. Then it pushed off the wall and circled once around itself, gazing up still, a sleek and elegant shadow that I felt more than saw against the dark grey ground. But what I did see was beautiful: its grace, its careful, soundless power, its cunning calculation. This was an experienced one, probably looking for sustenance to turn into milk for its young. In the teeth of its stare, its sheer majestic presence, everything was rendered utterly *here* and *now*. I felt viscerally seen by this creature that considered my body a tasty morsel indeed; and perversely, despite the fact that it and its ilk meant certain death for me and mine, being this looked at... it grounded me on my cold and comfortless perch, made me real, alive, *relevant* in a way that shook my soul. This hunter carried no malice in its bones. It *saw* me. It *understood*. It would kill, but it would *never* torment. We were equal in the push and pull of life.

"Well met, blood-bane," I whispered, and it froze, looking and looking and *looking* at me in confusion and—what? Curiosity?—until it spat a sound like a grumbling merchant, turned away and slipped off into the night.

I sank back against the stone, shaking all over and feeling giddy with it. Well, wasn't that one for fires and frying pans! I hadn't felt this good in years. I sat and stared up at a sky full of stars suddenly brighter and sharper than ever before, and I had to smother my laugh with both palms lest I woke the whole town—or brought the other pack back onto my tracks. But not long after, the Terrors' howls haunted the night, drowning out all other sound.

My grin lasted until the early morning, when I finally climbed back down to the streets and made my way to the smithy—only to find Aneste in a chaos of tools, the glass of the window strewn all over the floor, the coals flung about everywhere and black dust coating every surface of the workroom. I stood, too stunned to speak.

"They used the howls to cover their destruction. The forge is fine at least," my master said. She sat on a chair, vest and trousers stained, a dirty cloth in hand, looking sad and tired in a way that hurt. "So help me, if they'd gone for the bellows... But not even these shits are brash enough for *that*." She sniffed. "Be fun to see how well the town would like them putting us out of work for a week."

"Aneste—"

"Nevermind. It's not your fault," she cut me off.

"But it's my problem, and now I—"

"No." Her face set like a tempered blade. "You know what? I have *had* it. It ain't your problem. It's *theirs*. And by the sun, I will let them *feel* it this time." She whipped the rag she'd been squeezing between her fists and smacked it down across a counter, rising to her feet and storming past me, down the still morning-clammy street and towards the town square.

"Aneste—" She ignored me, trailing fury in her wake like heat off her furnace. I scrabbled to keep up. Aneste stormed right up to Council Ulga's front door and banged her fist against the solid oak. I tried to stop her, but she threw off my placating hands and kept up her thumping.

"Ulga! Wake up! Get yer ass out here and drag your feckless brood down with you, saves me some trouble with the stairs!" She hammered her fist against the wood again. "Ulga!"

A window creaked above us. Ulga, light brown hair dishevelled and eyes still sleep-glazed but alert, shouted, "Smith! What on earth is *wrong* with you? Has the heat finally cooked your brains?"

"Spare me the derision and get your flea-infested pups out here *this instant*. Trashing my shop in the early hours and running for it afore I can get them the kicking they deserve! I demand—"

"*Demand?*" Ulga thundered. "You come here full of poison and noise and *demand?* Of *me?*"

"And why should I not, seeing as I gave you my vote last year! Beats me why, you self-serving—"

"Aneste, *please!*" I pulled her arm, desperate now. "Please don't—"

"No, luv, it's time and past we went and said it as it is." She turned her face back to Ulga. "Fine *town guard* we have here, indeed, breaking into—"

Ulga's face vanished from sight, and Aneste sputtered to a halt, lungs still full of air and anger. "That utter—"

"Smith Aneste." Korr and his three compatriots came through the crowd that I only now saw had gathered to gawp and whisper all around us. "I must ask you to calm down now. You are causing a distur—"

He never finished his sentence. Aneste rounded on him and punched him in the stomach so hard he doubled over, and in the chaos that followed, I could only watch in helpless horror as an enraged Ulga ordered Aneste dragged away to the one cell our town boasted, already threatening the full mercy of our scant laws. *Justice*, she called it.

I walked home in a haze, drifting like a leaf on a forest stream, not knowing if people talked to me or shunned me. Ulga had told me to appear for the hearing, set for the next day because "heads needed cooling, as we all can see". And that left me... where?

I found myself standing inside the smithy, looking at the destruction, with not a clue to my name. After a while, my hands took over and saw me through the day and all the motions it required, from firing the forge to cleaning to taking customers' orders, but I was barely there. Aneste...

"*If found guilty of grievous assault, a punishment of no less than twenty lashes...*"

I have had it. I have had it.

Yes. So had I.

And it dawned on me that I, myself, didn't have to fight at all.

I lingered. I loitered. I followed four pairs of feet at a cautious pace. And then, when the day sank towards its end and they were just moving towards the gates to watch them get locked tight for the night, I stepped out of the nooks I'd been ducking into.

"Hey, Korr," I called.

They turned their heads and looked at me, surprised, for I had never addressed them this openly before. My back was turned toward the wall. My heart raced, but my feet were steady.

"What do you want?" he called back.

I walked casually away from the wall, my back now to the open meadow, the road leading out of there, curving towards the mountain. "Is your mother always this crooked?"

Korr's and Rufah's faces darkened. "You shut your mouth *right* now. As Council, she is—"

"Shut my mouth?" I grinned. "Nah, you'll have to shut it for me," I said, letting my grin slip into something wide and wicked and dirty. I felt the sun on my neck. Low as it was, it held power as it flooded its radiance through the still-open gate. "I think I know how you could do it, too—at the drop of a belt. What do you think, handsome?"

I was off before Korr's furious bellow had fully registered. The rest was almost too easy—how strange, to have such a hold over people who we all thought were controlling *me*, just because this time, I'd decided to make them angry and use their wrath to slake mine. It was like pulling dolls along on a string. The thrill of it was nearly sickening, nearly sick. I dashed across the fields and headed for the trees, flinging obscenities and coarse falsehoods and the occasional stick, laughing as I leapt over fallen trees and danced around the hollow halls of the beech forest. They kept at me for a good half hour, cursing and panting. I tugged them along, never too far away but never quite caught either, stoking their anger as much as I could, keeping the balance just on this side of not too much, not too obvious.

By the time they understood, it was too late. The gates were not quite shut yet... but they were a good two miles off.

The gurgling chirp that sounded off the trees ripped screams from their throats for the few moments they still *had* throats, and I smiled and sat down on the warm, damp, living forest floor and listened to four lives ending, four unjust, self-centred, conceited reigns ending, four burdens to probably dozens of people in my beloved town—finally, *finally* ending. At long last, I was well aware, my mind had snapped; not in a way that would make Aneste proud... but I was looking at its workings right then and found myself at peace.

A minute or two of eerie, absolute silence later, a huge presence rose up in front of me. I opened my eyes and met theirs, huge and green-yellow, the colour of teeth-baring vindictiveness. Muscles were bunching and tense under their glossy coat, lungs working, mane thrashing like snakes—heated, fresh out of a fight and not quite done yet. *Beautiful.* I grinned at the blood running down their throat, covering their legs and paws. I wanted more of that. I stood up and moved forward recklessly, hands reaching out, and the Terror barked and leapt forward, slamming into me and toppling me over into old leaves and dirt and moss with breath-taking speed and strength, pushing me face-down into sweet, clean rot and simmering potential. Its finger-thick feelers slicked over my neck, my skull, around my throat and into my mouth. My shirt tore down the back, and I wondered for just a heartbeat if that would make it easier to rip out my spine, but when I opened my mouth, what spilled out... was not a whimper of fear, at all.

Above me, the creature went motionless, snare-limbs barely twitching against my skin—waiting, scenting. Skin for skin and blood for blood, a Terror would make you pay if you fought back... but I wasn't going to. I lay there, panting and hoping and dreading, and then I made that breathy little sound again.

I hadn't known a Terror could croon, but they did then, and their hands came down on me, one spanning my entire back and pressing me down, the other moving to where their feelers were already busy pointing the way. They rid me of my trousers the same way they had done away with my shirt, leaving me lying in their combined ruins as feelers roamed my shoulders, my sides, over my thighs—I hadn't known there were so many of these nimble appendages on their kind. I hadn't known a great many things, it seemed: that I loved how good their slide felt, dry yet smooth, lethal yet enthralling; that they were dexterous enough to fondle and tease between my legs, along every seam, over and around my sex; that I could make sounds like that, sounds that bounced off the tree trunks and echoed into the night as the barrage of strokes and caresses crept ever lower and deeper; as they began to cover me suddenly in a prickling wetness; as three of those curling limbs pushed against my arse, slicking into me in a writhing ecstasy that rolled my eyes back in my skull.

I could feel them move inside me, all three, independently mobile, curling and smoothing over my flesh, warm and alarming and divine. I hiccupped a strangled laugh, moaning, and felt the Terror's nose pressing against my neck, licking the blood of my enemies over my cheek and my ear and my throat. I hissed, begging without words and not sure I'd be understood, and the feelers inside me tugged outward, spreading me, opening me in a deep, visceral pull so glorious I almost growled, almost sobbed—and then I did sob as something much larger than those feelers nudged against me, pushed into me. The unstoppable, near-overwhelming stretch arched my back and took my breath, it was so perfect.

The feelers inside me stroked around its own hardness, dozens more stirred again all over my whole body, cupping my sex and sliding up and down my shaking thighs, snaking under my body to writhe between me and the seething forest floor, and the heartbeat pulses inside me and the croons in my ear and the blood on my skin were almost too much—and not nearly enough. With my Terror's deepening pants against my hair, I keened, right hand flailing and grabbing on to their paw where it curled into the mulch beneath us. It held us close, massive body moving in tiny, torturous shifts and nothing more, their organs stirring hot and thick inside me, nothing but throbs and slithers and pressure, flattening my breath and spiralling me up and up until the devastating tension cracked and crumbled through the centre of whatever sanity I'd had left.

"Please." I pushed backwards with my hips, mindless, and again, whispering desperately against the barrier of habit and species and language, begging it to understand, and the Terror breathed a nearly question-like sound and pumped into me, three, four, five times, and I was gone, gone, *gone*, screaming and sobbing and sinking my teeth into the hard tendons of their arm as I came, feeling their own spend slick their skin and mine as it welled into me and all over me and everywhere between us.

I hadn't known that Terrors could purr, either.

THE KULWIN SIREN
EVAN NOREN

I watched the black waters spill onto the deck and wondered how it would taste. The sea around Kulwin Island had always been unkind, so I expected it to be especially bitter. I didn't bend down and cup my hands for a sampling in that moment, not with Mira nearby, but I would be proven wrong. It's like honey and brine—just like you.

Mira, at the helm of the ferry with her captain's hat on, laughed. I wore the same tired brogues from my father's funeral, and my feet slid along the teak veneered floor. Buster Keaton would've looked graceful next to me. I was more than happy to play the fool if it would make her smile.

Her face was painted by the sliver of sunset that cut through the gray clouds. Heavy rain droplets clung to her eyelashes like drowning men to flotsam. It had been over a decade since I last saw her, and she seemed entirely untouched by time. We clicked immediately, as though I had never moved away.

"The All Hallows Episcopal Church burned down a few years after you left, but besides that, it's all the same. Mosquito swarms are still thick as mist. The Blue Shard Bar still stands. People still walk the shoreline to find a private tidal pool to fool around in." The wheel spun in her hands, like a clockwork ballerina in its box. "I can give you a tour once we're on land, if you're interested. We can relive some good memories."

She took hold of the handles at just the perfect moment to see us through the violent waves. Mira was the last face I expected to encounter when I boarded the ferry, but seeing her there in her element made it hard to imagine her being anything other than a sailor. I told her she made my father look like an amateur. He'd never had any luck with the sea around Kulwin.

"I actually asked about that right after I started working on my first boat. From the way the older sailors talk of it, your dad just didn't gel. Didn't want to pay his dues or follow the rites. If he did, then the waters would have been kinder to him."

The swells calmed as our destination grew near. The lights of the harbor were pale, like the overhead fluorescents in a mortuary. Their glow revealed the faces of their ugly buildings—the deteriorating walls of a bait and tackle store, the swollen front door of a shanty, and the grim remains of an abandoned whaling station. Above them all, the Blue Shard Bar's neon sign shone down like God rays.

I made a rectangular frame out of my thumbs and forefingers, held it to my eye, and attempted to fit the entire town inside of it. "This would be a great spot for a Thalassotherapy retreat. It's a trend at the moment."

"See, Clark, that's the problem with you realtors—you're always saying some stupid shit like that. Always acting like you want everywhere you go to be chic or metropolitan. There's nothing wrong with appreciating a place for its hard edges and its harsh winds. No offense, of course." She always had a way of cutting me with a smile, even back when we were kids making out behind the columns of the church transept. A crease in her lips was all the antiseptic I needed.

We docked. The wheel went still. I had returned to a town that was never meant to be. It rested at the inlet of an island known for storms and shipwrecks. The dirty secret of the Pacific Northwest. Timeshares would never line its coast. Cruise ships would never ride the horizon's edge. Oil would never stain the shore.

The past had called to me from across the ocean and told me to come home. After my father's funeral, memories of our time on the island played on a loop in my mind like a bad earworm. Its verse was the boardwalk scorching my bare feet in the summer. Its bridge was the foul salt air. Its chorus was her—or had it always been you from the very beginning?

Did you watch us from the rocky shore? I imagine your black eyes caught the moonlight and glowed above the water like will-o'-the-wisps. If I had made the journey alone, would you have broken through the hull and dragged me down to the seabed?

I hope you take my words here as you would a tithe.

We walked past tired fishermen as they gazed off into space with glazed smiles and cold stares. Each one had the viscous vibe of someone out of step with material reality. They seemed happy to be far away from the rest of the world. Mira took my hand, wove her fingers through mine like mooring rope on a pier, and led me toward the beach. Away from all the artificial glow and into the burgeoning night.

Round stones cried beneath my feet as we walked. "You ever think of leaving?"

"I can't be far from home for too long. I get sick. Ugly sick. Must be something in the air on the mainland." She brought me to a place where the shore was thin and trees grew just beyond the inlets. Bottle caps, spent cans of sunscreen, and used condoms were littered among the tidal pools. There was so much detritus that I didn't ascribe any intentionality to the line of beer bottles that stood against the current. Not until I noticed the weathered scrolls of printer paper stuffed down their necks. Mira pulled me away from them toward the trees. "They're part of the rites. It's silly."

I pinned her to the trunk of a manna ash and pressed our lips together. Hook, line, and tongues. Spindrift coated her teeth like winter mint. She clawed at the pale lichen that tickled her back. We were young again, hiding behind stone columns, mixing tender petting with hard surfaces. The wind was soft against our cheeks, blessing our reunion.

Distant light pollution clouded the clear night like cataracts on a pupil and highlighted the contours of her body with silver. The order of our touch was a recreation of our past, like following an ancient ritual. Radiant heat rippled across her flesh. She arched into coarse bark as my feet dug into the soil. She pressed my hand to her, harder, and told me to pray.

Mira never looked at me. Fingers tight around locks of my hair, keeping me on task, but her face turned away. When her eyelids were open, she watched the sea. What little ragged breath she had in her was given to the lapping waves. She faintly whispered, "I missed you."

If I had followed her gaze a bit further, I would have seen your back cresting in the dark. I would have seen the ridges of your spine cut the horizon. I could have watched as a bottle, the one she left for you, was pulled out toward your wanting grasp by the tide.

Do you read your love letters through the amber glass? Or do you shatter them and let the ink bleed off of the page?

What remained of my childhood home was a rusted chain-link fence surrounded by overgrown dandelions and blackened ruins. It had been lost in the same fire that took All Hallows. Mira stayed at my side, kicking at crabgrass in the gravel driveway. "I thought about telling you sooner, but I was worried you'd want me to turn the boat around."

"I would have stayed for you anyway." It was a delightful bit of selfishness that made her more endearing, not less. Reminded me of how she would come up with any excuse to see me whenever she talked to my parents—community service, Bible studies, and tutoring to name a few. I don't think they ever bought it. My grades were awful, and I couldn't remember a verse to save my life.

Charred stacks of brick stood before us like cheap grave markers. The only sign there had ever been a fireplace on the plot. That there was ever warmth or family. "Think I can fashion a place to sleep out of weeds and ash?"

Mira's apartment didn't have a fence, or a yard, or a fireplace, but it was alive. We spent most of the night naked and nostalgic while making the most of our reunion. "Is the school still the same? It was so small, just a glorified house." I wove my legs through hers until we were tangled and inseparable.

"They have laptops now." We laughed as if it were an anachronism. Time wasn't supposed to move here.

Long after midnight passed, as we were fighting sleep and staring at each other through half-lidded eyes, something changed. The air became charged. The smell of ozone bled through the walls. She got up and stood naked in her window, looking out toward your holy site, past her own reflection through rain-marbled glass. Color drained from her irises, washed away like ocean foam. You were singing to her. A captivating song that made it so she couldn't even hear me call her name as she left the apartment. She stepped out, nude in the witching hour.

I followed her through the woods to the very spot where we had kissed and fucked in the twilight. You stood on the rocks like a ship run aground. You were waiting for her.

Your body is like no other. A siren, like a grotesque fairy tale, or Poseidon's rejected spawn. Just your human half alone stood above the beach as tall as a fishing boat. Your tail stretched behind you, scales shining like distant constellations until it vanished beneath the waves.

Mira fell before you, onto her knees with hands clasped as if at a pew. You craned down to meet her face. Your back was riddled with spears and flensing knives, with barnacles formed around the wounds like scar tissue.

I would learn later that there were steps to this. Scripture, hymns, and sacrament. Bottles, songs, and sex. But the moment you spotted me hiding behind the tree line, the order of operations changed. The regular ritual worship was abandoned. You, and Mira, beckoned me with open arms.

You were far more immense up close. You blotted out the sky. A whirl of stars above your head made for a dark halo. Your ears pierced with hooks from countless ancient mariners. Nets caught in your hair that draped across your face like a black wedding veil. There were so many places to tangle and trap our fingers as we stood to kiss you. Our dry, wanting tongues searched for your lips. We found no purchase, no defined rim, just more scales and skin.

Stiff, seaweed-green claspers jutted forth from your groin, as thick as fallen tree branches. One for each of us to glorify. If it weren't for Mira at my side, her

81

hand in mine as she showed me the steps to this new ritual, then I would have frozen.

Your sharp pelvic fins cut into our thighs. Hurt must be the inevitable consequence of loving you. We rode and writhed until we lost our minds, spiraling down a dark maelstrom.

From there, on top of you, I could hear your song.

I could hear you sing through her.

My voice joined hers.

I didn't know your name, but I had the many names of God to use in its stead.

The ceremony went till daybreak. Our bed was your body and the rocky shore. You were gone in the morning, leaving us bruised and naked.

In the daylight, the scales fell from Mira's eyes, and she began to cry. She said it was especially cruel of you to call on her while we were together. That night, of all nights. I kissed her to cut through the tears and gave my oxygen to her breathless lungs. We broke apart as she calmed down. "You taste like sweet brine."

No one paid us any mind on our walk back into town. Naked, hand in hand. Everyone we passed turned away, their eyes shining like sea glass with the sunrise. As if your touch never truly left them.

I tried leaving Kulwin. No offense, truly. It was all just too much for me. Mira ferried me to the mainland across still waters, and there wasn't a moment of silence between us the entire trip. We exchanged contact information and talked about our dreams and far off futures.

"What about your dad's land?"

"Just leave it as is. The decay makes it feel lived in." That made her smile, but it didn't ease the sting.

"I don't want to keep anything from you, Clark. If they want you, then they'll try to keep you. It'll hurt. It's why I can't—" She kept the wheel steady, our course locked. "But you don't have to leave. You can stay. With me."

She had already turned a sickly green by the time we docked. I helped with the mooring so that she could stay in your domain. I gave her a weak salute. "Captain Althusser."

"Mr. Eisen." She leaned over the starboard side, her weak grin a parting gift. "If you come back around, just don't bring any mainlanders with ya. Don't want them to drink up all of our seawater. Thalassotherapy is bullshit anyway." The rope fell from my fingertips, and she was all yours again.

I didn't make it far. Just barely held myself together long enough to get a hotel room. My vomit was black, wretched bile dappled with barnacles that poured down my tongue. I ruined the bathroom until it looked more like a necrotic gaping wound inside the body of the Embassy Suites. Did you hear me crying? I kept whispering desperate apologies into the toilet bowl.

It took all the strength that my pale, trembling hands could conjure to hold my phone. Mira's number was just barely visible through the ichor that blotted my pupils. I think she could smell my sickness through the receiver.

She had been waiting for me to call. "I had this hollow feeling in my chest when you left. It only got worse the further apart we went, so I decided to anchor for a bit. To wait for you." She came back for me, took me aboard, and wiped the brackish streams that stained my face.

The creek that runs into your bay echoes your voice. I can hear it from our bed. You pollute everything. Even me. Now I live with Mira, right next door to your most fervent devotees. The ones willing to raze and burn for you. I sleep with Mira, I eat at her table, and I call her home. She's a silver lining and a beautiful lure.

Mira's faced twisted with grief when I told her I intended to participate in your rites. I explained I couldn't afford to fall out of favor with you if I wanted to work on the ferry—if I didn't want to be a burden to her. I didn't tell her I can't blind myself to you, to what you do to the people who live here. I didn't tell her that your taste still lingers in my throat.

When you take this bottle, this offering, and summon me to your side—be as gentle or cruel as you like. Just make it worthwhile. Make my new prison feel like paradise as I drink you in.

EARTH SONG
MONICA CHEN

They say no woman shall enter the mountain, lest she upset the jealous goddess who lives within. It is said the goddess cannot bear the sight of other women—she will curse the earth, rattle the stones, and set fire to the trees if she is crossed.

Yisa first saw her at the edge of the river, where women weren't meant to be.

Shei stood ankle-deep in the water, her skirts hitched high and her hair half undone, skin aglow in the dying light. The men hauling nets nearby didn't look at her. Not once. Their eyes slid off her the way one might avoid a shrine to something long-forgotten. Sacred. Unspeakable.

Yisa watched from behind a tree, breath caught somewhere between curiosity and the heat that settled low in her belly. Shei was a widow, they said. Shei was trouble, they whispered. Shei didn't wear shoes in the village, only thin socks, and never spoke unless spoken to. Her house on the slope above the trees had no husband and never locked its door.

Shei turned her head slowly, as if she had known Yisa was there all along.

Yisa was known in the village for being wild. Wild and, to the old women, cursed. Men spoke her name in low tones, especially when tremors came in the night. Her father—a respected merchant and a superstitious man—tried to keep her busy and bound. He burned her walking shoes once when she snuck out. He threw salt across her threshold when she returned muddy-kneed from the treeline.

"The goddess sees you," he hissed. "She sees you, and she'll see us next."

It wasn't uncommon, the fear. The mountains were holy and wrathful. Women were warned never to cross the ridge alone. Once, an old washerwoman had wandered too close to a stream at the mountain's base. That night, a tremor split the well in half and swallowed two goats whole. The village priest had declared it divine punishment and demanded three days of prayer.

So the women stayed away. Or if they went, they didn't speak of it. And when girls like Yisa stood too long at the forest edge, mothers pulled them back by the wrist.

"Don't tempt the mountain," they whispered. "She doesn't forgive."

But the mountain called to her, and Yisa had never been good at ignoring the call.

She wondered about Shei more than she admitted. Wondered what her skin felt like, what she whispered to men to make them come to her door at night, heads bowed like pilgrims. There were stories about what happened inside that house. Shei the widow. Shei the unchaste. Shei the woman who ran alone at dusk and came back with leaves in her hair and bruises no one asked about.

And yet, when Shei looked at her, it was without judgment or indulgence. Just a gaze like the wind across a cliff—measuring whether you could stand before it or fall.

"You're not very subtle," Shei said one afternoon as Yisa trailed after her to the edge of the trees.

Yisa didn't pretend not to know what she meant. "And you let me."

"I was curious how long it would take you to stop pretending," Shei said. Her tone wasn't mocking. Just... observational. "Some girls stare at the mountain because they're afraid of it. You look at it like it's waiting for you."

"Maybe it is," Yisa said, surprising herself. "I like to think it is."

That made Shei smile—small, crooked. "Then maybe you're the right kind of wild."

A silence stretched between them, not awkward, but taut with something unnamed.

Then Shei said, "The mountain wants offerings. Your name. Your fear. Your story. If you're not ready to lose them, don't follow me."

Yisa stepped forward anyway.

"I'm not here to be safe," she said.

Shei's gaze softened, just a little. "Good."

The invitation wasn't spoken. It came with a glance, a pause in the path, a hand extended in moonlight. Yisa took it. Of course she did.

She followed Shei up the slope into blackness, past where the village lights stopped and the air turned colder. The forest grew thick; the path disappeared. The sky seemed to lean down and listen. Somewhere far behind them, a dog began to howl—and then stopped.

There were others waiting. Women. Half-glimpsed in the dark. Faces hidden behind pale, expressionless paper masks that glowed faintly in the firelight.

None of them spoke words, but they were not silent. They whistled low, fluted melodies in a strange, elegant language. The notes rose and fell like bird-song—piercing, coiling, and oddly joyful. Each woman had her own tone, a partic-ular pitch pulsing through the trees like an echo that knew the way home.

They didn't speak, but they *sang*—greetings, warnings, laughter. A language forgotten by men but remembered by wind and moss.

"Names are dangerous here," Shei murmured, tying a red cord around Yisa's wrist. "You'll leave yours behind if you want to keep it."

"And the masks?" Yisa asked. "So the goddess won't get jealous?"

Shei looked at her, bewildered. "What does a goddess get jealous of?"

"Beauty?" Yisa shrugged, unconvinced.

Shei cackled. "Beauty is mortal. The goddess doesn't care. The mask is for *everything else.*"

She gave her a mask, fresh paper, soft against her skin. The string was damp. Yisa tied it behind her head, fingers trembling.

Yisa's first night on the mountain was filled with strange sounds. Low moans of shifting stone. Cries of beasts she could not name. The other women lay together in the open, pressed shoulder to shoulder like sisters in a grave. No one removed their mask. Not even to sleep.

The ground pulsed beneath them. Like a countdown.

She dreamed of something huge breathing beneath her and woke with the taste of moss on her tongue.

The next day, they ran. They ran through dense underbrush, down slippery slopes, along leave-paved animal trails. Yisa fell, twice. Scraped her palms bloody. No one helped her up. But Shei waited at the next ridge, silent. Watching. Measuring.

They taught Yisa how to listen—to the birds that went silent too quickly, to the pressure behind her teeth before the ground shook. To the tingle in her toes when the mountain turned. They taught her how to place her feet so she wouldn't be heard. How to blend her breath with the breeze.

They bathed in cold rivers, scrubbed their limbs with clay and salt. They learned not to flinch at the sound of bones cracking. Sometimes it came from the forest. Sometimes from within.

At night, Shei lay beside her. Their fingers brushed in the dark. Unable to resist her, Yisa turned her head and whispered, "Why me?"

Shei didn't answer at first. Then: "Because the mountain wants you and you want to be wanted."

Yisa turned over, searching her face in the dark. "And you? Is that why you stayed?"

Shei exhaled slowly. "Yes. Because once the mountain touches you, it doesn't let go."

Later, when the others slept and the stars blinked coldly above, Shei reached out and tucked a strand of Yisa's hair behind her ear.

"You're louder than you think," she murmured. "Even when you're silent."

"I like to know things," Yisa whispered.

"I like your questions," Shei replied. "But ask too many, and the mountain will start answering."

Yisa smiled against the earth. "Then I'll learn to listen."

The tremors began days later.

Soft at first. Just enough to shiver a cup on a table. Then stronger—rattling roof tiles, cracking open a grain store wall. The village men muttered about women going too near the peaks. About omens.

But the masked ones already knew. The mountain was shifting. Neww was waking.

They chased the river spirits in the morning mist—white slithers of holy snakes flashing between stones. These were no ordinary creatures, but omens of shifting terrain, whispering signs in the flow of water and soil. The masked sisters called them the daughters of erosion, messengers of the goddess's unrest.

Each time one vanished beneath a rock or slipped into a hollowed tree root, they would halt and listen—heads tilted, hearts pounding—not for the sound of the creature, but for the silence that followed it. The silence of diverted water, of a drowned root system, of something vast turning slowly below.

Yisa learned to see the mountain like a map of veins. River paths, trickling currents, soft patches of wet earth where the roots no longer held. They read the land the way one reads fever in a body—watching for heat, color, displacement.

Following the swimming snakes, they reached a collapsed riverbed, the stones dry and the water gone. Where the snake had vanished, they found trees bent at wrong angles and the scent of iron in the mud. One woman, older, placed her palm to the ground and whispered, "He passed here. He is close."

They fanned out, barefoot, running as quietly as fog, weaving between trunks and ducking under low-hanging branches. The whistling shifted into silence. They were no longer singing. They were *hunting*.

Yisa ran barefoot now. She was fast. The mask no longer felt heavy. Her legs carried her like wind. Her breath matched the rhythm of the forest.

And then the ground ahead trembled, and every bird took flight at once.

They found him near the heart of the mountain, where the trees grew twisted and the soil steamed. Neww towered above them, barely visible through the rising heat. His back was a range of black ridges, uneven and terrible, like the spine of the earth cracked open. The curves of his form were not of flesh but of geography—spinal peaks that looked like stone worn down by time and tremor.

The air was thick with humidity, and something else—expectation.

Shei knelt first. Then the others. The goddess arrived last, crawling from the fog, limbs too long, eyes too bright. The goddess Mey's body shimmered with wet moss and glowed with unclean grace. She moved like something half-remembered from a dream of prey and prayer.

They circled him, the women chanting in low hums that vibrated under the skin. The ground quivered.

Mey climbed Neww's back like a spider, mouth to the earth. She whispered to the cracks in his spine. Steam hissed. Bark peeled from trees. Something ancient stirred.

Yisa stepped forward when Shei looked back.

"Are you afraid?"

Yisa's heart thundered. Her thighs trembled. "No."

She didn't remember undressing. Just warmth. Hands, maybe. A pressure in her chest like falling—but slow, expectant. The ritual was never instructed or directed, only understood, handed down in instinct and breath. The others stepped back. The goddess Mey disappeared into the mist, as if her presence was no longer required.

Neww did not speak. He rumbled.

The ground beneath Yisa's feet hummed with restrained energy as she approached him. His ridged back shimmered faintly with subterranean heat, and when she laid her palms against it, it was like touching the skin of the world. There were no clear joints or flesh—just the suggestion of form, movement in shapes that shouldn't be able to move. His breath was the draft in the cavern, slow and deep, scented like stone soaked in storm.

He turned toward her, not like a man, not even like a beast, but like a continent shifting under its own pressure. He pressed forward. Her knees buckled. She landed not in pain, but in reverence.

His hands—or something like them—gripped her hips, rough with soil, hot with pressure. He moved slowly at first, like sediment rolling through a fault. There was no rhythm but the mountain's own. She gasped, the sound torn from her throat like ripe fruit ripped from a tree.

His body opened around her. Not with cruelty. With inevitability. Every motion was tectonic: ancient, deliberate, and utterly final. He surged, trembled, pushed deeper—until there was no distinction between her breath and the steam rising from his back, between the pulse in her throat and the groan in the earth.

Shei watched from the circle, mask in place, but her fingers twitched.

Yisa moaned once. Twice. Then forgot the sound of her own voice. Her body arched, caught in a quake of pleasure and terror so deep it unspooled something holy inside her. Her thoughts stopped. Only sensation remained. Soil. Heat. Pressure. The weight of a god not crushing her, but making space for her in the mountain's memory.

And Yisa let him.

The sounds she made were not entirely human. The earth joined her chorus, branches shivering, birds scattering into the sky. Beneath them, the ground pulsed like a second heartbeat. The mountain held its breath.

And then, at the height of it—release. A roar, a quake, and soil collapsing inward, pulling Yisa under.

She was buried in darkness. A layer of soil above her chest. Another over her thighs. Over her face, her limbs, her sex.

She couldn't move. She couldn't scream.

But she didn't panic.

She had felt it. The mountain's breath. The weight of something older than gods curling around her soul.

She dreamed of root systems threading through her lungs, of stone pressing close like a lover. She didn't feel fear—only belonging.

Hands broke through. They pulled her, gasping, out of the earth into fire-light.

Shei leaned over her, mask discarded.

"You're one of us now."

Yisa blinked up at the stars. They looked brighter. Closer. Proud.

She was. She belonged to the mountain now.

The mountain slept again.

They say no woman shall enter the mountain, lest she tempt the goddess's rage. But the truth is simpler, stranger, and far older than the village dares speak aloud: Women are welcome in the mountains. But only if they come without names. Without faces. Only if they come ready to be unmade—and made again in stone, in soil, in song.

SWEETHEART
DC VALENTINE

Rhys read online that a beehive's buzz—the collective hum of tens of thousands of workers and drones serving one queen—tends to coalesce into a single note, usually one in the key of C. Once, while Parker was sleeping, he grabbed his pitch pipe to test that, and goddamn if the gentle drone from his chest wasn't a perfect E-natural.

Parker and Rhys didn't really know each other when they agreed to live together for their last semester of college. Parker was Rhys's ex-boyfriend's roommate's brother. They'd met maybe half a dozen times.

During the last weeks of what *would* have been their final semester of school, the two learned through those tenuous mutual connections they were in the same situation: that one really hard class in their respective majors—the one with the professor everyone hates—really was that bad, and now they both had classes to retake that weren't offered in the summer or available online.

They both needed a place near campus for the fall semester. They both needed at least one roommate to make rent. They both were running low on friends, their respective circles graduating and moving on.

They were both the best the other was gonna get, this late in the game.

For Rhys, it still stung bad that his ex—a junior that fall—wouldn't put him up at *his* place for just those few months. Rhys knew he had the space.

"Can't we be adults about this, Micah?" he'd pleaded with him. *"I know you're already getting serious with Alex and that's* fine. *I'm not trying to play home-wrecker and I'm not gonna be weird, I swear. I just* really *need a place to live."*

"I don't wanna have that conversation with Alex," was Micah's reply. Rhys hated that he'd have said the same in his shoes.

Rhys had noticed Parker before, the few times they'd met. Since, at the time, he'd been with Micah—and figured Parker was straight anyway—he'd never *done* anything about it, and he didn't expect that to change when they moved in together.

He did a lot more noticing, though.

He noticed Parker's tendency to wait too long to shave, how half the time he went around with a scruffy five o'clock shadow that Rhys longed to drag his lips across. He didn't know if the scruff was an aesthetic choice on Parker's part or if he just couldn't be assed to shave daily. Either way, it worked on that face.

He noticed the curls at the top of Parker's haircut and daydreamed about twirling one around his finger. He noticed how quickly Parker's cheeks went red whenever he drank, how ruffled and flustered he looked after just one beer, even though he'd put away *way* more than that before he got sloppy.

(It was disturbing how quickly they got acquainted with each other's drinking tolerances.)

They were drunk when it finally happened, barely four weeks into their cohabitation. Not *drunk* drunk. Just a couple of beers apiece. Enough to give Parker that delicious hot-and-bothered look, which wasn't much at all. They got to talking.

Turned out all that noticing Rhys did wasn't so subtle. Turned out Parker wasn't *that* straight. Something something, *"stress relief,"* something, *"no strings,"* something. And then Parker was sitting on the couch, knees spread, pants around his ankles. Rhys knelt on the floor in front of him, one hand on Parker's knee and the other resting at the base of his shaft, pulling him out of the front of his boxers so he could coax him to full hardness with his tongue and lips. It didn't take long.

Rhys had known for years he had an oral fixation. Normally, that mostly meant stocking up regularly on candy in all the best textures, but it came up on other occasions. He *really* liked using his tongue.

Sucking cock was *fun*, it felt *good*, the same way it felt good to whittle down hard candy or crush a Cheetos puff against the roof of his mouth. It felt good for the other guy too, of course.

Parker was adorably shy about it, biting his lip, clenching his fists, huffing out desperate little puffs of breath. Shy wasn't Rhys's usual type, but something about the sound of Parker trying to hold it together hit *hard*, and he let go of Parker's cock to palm himself through his jeans, start fiddling with the button. In case Parker missed that hand's attention, Rhys relaxed his throat, slackened his jaw, and dipped *way* down, touching the tip of his nose to the fabric of Parker's boxers once, twice, three times for luck, before sliding back up to reassure the head it was the star of the show.

"*Ngh,*" was Parker's eloquent appraisal of this maneuver, and Rhys's newly freed cock twitched in his hand.

The show went on for a couple more minutes, Parker so audibly impressed with Rhys's work that Rhys almost finished himself off just from those strangled little noises. Parker beat him to the finish line, though. With one more emphatic "*Ngh!*" he grabbed Rhys by one shoulder, held on for leverage, and yanked himself out of Rhys's mouth, making a perfect lollipop *pop* upon breaking suction.

Rhys frowned petulantly. Parker didn't get him in the *face* at least, instead veering off to splatter his right shoulder. But *still*. He'd planned on getting another day out of this shirt. He sighed.

"What?" said Parker, avoiding eye-contact.

"*Dude,*" said Rhys, awkwardly swiping at the mess on his shoulder, trying to scoop off the worst of it, "I was gonna swallow." Was it dumb that the thought of altering his laundry plans for the week annoyed him so much he was going soft?

"Gross."

"*Gross?*" Rhys laughed. "What's *that* supposed to mean?"

Parker muttered something inaudible and scooched farther back into the couch. Rhys rolled his eyes, then held his sticky hand up to his face and licked his lips, just to see Parker's reaction. Parker recoiled dramatically, sliding all the way to the next couch cushion over. Rhys snorted.

"Oh, grow up," he said. "You're fine sticking your dick in my mouth, but *this* is where you draw the line?"

"... It came from inside me," Parker mumbled.

"And now it's going inside *me*."

After telling Parker to grow up, Rhys was suddenly feeling way more childish. He stuck his tongue out and licked his hand in a slow, theatrical swipe, like he was licking a donut to claim it.

And that was how he found out. That was how Rhys knew.

He froze mid-lick, honest-to-God *startled* by the sensation, so shocked he almost didn't notice how much he liked it. *Almost.*

"Whoa," Rhys whispered, "What the fuck?"

"The fuck you mean *what the fuck*?" Parker was visibly struggling not to gag. "*Y-you* what the fuck?"

Rhys snorted at his flustered phrasing, then grew serious.

"This does *not* taste right, man. You have diabetes or something."

"What do you mean it doesn't taste right?"

"What do *you* mean, what do I mean? I..." Rhys shook his head. "Sorry, I guess, but that's not the first cock I've sucked, I know what this stuff tastes like—"

"Gross."

"—and yours tastes wrong. It shouldn't be that sweet." So sweet he wished he could sit on the couch eating it straight out of the carton with a spoon. And yeah, wrapping *that* thought around it was, to steal Parker's parlance, *gross*, but still Rhys's mouth watered.

Parker looked at him like someone trying to figure out what kind of animal a scrape of roadkill used to be.

"*Wow*, man."

"*Whatever*, dude, go throw up about it, and then go get a blood test, because you definitely have diabetes." At that point, Rhys wished he had a better poker face and just hadn't reacted to the unexpected taste.

Was that messed up?

"I *don't* have diabetes," said Parker, sounding strangely certain.

"Prove it. Literally. Go get a blood test and prove it."

Instead of arguing further, Parker bent to grab the waistband of his jeans off the floor, flopping back on the couch in an awkward back-arching maneuver to get his pants back on instead of standing.

It was mesmerizing.

Goddammit.

The guy *just* called Rhys "gross" after he got done blowing him, and here Rhys was, already hoping he'd let him take another crack at it. Didn't help that he was still half-hard. *Really* didn't help that the sticky mess on his shoulder still needed attention, and he kept imagining licking himself clean like a cat just to get another taste.

He wouldn't *actually* lick any more of it. At least, not in front of Parker.

Rhys bet it tasted better straight from the source, anyway. And, if he played his cards right, maybe he could make that happen. No one'd had any complaints about the way he swallowed before, after all. Parker might like it too if he gave it a chance. And if not? They could try something else Parker might like. Rhys had some ideas.

Not long after that, Rhys started to notice the bees: a buzz near his ear while on his way out the door, a blur in the corner of his eye that disappeared by the time he looked. The first time he *saw* one was in the kitchen while he and Parker waited for their geriatric coffee pot to spit out their daily caffeine fix.

Rhys had squinted at the kitchen counter for a full five seconds, wondering when and why a lone purple grape got abandoned by the sink, when the thing twitched its wings, revealing itself to be a big, bulbous bee preparing for takeoff.

Parker barely reacted while Rhys cringed his way to the farthest wall, pointing. Rhys wasn't *afraid* of bees—he wasn't even allergic—but it was too early in the morning for this shit.

Soon enough, seeing the bees became a daily occurrence, usually in the kitchen or the bathroom. They made Rhys uneasy but never acted aggressively, so they were tolerable. Parker didn't react to their presence at all.

Rhys wondered what species they were but never could Google the right terms to find out. He'd never seen bees like them before. They were huge, but it was their color that really stood out. Sure, they were black with yellow stripes, but the stripes were *too* yellow, a bright, electric hue, more like a child's crayon drawing of a bee than anything from nature.

"Maybe they're in the walls," he said to Parker once, after spotting six in one day.

"Maybe," Parker replied with a dismissive shrug.

"Should we call Maintenance?" Annoyingly, calling Maintenance in this complex meant literally calling an actual phone number instead of putting in a request online.

"Don't wanna," said Parker simply. Rhys didn't wanna either.

Later that night, Parker mumbled something about *"stress relief"* and Rhys blew him again. Parker didn't pull out this time, though he *did* make a judgy face while Rhys sucked it all down. It tasted even better than last time, so good Rhys finished in his own hand while savoring it.

He'd always loved sugary snacks, but Rhys never thought he liked food *that* way. The more he sucked off Parker, the truer it got, though, and he did that a *lot* now.

Most times, Rhys finished just from the taste. It kept getting better, no matter how many times he came back. The sweetness was that dangerously potent kind, hitting his tongue so damn *good*, like licking the buttercream frosting off a Costco cupcake.

It was *so* good Rhys craved it when Parker wasn't around. In class, at the library, in his room waiting for Parker to get home—whenever, wherever. His mouth watered, his dick twitched, and he had to do breathing exercises or else turn into a drooling pervert. Luckily, once they were both safe in the privacy of the apartment, Parker was always just as ready to go as Rhys was.

When that taste alone wasn't enough to get Rhys off, he pulled himself onto the couch after and Parker gave him a hand. He gave Parker shit sometimes about never reciprocating the *extensive* oral attention he'd received—not that Rhys was surprised—and one day that led to some mumbled questions that led to Rhys picking up some condoms and lube, and a new kind of *"stress relief"* was added to their repertoire.

Now they could leave the couch and go to Rhys's bedroom, where Parker laid back and played with himself while Rhys grabbed him by the hips and pounded his way home.

Rhys had never been a fan of missionary before, but now it was the only way he would do it, drinking in the sight of Parker hiking his knees up and arching his back like a porn-star while *still* biting his lip to muffle all the sounds Rhys could fuck out of him. Rhys always finished first like this, but watching him get there pushed Parker over the edge soon after.

Then came the best part, when Rhys backed up, dipped down, and licked Parker's splattered chest and stomach clean. It was why he insisted on missionary—despite the extra effort—because he wasn't about to drag his tongue over his own rough, unwashed sheets. Parker didn't even have any chest hair to mess up the texture. Besides, he loved the way Parker twitched ticklishly under his tongue, whispering, *"Jeez,"* as he tried to hold himself in check. *Jeez.* Fucking precious.

Things got weird in October, when Parker suddenly started shaking his head at Rhys's advances.

"Maybe later."

"Not tonight."

They went back to just third base for a while, then indulged less often, and *then* stopped altogether for four full days. (Rhys knew that wasn't *really* a long time, but it was for *them*.)

He was worried about what was going on with Parker. He *was*. But, way, *way* more than that, he wasn't ready to go cold turkey.

"So, what *is* this?" he asked sharply one afternoon after a rough midterm. "Are we just *done* now or what?"

"We could be," said Parker, voice so flat he sounded fucking *bored*.

"What?"

"We could be done," said Parker slowly, "or I could show you."

"What?" Was Parker telling this to Rhys or to himself? "You could 'show' me what?"

"You don't wanna see." Parker's tone had gone even flatter, robotic.

"I—what? Parker..." Rhys couldn't guess what the context here was, but he was pretty sure it was fucked.

Parker said no more.

"Well," Rhys restarted, "do *you* want to show me?"

"I... don't know."

"Do you want... us to be done?"

"... No." He said it so softly. That same special whisper-breath he used to say, *"Jeez."*

"Show me."

Parker nodded, stood up from the couch, and walked to Rhys's room. Rhys followed him and watched as he lied back on his bed—clothes on, for once—gripped the bottom of his T-shirt, took a bracing breath, and pulled it up to show Rhys his chest.

"... *How?*"

It wouldn't be the last time Rhys asked. Parker always gave the same answer: "I can't tell you."

Rhys never knew if Parker meant he was unable to explain, or forbidden. Maybe he was lying.

Parker's chest was covered in holes, from a couple inches below the collarbone to just above the belly button. Each hole was the size of a quarter and shaped like a hexagon, all slotting together perfectly. Honeycomb, unmistakably.

"The bees...?" Stupid question.

Parker nodded.

"And that's why..." Stupid *and* "gross". This was why Parker's cum tasted so sweet. Funny, Rhys had always thought it tasted like sugar, but never guessed *honey*. The stuff these bees churned out was more refined than any honey *he'd* ever had. More *potent*.

Each hole in Parker's chest was so deep its bottom was lost in shadow. Some looked clean and dry, but most oozed shining beads of discharge from their walls. Several were full of the stuff, spilling over the dividing membranes of flesh into neighboring holes.

The colors on display were *so* wrong. Nothing like honey or beeswax *or* healthy human skin. The discharge reminded Rhys of what he spat in the sink after brushing his teeth too hard: Splashes of frothy white, shot through with dark red threads, seeping out sickly swirls of pink.

The skin around the holes was a swollen, hot red in some places and dirt-dark purple in others. One of Parker's nipples straddled a hexagon's corner, looking like one of those malformed strawberries where the bottom pinched into multiple sections. The other nipple was missing entirely.

The smell was gnarly too, once Rhys got close enough, a sharp, copper-tinged mix of sulfur and ammonia, with a lilt of floral sweetness on top, like someone'd sprayed the rotting wounds with a single spritz of perfume.

That *was* what he was looking at, right? Wounds. Injuries. Violence. (Self-inflicted?) This *wasn't* a honeycomb, they were *holes* in a *human*.

"Parker, this... You gotta go to a hospital, man."

"What would a hospital do with *this?*"

Rhys didn't like that tone: cool, matter-of-fact, *patronizing*, like *obviously* he was never going to go to the hospital for this, and Rhys was annoying for suggesting it.

"Dude, I'm serious..." said Rhys weakly. It *was* obvious, wasn't it?

"Yeah."

"I mean, shouldn't you at least...?" At least what? *Put some Neosporin on it? Buy some Raid?*

"If you want me to show this to a doctor, make me."

"*What?*"

"Make me."

That toneless robot voice. Not sad, pissed, or even smug about the argument he was winning.

Rhys sighed. How would "making" him even work? He couldn't pick Parker up and carry him to a doctor. He couldn't call an ambulance and expect *them* to forcibly remove a grown-ass man from his own home, especially if he just pulled his shirt down and went back to looking perfectly healthy. What options were there? Force him at gunpoint? Not fucking likely. And, hell, would the threat of a bullet wound mean anything to someone with dozens of torso-holes already?

"I'm not gonna 'make' you."

"I know."

"Dick."

Rhys watched a fat bee emerge from one of the holes. He wished it surprised him more.

"... Does it hurt?"

"Yeah. Feels good too, though."

The bee flew over to land on Rhys's hand. Rhys tensed but studiously kept from moving. He wasn't allergic, but he still *really* didn't want it to sting him.

The bee crawled a few steps across his skin, and the sensation twisted Rhys's guts so hard he damn near puked.

"Problem?" asked Parker.

"*Why is it wet?*"

Rhys couldn't help it. He jerked his hand up and shook it so hard his joints clicked. The bee didn't sting, just fluttered back into Parker's chest while Parker laughed, a wheezy, painful sound, quiet and cold.

After that, Rhys *was* ready to go cold turkey—for a few days at least. *Parker* was showing interest again. Rhys didn't know what to make of that.

Despite how they left off, Rhys didn't give up entirely on getting Parker help. *He* couldn't make Parker go to a doctor, but that didn't mean *no one* could. One Sunday morning, while Parker was sunken into the couch playing Call of Duty,

Rhys plopped down next to him and asked, "Hey, I've been wondering, how's Kirk doing lately?"

"Uh... fine?" Parker squinted at the screen. "I guess? Still living with Micah..." He frowned, probably trying to figure out why, aside from proximity to his ex, Rhys would care what his roommate's little brother was up to.

"Hey!" Rhys chirped, aggressively casual. "Doesn't he play too?" He pointed at the TV screen. "Maybe we should have him over for a game night!" *Maybe*. Like he hadn't already bought a third controller for the occasion; nevermind that he'd pawned his guitar to make rent this month.

"Oh," said Parker. He paused the game but still stared at the screen. "I already told him, if that's where this is going."

"What?"

"Yeah... Here." Parker grabbed his phone from the arm of the couch, pulled up a text chain, and passed it to Rhys before unpausing and getting back to playing.

Rhys stared at it a long time.

The brief text exchange took place the previous day. First, a message from Parker to Kirk: *FYI*. Then, with no further warning or context, a photo. It was a bathroom mirror selfie of Parker, holding the bottom of his shirt up to show off the pink, puffy sieve of his chest, like some grotesque parody of a gym bro's profile pic.

Funnily, Parker's honeycomb looked a lot better in the picture than it did when Rhys last saw it. The wet discharge was gone, and the skin around the holes looked healthier. Not *healthy*, but, maybe, healing? The holes were still *there*, though. Still dark, deep, perfect hexagons.

Kirk had responded to the image with two messages: *Fuck you*. Then, *Not my problem*. Nothing more.

"What...?" Rhys didn't know where to start. Parker stayed focused on his game.

FYI.

Fuck you.

The unhinged exchange made no sense. Unless...

"... Kirk knows what this is, doesn't he?"

"Yeah." Still gaming.

"And how to stop it?"

"... Yeah." Not even bothering to pause.

"But..." But he wouldn't. It wasn't his problem. "... he seems pissed."

Maybe it made him an asshole, but Rhys wished Parker would act more upset. He paused the game again, at least, eyes still glued to the screen.

"Yeah. I... Yeah."

"Okay." God knew what *that* meant. "... Is it... too late to stop?"

"No," said Parker softly, "not until the queen gets out."

"*What?*"

No elaboration.

"Well," Rhys blinked rapidly, "how long until *that*, then?"

"I can't tell you."

Of course not. Rhys watched Parker's face as he un-paused again. His cheeks were red, like he'd been drinking, but there weren't any empties nearby.

It should have been a relief, knowing it wasn't too late to stop this, but Rhys felt like shit. Roping Kirk in had been his entire plan *for* stopping it, and Kirk made it clear that Rhys and Parker were on their own. *Now* what?

He asked Parker if he was down for some Sunday morning *"stress relief."*

He was.

The days blurred together into what Rhys internally dubbed Bee Island. His world shrank to campus, groceries, and the apartment. Where now, everywhere he looked, any time of day, he saw them: slipping in and out of the windows Parker left ajar, grabbing a drink from the wet counter by his bathroom sink, crawling in dozens over any food left unattended for more than thirty seconds, especially the sweet stuff.

Going to class was an exercise in tedium and confusion. The three-times-a-week graveyard shift Rhys worked at the campus library was hours of sleep-deprived silence and not much else. He only ever went for groceries *after* those shifts, when other graveyard shift zombies were the only ones around.

Everything outside the apartment was a dimly lit stress dream. He and Parker were the only people on Bee Island, and neither had an escape plan.

Parker's chest holes continued to heal. Not *close*, but heal. The swelling went down, the redness faded, and the smell and excess moisture disappeared. Now they looked like they'd always been there, no more foreign than his arms or legs. Rhys hated how fast he got used to seeing them.

At first, he wouldn't touch them, but inevitably, one night Parker came so hard that it all shot right past his stomach and splattered into the honeycomb. (Parker seemed to enjoy missionary more than he used to lately.) Rhys stared at it, gnawing hungrily on his lower lip, until Parker smirked up at him and said, "You know you wanna."

The shock of *Parker* saying something that saucy, without even dodging eye-contact, hit Rhys so hard he forgot to get embarrassed. He *did* wanna. But...

"Won't the bees... not like that?"

"The bees like you fine," Parker replied. Rhys didn't enjoy hearing that. Still, he found himself dipping back down, tongue already out from muscle memory.

It was *so* good.

The honeycomb's inner walls were the texture of hard candy, warm and smooth and sticky. It was *painfully* satisfying to let the tip of his tongue swirl round and round the perimeter. To touch all six corners in succession. To lap up the remnants of Parker's pleasure from the welcoming depths. His tongue easily found what felt like the bottoms of the holes, but that couldn't be right. It had to be some kind of closable membrane, protecting the bees from all this mess.

After that Rhys sometimes stuck his fingers in them, carefully testing how hard he could press that membrane. He tried not to think about what else he might stick in there if the holes were wider, deeper...

Rhys felt guilty for all the pleasure he took in something that had to be bad for Parker, but it wasn't like he could stop it, right? And Parker clearly *wanted* the bees building their hive in his insides, just as much as he wanted Rhys to keep coming back for *"stress relief"*, just as much as the *bees* wanted to keep feeding him through Parker's cock.

And the bees *were* all too happy to do that.

He could tell by the way they'd come flying out of Parker's chest while he fucked him, landing on his back, where his sweat pooled. (Rhys *almost* didn't flinch at that feeling anymore.) They'd crawl along his damp skin, tasting the salt. (He'd read online that bees tasted with their feet.) When they did, Parker licked his lips.

He could tell by the way Parker didn't pull a face anymore when Rhys sucked him off and swallowed, instead groaning out a loud, lurid, perfect E-natural while Rhys drank it all down.

He could tell by the contented hum he heard from deep inside Parker's chest when he licked him clean. He didn't whisper, *"Jeez"* anymore.

Parker changed in other ways too. He walked to campus for his class instead of driving. His groceries started to include more fruit. He shaved every morning, never giving that familiar scratchy layer of scruff a chance to return.

For a little bit, Rhys thought maybe the bees *were* good for Parker, but that illusion shattered the day he came home from class, went to his room, and found Parker restlessly perched on his bed, naked, waiting to show him his newest addition. His newest subtraction.

Parker's left eye was gone, an empty hole in its place. Not a round socket, a *hole*, just like the ones in his chest, dark and dry. At least this time there wasn't a bloody pus phase, but still, it was so much worse than the chest holes. Why was it so much bigger? *How* was an empty eye socket reshaped into a hexagon? Where did his eye *go?*

He tried to ask Parker but got, *"I can't tell you,"* as per usual, extra dismissive this time. Parker was happy, *excited*. He was in Rhys's room for a celebration smash, half-hard the second the door opened. Rhys told him no, and Parker left with a playful pout.

Rhys needed to figure out what this meant.

Parker didn't bother explaining *why* it was so wonderful. He acted like it was obvious he'd love this development, as if Rhys had come home to find Parker had adopted a puppy and *he* was the asshole for asking if it was housebroken.

It had to be good for the bees somehow, because it sure as hell wasn't good for Parker. He stopped going to his class, stopped going out altogether. Which made sense with his face like that, but it wasn't like he could do this for the rest of his life.

Unless that wasn't long.

Rhys remembered what Parker said about when it'd be too late. *"Not until the queen gets out."* The hole in Parker's face was bigger than the ones in his chest. The queen was always bigger than her workers and drones. Was this how she *got out?*

He considered trying again to get hold of Kirk, learn whatever he knew, but he'd need to get his number from either Parker or Micah. He didn't wanna have either of those conversations. It wasn't Kirk's problem anyway, right?

It didn't take Parker long to get Rhys into *"stress relief"* again.

Rhys couldn't stop staring at the new hole while they fucked. He wondered if his dick would fit in there, what it'd feel like. It was less *desire* than a hot, itchy *urge*—the kind of compulsion that made him chew his lip bloody a couple times a year—but the thought of it made him hard all the same.

The way Parker grinned at him whenever he caught him looking told him he knew what he was thinking. Even so, when the time finally came, Rhys wasn't ready.

It was close to the end of the semester. Another couple of weeks and it'd be over. Rhys was halfway sure he'd fail his class again, but he'd decided he wasn't coming back to school in the spring either way. He didn't know what Parker's plans were, and he couldn't make himself ask.

They were sitting on the couch, drinking. Parker said something about *"stress relief"*, and Rhys started to get up to head for his bedroom, but Parker stopped him with a heavy hand on his knee.

"Stay," he said, a playful lilt in his voice. Then he scooched off the couch and onto the floor, crawled between Rhys's knees, grabbed the waistband of his sweatpants, and yanked.

(Rhys didn't wear jeans often these days. The only pairs he had were too small.)

Parker's mouth was wet and sloppy, moving on Rhys with more enthusiasm than direction. It was enough to get things started, but finishing might be a challenge. Rhys didn't wanna be an asshole, but he was dangerously close to informing Parker that the goal here was *not* to just cover the shaft in slobber when Parker stopped, pulled his mouth off, and took the end of Rhys's cock between three fingers.

Wait.

He guided the head up to rest on his cheek, right beneath his new hole.

That wasn't a blowjob. It was prep work.

"You know you wanna," Parker said.

"No..."

"Liar."

"... Yeah." Rhys didn't *want to* wanna, but that didn't mean much.

"Please? *I* wanna."

Why was that so damn gratifying to hear?

The first inches went in easy. The hole was so wide at the front, the walls barely grazed him. Would this even feel good?

Farther in, though, where Rhys was halfway sheathed, the walls squeezed closer. They were warm and sticky, the same texture his tongue was used to finding in the honeycomb of Parker's chest. It wasn't *bad*, but he was glad Parker got him nice and wet first. Going in raw, he would've been scared of getting stuck as the walls held on tighter, tighter...

Maybe Parker's spit *wasn't* enough to make this feel good. Rhys stopped.

"Parker..."

"Just a little more? Please?"

Parker blinked up at him with his one good eye, the rest of his head anchored all-too-firmly in place. If Rhys made it the rest of the way in, all there'd be left to look at would be those soft, springy curls on top.

Rhys wanted to get the rest of the way in. Even if just to pull out and never touch Parker's face again.

He gently carded a hand through Parker's curls before slipping into a firm grip on the back of his head. Parker gave a hum of approval, and Rhys felt the vibration of it, almost as good as it'd feel in his mouth. Maybe this *could* feel good.

Holding Parker's head in place, Rhys sank in another inch before hitting the back.

"Oh." Rhys didn't mean to sound disappointed, but, well, he'd expected deeper. He'd expected to use his full length. Parker's head *was* pretty big, if that mattered. But maybe this was for the best.

"Harder."

"W-what?"

"You heard me."

Yeah, he did. Parker wasn't the shy mumbler he used to be anymore. What happened to *"just a little more"*? And yet...

"Say it again."

"*Harder.*"

Fuck, that was hot. Maybe that was messed up, getting off on Parker being un-Parker, but there was no dismissing the sweet pulse it sent to Rhys's cock.

He gripped Parker's curls, pulled out a couple of inches, and thrust back in. Then did it again, this time accidentally yanking Parker's head back in his struggle to pull back farther.

"*Yes,*" Parker hissed, and something inside Rhys took that as the signal to go fucking feral.

He clamped Parker's head with both hands and started thrusting like it was his ass and not his face. Turned out Rhys *could* overcome the resistance of Parker's strange texture with enough brute force, and the harder he worked, the better it felt. Same went for Parker, judging by the damn-near-melodic litany of *"yes, Rhys, yes"* from below.

As he finally established a rhythm, Rhys found the back of the hole wasn't as solid as the walls. It was softer, less sticky, and yielded a bit when he hit it hard enough. It felt like the protective membranes in Parker's chest cells. He thought maybe it was dangerous to risk damaging it, just as his cock punched through.

Rhys stopped thrusting with a yelp, caught in the full body stutter of missing the last step on a staircase, but with no way to get his balance back. It felt too damn wrong, balls-deep in Parker's skull with zero warning. For several sick, hazy seconds Rhys worried he'd *killed* him. The head of his cock was sunk deep in something horribly warm and wet. He pulled out of Parker's head and grimaced at the thick, pearlescent fluid coating his last inches.

It wasn't the same color as what came from Parker's cock. That stuff had started out white, but shifted to dandelion yellow over the past few weeks. *This* stuff was an off-white, marbled with swirls of strawberry milkshake pink.

His grimace deepened as Parker took his cock in hand and hungrily lapped up the goo. Once he got most of it, he paused his ministrations and sat back, taking in Rhys's expression with a smirk.

"Grow up," he teased. "You're fine sticking your dick in a hive, but *this* is where you draw the line?"

Hard to argue.

If this wasn't Parker's honey, what was it? Rhys thought of all his online reading on bees, recalled an image of larvae sealed into cells full of sweet, white slime.

"Is the queen in there?" Rhys asked, guts seizing and sinking.

"Yes. Do you wanna meet her?"

"*No.*"

"Not today," said Parker with a nod, like he was agreeing, even though that was *not* what Rhys said. That was how Rhys knew.

Either he stopped now and, probably, Parker was done with him, or sooner or later, Rhys would see the queen get out. He'd see whatever happened next, whatever "too late" meant.

Parker ducked his head to suck the last of his jelly off Rhys's cock. Rhys thrust into his mouth without meaning to.

Huh. Still hard.

Parker had no complaints, just kept sucking. Already, it felt better than last time. Rhys nestled his hand into the curls on top of Parker's head, twirled one around his finger.

Not today. But he was going to meet the queen.

THERE'S SOMETHING IN THE FOREST
MANDY S KNIGHT

There's something in the forest.

That's what they keep telling me. I don't believe them at first; it doesn't make sense. There are lots of things in the forest. I've only just arrived here, wherever *here* is. Although they kept assuring me I wasn't, I was convinced I was dreaming. Now, nine hours later, I'm not so sure.

It's gone on for too long.

It's my first night; when Starrick builds the fire, he promises us the light would keep the forest away. I laugh. *That's ridiculous*, I think. I don't believe him.

I lay curled beneath the thin robe they gave me, tucked in tight to keep the cool night air off my skin. Starrick keeps watch, letting me and the others sleep. That's when I hear it.

There's something in the forest.

Something unholy.

Something shrieking in the night.

Screams—the noise enough to rouse me from a dead sleep.

A shiver runs down my spine.

I believe him now.

THERE'S SOMETHING IN THE FOREST

The second night, I stay awake. I want to hear it again. I keep the fire alive and watch the forest, wrapped in my robe. Sleep is impossible. A thin layer of fog covers the woods, settling low to the ground. Fingers and wisps reach toward me across the clearing, shrieks and screams riding them.

Closer. Closer.

My blood chills. The mist rolls over our camp, permeating me to my core. The haunting cacophony reverberates through my head, driving me to the brink of madness.

I fall into a waking dream of rushed emotions and shrill noises. Shadows trace over my sensitive body. Breathless murmurs and puckered flesh. The forest closes around me, nestling me in its leafy embrace.

By morning, I'm flushed. My breath is shallow.

Starrick puts his hand on my shoulder and I jump, wrenched back to reality. I look up from his brown steel-toe boots into his charcoal grey eyes, his wild salt and pepper hair even more dishevelled from a restless sleep.

"Are you well, Ayla?"

How can I explain to him I am *more* than well? How can I possibly explain that the noises from the forest do things to me that I just don't understand?

I shiver, plastering a hollow smile on my face, and nod. "I'm fine, Starrick. It was a quiet night."

It wasn't a quiet night, but at least no one from our camp was taken. I turn to the trees. Is it just me, or— "Did it move closer?" I ask, intrigue crinkling my brow.

Starrick follows my gaze and nods. "Aye. It does look that way."

Impossible. How can an entire forest move closer? "Do you think we should move on today?"

"I fear we've overstayed our welcome in this clearing," Starrick agrees with me. "We were here a few nights before you staggered in. It seems to be moving quicker than before."

Goose-pimples rise up my arms, and I rub them beneath my robes, staving off the chill from my bones.

I don't remember arriving here. Starrick says I stumbled in, screaming, covered in blood and babbling incoherently. The camp mother washed me, searched me for wounds, but the blood wasn't mine.

I don't know what happened.

It doesn't take us long to pack our camp. Tents and blankets are rolled away and stowed on the ass. Pots and water-skins, too.

I don't have anything. It's just me and the robe they gave me, and this strange feeling inside. I watch the forest, but it stays quiet.

Starrick kicks out the fire. "Time to go, lass."

I startle, having been lost in the eerie depths within the trees, trying to find the source of my discomfort. My temptation.

We walk only a short distance. It doesn't feel like far enough, but they assure me it is. Another clearing facing the woods, another chance to live through the night.

We gather around the fire before full dark, roasting squirrels and rabbits on a spit. Camp Mother tells us our history.

"It came for us one night. A night, much like this one, when we were many instead of few. We didn't roam as much back then. We were trying to make a life. Make a home outside the forest.

"When morning came, one of us was gone. We found his shoe halfway to the woods. We found his head a little farther on."

I shiver as dusk settles over us. Starrick builds the fire higher, banking out the night.

"We found his body right at the treeline. Without a head and gutted like a fish. We brought him back to camp, buried him close by. We thought that was the end of it.

"When dawn next broke over our camp, another was gone. It had come for us again. We found his foot, halfway to the forest. We found his head, a little further on."

Night sounds and crackling fire break through the silence that has settled in the stillness of her words. Crickets chirp, fireflies glow. Camp Mother continues.

"We didn't find his body, but that night, we heard *it*. The shrieks, the screams, the moans and groans. Coming from out there. And that's when we knew.

"There's something in the forest. That's why we move."

I sleep that night. Troubled dreams of dark creatures and uneasy growls. Dark wisps explore my fevered skin. Pulling, tearing, pushing at me. Shadows lock around my body, drowning me in their murky embrace.

I awake with the dawn, flushed, rushed... *piqued*.

He's gone.

The man who camped beside me. I'm ashamed to admit I don't know his name. His bedroll is empty, crumpled, like he left in a hurry, leaving behind only a memory of his presence.

"It's happening again." Starrick runs his hand over his face, exhaustion lining every bit of his skin. "It shouldn't happen so soon."

I look over the field between us and the forest. He points out what I'm missing.

His boot, halfway to the trees.

I walk into the field; I need to see the truth for myself. It's right here, his leather boot. I nudge it with my foot and it turns. White bone sharp where it juts from the opening, cracked and bloody, it faces the sky.

There's something in the forest.

It's watching. I feel its eyes slither down my body, as curious about me as I am about it. I watch it back, lips parted, and reach my hand to my neck, fingers tracing the hard lines of my taut muscles.

I quiver at my own touch. My breath grows heavy.

"Ayla!" Starrick shouts. I drop my hand and the feeling fades. "Come away from there. We need to move."

I don't want to, but the protest sticks in my throat. Slowly, I tear myself away and head back to camp. They're ready to go.

My feet drag this time, more reluctantly, but I follow. I don't remember how I got here, but these people are all that I have. I have to stay with them.

I want to understand this lure. This curiosity to the forest that devours our few.

The blood I wore when I arrived, whose was it, if not mine? The scream that tore from my throat, where did it come from? What was I saying that night? Do they remember? I wish I did.

This part of me that's missing, that dreams of dark things in the night—it has to come from somewhere. *I* have to come from somewhere. I'm the unknown, the missing, the found. Starrick calls me Ayla, but who am I? Where do I call home?

I walk in silence. No one speaks, but branches snap and satchels rustle and the ass brays.

Still, I feel *it* looking at me. I idly stroke my skin, my touch searing a reminder into the charged flesh.

Farther, tonight.

We make camp, pitching tents and unrolling blankets, the distance between us and the forest greater than before. There's a free blanket now; he won't miss it. I claim it as my own, wrapping myself in the warmth of wool, and hunker down for the night.

It's fully dark when I awaken. The fire is low. Whoever is on duty will be in trouble for endangering the camp.

There's something in the forest. I hear the shrieks. I hear its screams. My blood surges and I stand. Heart in my throat, I tiptoe to the edge of camp, and I look.

I see Starrick—he's there. His back is to our camp, so he doesn't see me, his disheveled hair glinting in the moonlight. The fog reaches for him, swirling toward his legs.

I can't let him die, too.

My feet are swift as I rush over the grass, but it's too late. Something grabs him, severing his leg. It spins and pauses in the air. Then... it drops and he's gone, pulled into the trees. He doesn't make a noise, but the forest is alive.

THERE'S SOMETHING IN THE FOREST

There's something in the forest. I have to see what it is. I follow its call, tracing his trail.

I find his brown steel-toe boot halfway to the forest. Tattered flesh vivid red in the dark, and white bone, marrow seeping out.

I find his head a little farther on. Mouth open in distorted fear. *Goodbye, Starrick, you were kind to me.*

The forest sounds near. Screaming, shrieking, crying out for me.

I keep going and it looms, towering above me. I take one last look at our camp, fire low without its keeper. *Please, let them be safe.*

There's something in the forest. This time, it's me. I enter its domain when I step over his body.

It's quiet here. The sounds I heard from camp are still. The air is heavy and dank, but light on my skin as I brush through branches and stumble through the shadows.

Darkness caresses my cheek, and I sigh. "Why do you do this to my people?" I ask out loud. Wisps pull at my robe, and I clutch it tighter to me.

I continue into Darkness, led by an unseen force. It whispers in my ears, tickling my skin. It's warm here; I'm flushed, heated from this desire that I can't explain. A touch traces down my back. This time, I let it take my robe, relishing the damp, cool air as it clings to my fevered skin.

Almost there, it seems to be saying, urging me forward. *Keep going.*

I stumble on through branches and brambles. They catch my skin, but I don't stop, not until I'm there. The scrapes and cuts feel like a balm, soothing the frenzy surging inside me.

A small clearing opens before me, and she awaits. Darker than shadow and denser than night. She turns, suspended from the trees, vines connecting her inky body to the forest around her. They lower her to the ground, her bare feet sinking into the loamy undergrowth, and she beckons me closer, threads of darkness swirling around her hand.

"There you are," she says, and pulls me close. "You've been gone too long." Her voice is a sultry lure to my senses.

Hair of leaves wraps around her head, trailing down her back and rooting to the woods surrounding us. Her nakedness disguised with foliage, black and grey in the shadows of the night. The heated look in her fathomless eyes captures me, compels me.

Yes, I remember everything now as I gaze tenderly at my love. I belong to her, and she to me. Her hand trails down my cheek, her touch cool, bearing the softness of new growth, and I tip my face toward her.

She leans forward, kisses me, tongue taking what's hers. It strokes mine, strong, secure, wanting. "I'm home now," I say when I break our kiss, pulling back to rest my forehead against hers.

Dark shadows streak around us, pushing us closer, before creepers pull me back.

"Let me look at you," she says, and rakes her hooded eyes down my bare body. I shiver, quivering under her intense gaze. "You're beautiful," Darkness of the Forest tells me, a heat glowing in her eyes. A matching throb pulses between my legs.

I know what comes next.

There's something in the forest and I couldn't stay away. *She* is the forest. My heart, my soul, my lover.

I find a stump and slide onto it, spreading my legs wide for her. I know what she wants. It's time for Darkness to feast.

"You've been busy," I murmur as she comes closer, toes skimming the moss, her eyes never leaving mine. She stops between my thighs, tendrils of shadow caressing my breasts.

"I wanted you home," she admits. The power I have over Darkness makes me wet. She can smell it, musky but sharp. She inhales, taking my scent deep inside. "I knew you'd come back if I took more of the men."

I lean back, baring myself to her. She's right. I couldn't stay away; I had to learn the truth.

Her shadows swirl over my nipples. They're cool and light, and I peak at her touch. A moan escapes my lips and I meet her eyes.

"I missed you, too."

THERE'S SOMETHING IN THE FOREST

We've played this game for as long as I know. My light to her darkness, my obsession for her touch. I forget, I fear, I tremble and shake but always lured in. A moth to a flame, a woman to her lover. It never matters how far the camp moves, she always comes for me. Fog reaching. Pushing, pulling, pulsing, taking.

Feeding.

Darkness kisses me again, her tongue flashing deep inside my mouth, brushing my throat as she delves deeper and deeper. I choke, and her hand is on my neck, squeezing. "*You're mine.*" Her voice inside my head, as deep as her tongue is in my throat. "*I want to hear you say it.*"

Shadows twist up my thighs, finding my wanting centre to stroke my aching pussy. My head drops back, and I'm free from her tongue.

"Say it," Darkness growls as she pushes herself into me.

Tendrils of shadow merge with her hands and she's deep inside me, stroking my core. She pulls out and splays me wide, fingers pulsing my entrance.

I'm alive at her touch, a fire building within me. Searing my veins, scorching my soul. A deep ache fills me, wanting her. Nothing but her.

I reach for her, desperate to feel her skin, but my fingers only glide through silken shadows.

"Say it," she demands, her fingers rocking into me again, nails dragging on the soft flesh within.

I groan. It hurts so bad but feels so good. "I'm yours." My voice is barely a whisper. "I'm fucking yours and no one else's."

Darkness drops to her knees. "Good girl," she whispers into my pussy before sliding her tongue through my wetness. She circles my clit, and I'm panting already.

My back arches me into her lips, and shadows claim my tits again, squeezing and flicking and making me moan while she's deep inside, fucking and sucking and bringing me to the edge.

"*Not yet,*" she warns, but doesn't stop. I have no control; she has all the power here. I try to hold off.

I count to ten, I think. I try. I've lost count. I try again, but she's driving me to madness. Her tongue enters me, too; her shadows stretch me wider.

I'm full of her. Her fingers, her tongue, her darkness. Stretching me wide, fucking me deeply, her shadows relentless in their mission. My pussy an endless chasm for her to explore as she pours more, more, *more* of her shade inside.

She slides in and out, slowly, then fast. Every inch of me is consumed by her, I'm surrounded by her shadow, muting my other senses. All I can feel is her. All I am, it is hers. Full of her, full of her touch, full of her dark delight.

I moan, the sound earthy and desperate, needy for release. I can't take much more of this. My breath comes in little puffs as I try to catch it, my heart beats too fast. I'm coming apart at the seams, but I hold on.

Not yet, not yet.

Faster and faster, she moves. Deeper and deeper, she seeks. Fuller and fuller, she pushes. Until *finally*.

"Come for me."

I shatter, obedient as always. A shriek pulls from my lips as I'm torn apart; where I end and she begins, I don't know. She doesn't waver. She makes me ride this high, wave after wave. I scream, I think I'm crying, I moan, I think I'm drowning, I laugh, I'm coming up for air, and she stops.

Darkness pulls out her tongue, slides free her hands. Her shadows stay deep, stroking the molten depths of my core as I pant, I whimper, I follow the aftershock.

Her lips meet mine. I can taste myself: salty, musky, sharp. She's cut me, I realise; the taste of my blood mingles with the taste of me.

My arms snake around her, hands creeping up her body to cling to her vines. Thorns pierce my skin, marking me again as hers, and I cling to her mouth, desperate for one more kiss. Her lips ghost mine.

"I hate when you leave me." She pouts as she pulls away, shadow and body. I'm empty, deflated, but lay there spread, still for her.

"I hate when I leave you, too," I admit. "But it has to be this way. We have to feed the Forest." I have to feed the other parts of her, too. My flesh only satisfies her soul. The men, their flesh satisfies her hunger.

Darkness of the Forest frowns, but nods. She understands. "I left his body for you," she tells me. "Near where you came in."

THERE'S SOMETHING IN THE FOREST

I nod sadly. This is it, I think, remorse pooling in my stomach, the culmination of our game. It's time for me to leave the forest and lead them away, to begin our deceit again. I don't want to, but the Forest needs to be fed. My bottom lip trembles, knowing once I leave her threshold, I forget who I am.

I forget *her*.

Vines carry her as she walks me through the trees, still and quiet in the pre-dawn gloom. Before I find him, Darkness pulls me close, ivy and shadow wrapping around me.

"I love you, Light," she whispers into my lips before meeting them, her touch gentle. Caring. "Until next time."

She stays while I continue, vine's touch lingering on my skin. I turn back when I find him, but she's already aerial, melting into shadows. I raise my hand in a final farewell and touch my lips, remembering.

There's something in the forest.

But she's quiet now, sated and fed. For their sake, I hope for a long time. For mine, I hope she hungers soon.

I turn to Starrick's body and kneel, dipping my hands into the empty cavern where his stomach used to be. I coat my arms in his blood and wipe them down my face, my breasts, my legs.

Goodbye, Starrick. You were good to me once.

I stumble into the light, the morning sun blinding me. I look around. A field, a clearing. I turn wildly. A forest looms over me. I cry out and stagger towards the camp I see in the distance.

I'm crying. Whose blood is this? Tears streak down my face as I run towards safety.

"Ayla!" a voice calls, but I don't know it.

Are they talking to me?

"Ayla, are you okay? Where have you been? What happened?"

Strong arms pull my naked, bloody body close.

"We need to take you to the camp mother."

There's something in the forest. It calls for me, even now.

IN THE BLOOD
JOACHIM HEIJNDERMANS

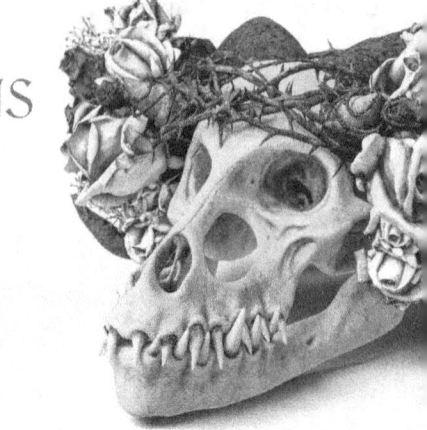

I have always been afraid.

As a child, I feared the dark and the monsters that lurked within. Between youth and womanhood, I became terrified of the boys and their eyes, their hungry gazes and their fingers, daring to grab and touch my skin without my approval. As a grown woman, yet still small and so rake-thin I am often mistaken for a boy, it was the solitude from being an unwed maid with no family to protect me that now fanned the flames of my terror. Being alone was mortifying. Or rather, it was the not knowing for certain if I *was* alone.

I would steal glances at the shadows.

Always on guard.

Always expecting to see eyes.

Eyes.

Eyes everywhere.

Always watching me.

Preying on me.

I've always been prey.

Only *now* do I feel some modicum of safety. Ever since the vampire crept into my home... and into my bed.

The wind howls through the windowpanes.

IN THE BLOOD

Rain hits the thatched roof; droplets of water seep through the holes I have yet to repair.

I sit by the fireplace. The flame in the hearth is dying. Soon the darkness will engulf me.

The vampire sleeps in the bed upstairs.

No eyes watch me.

I inhale deeply, gripping the air within my lungs. This peace... I hope it lasts. I pray it does. Yet, I know it cannot. This is the only house for many miles around, so travelers are bound to come by.

My solitude lives on borrowed time.

I gently bite down on my lower lip, just enough to cause pain, but not so much that I draw blood.

I mustn't bleed.

The vampire will smell it.

They came the first time because they smelled the open wound on my arm. Compliments of a nail I hadn't seen until my skin already scraped against it. They entered my home, cold and hungry after a long journey from Lord-knows-where, tasting the scent of me in the air.

My blood.

The *only* blood they feed on.

I... I do not know why just mine.

Others have passed through, but the vampire does not want their blood. Only mine.

They must love the taste of me.

And considering what they give... What I feel in return...

It's the wickedness.

The evil.

That sultry, sinful, ravenous part of me that has marked me for the pit.

That, what I cannot rid myself of.

That, what is in my veins.

With all my strength, I force my teeth away from my lip. It is bad enough that the blood of my body's cycle draws the vampire to me, so for the sake of my soul I mustn't lay before them more temptation. Their hunger will be ignited. Their other desires will awaken. They will want me. They will feed. Subjugate. And... and—Lord, help me—I will want them to.

I am a wicked woman. *Sinful*, as the pastor would say, were he to know what I do, hidden away in the home that was once a place of good and honest people. I could always say it was because of the vampire that I descended into carnal decadence. That I became the blood-drinker's harlot under pain of death.

But that would ignore that it was *I* who lured *them* into my chamber. *Mother Mary, forgive me*, but I did not even do *that*. I glance at the table whereupon I had laid myself down, dress hoisted, legs parted, cunt eager and willing for the vampire to use.

Lord, forgive me for my sinful desires.

Lord, forgive me for sheltering the monster.

Yet, for all the sins I have committed with my monstrous companion, that fear, that paralyzing fear that has gripped me for so much of my life, is dulled within their presence.

Is it love? No, I doubt what I feel is anything so powerful.

Security, then? Perhaps. That feeling that I am protected by a powerful force, if only as compensation for supplying the vampire with food and delights of the flesh? I cannot confirm what makes my fears melt like snow in the sun, but at least I no longer feel eyes upon me.

I look up at the cross my grandmother carved in the wood above the hearth, so this home would forever be guarded over by the Almighty. It failed to keep the vampire at bay. Perhaps the cross does not work on those who cannot see it? Or perhaps the Lord brought my "guest" as some sort of protector, to relieve me of my fears of being alone? No, a fanciful thought. The vampire is not of this world. And what we do? It cannot be anything *but* a sin, a terrible act I must discourage at every turn.

It takes all the strength I can muster to ignore the yearnings in my heart... as well as the ache for the vampire's touch.

Wait? What was that? That was not the creaking of wood. The vampire sleeps still. Was that... No, it could not be footsteps, could it?

A knock at the door.

I leap up, pressing myself against the wall.

Dead silence as I hold my breath.

Another knock.

"Hulloh! I say, I saw a bit of smoke from the stack. Is anyone home?"

A man's voice. I dare not answer. I know what men want. *All men.* They take. They take it all. Food. Property. Flesh. And they'll hurt me to have it.

"Beggin' pardon, but is anyone home?"

I make myself small. If I stay silent, he'll leave.

Unless there's more than one?

Brigands! A rabble! An entire group!

They'll break in! They'll take all I have! They'll take me! I am not safe!

I!

Am!

Not!

Safe!

Closing my eyes, I think of anything else.

The warm fire in the hearth.

The silence once they leave.

The vampire in my bed.

Our bed.

Despite my fear, I dare to look again.

Eyes!

Eyes, peering through the window. A man with a beard so thick it enlarges his face, making his jaw massive. Droplets of water dangling on the edge of his thick brow. He looks more beast than man, calling to mind the bears and wolves that once roamed the land. With starving eyes, he leers at me, no doubt eager to plunder and use me.

I am the lamb in the sights of the wolf.

At his mercy.

Prey.

"Hulloh," he says again, his face contorting to a smile. "Please, ma'am, might I come in to shelter from the rain? I can pay for my lodgings."

I tremble. I dare not look away. I should deny him entry and hide.

But then he'll storm the door.

He'll break the glass.

More will come in.

They'll have clubs.

Knives.

They'll take me.

Hurt me!

"Ma'am, please," he mutters shyly while rummaging through his purse to pull out a shilling. "I have money. And food. I shan't ask anything from you. I just need a place to find shelter." He suddenly drops the shilling, reaching down and mumbling to himself as the rain drenches him. "Bloody 'ell, almost lost me wage there, dinnit?"

He's laughing.

Smiling. Smiling despite being cold and wet.

The fear that grips my body grants me a moment of lenience. I feel the blood return to my arms. It's not the offering of coin, but the clumsy way he holds it.

Am... am I safe?

I... believe... believe I can trust this man.

With a gentle step, I approach the door. Having no weapon, I take a risk in allowing the man into my home. But it might not be hazardous. If anything should happen, the vampire might come to protect me.

Might.

With a pull, I open the door and allow the stranger entry. This place could hardly be considered hospitable. One small fire and the only sleeping place is currently occupied by the vampire. A part of me hopes the man will balk at the sight of my home and scurry off to find shelter elsewhere.

Alas, he's too drenched and cold to say no to any reprieve from the rain. He even smiles at me as he enters... our eyes meeting.

Eyes.

Eyes on me.

Looking into me.

Seeing my fragility... my weakness.

Teeth.

Teeth like fangs.

I have let the wolf into my home.

"Thank you, ma'am. May the Lord bless you for your kindness." He holds out the coin, gesturing at me. "Here you are. For your troubles."

Through some unknown strength, I grant him the slightest of nods. I even force a smile, though I am more inclined to scream.

With a trembling hand, I take the coin.

Any moment now, he'll grab me.

He'll hurt me.

Yet again, he takes his time, marching over to the hearth and warming his hands by the dim flame.

"Ma'am, your fire is dying. Permit me to reignite it?"

Do I answer? Do I grant him this request? As mother would say: "*give them a finger, and they'll take the hand*". What further boundaries will he push? What more will he take?

"Ma'am?" the man asks.

"Yes!" I cry out. He jumps, startled by my outburst. I hadn't meant to shout. I didn't. But the fear is stronger now. My nerves a strand of wool, grazing against the knife's edge. I must try to soothe the situation. "I mean... Please, do... do as you like."

"Ehmn, yes. Of course. Thank you, ma'am."

As he tends to the fire, I make my way back to my chair. He sits close to it. Too close. Part of me does not dare approach him. I ought to take my leave and hide within my chambers.

But he would question that. Or worse, consider it an invitation.

He would follow me.

He would see the vampire.

No, I brave the terror that grips me and approach him. He appears to have only eyes for the fire, which calms my nerves. Perhaps I am fortunate. Could this be a simple man? A kind man? One with no ill intent, who will leave once the rains stop?

He looks at me and smiles.

My jaw clenches.

My heart races.

I nearly dig my nails into my skin, but I dare not wound myself.

Blood cannot be drawn.

I mustn't wake the vampire.

The man speaks. "Are you here all alone, ma'am? I don't mean to pry, but I don't see anyone else present, or evidence of anyone having been here at all."

Do I tell the truth? No, that would reveal the presence of my companion. But if I lie, do I create the illusion that I *have* been here alone? That I am vulnerable?

How do I answer?

What do I do?

What?

What!

Lord, give me strength!

A memory returns to me.

A strong body atop me.

My blood being drawn.

Teeth in my flesh.

My wickedness.

The sinful part within me that I cannot escape.

That evil in the blood.

"I... I am alone, ever since the passing of my mother and father."

"Oh, my apologies. May the Lord keep them," the man says humbly. "I take it there's no husband to care for you then?"

He mocks me. Surely, he's aware of my appearance. Pale of skin. An overbite that would never encourage any boy to steal a kiss out of affection. A flat chest. No, never would a man be tempted to wed a woman that looks like me. Women like me only draw predators, men who inflict pain on easy prey. A woman like me can only find solace in the presence of monsters, and even then, we're left bleeding.

My silence confuses him. With a cough and a mutter, I answer. "No, there is no one."

"More is the pity, then," he says with a smile. My expression must have betrayed my horror at his remark, as he immediately begins to recant his words. "I mean—what I aim to say—oh, blast. My apologies, ma'am. I had no intention of putting you on the spot."

So frozen am I by terror, I fail to realize I have buried my nails into my palms. In a panic, I check for wounds. If the vampire smells a drop—

"Ma'am? Are you alright? Is everything in order?"

My jaw clenches.

Sweat pools underneath my clothes.

Fear stings my heart... just under where the vampire has left me my scars.

"I... I—" I mutter.

The man holds up his hand. "Please, ma'am. I can see I disturb you with my presence. I cannot say what it is I could have done to upset you so, but whatever my transgression was, I sincerely apologize," he says, nearly whispering. "Do I frighten you? I mean you no harm."

He rummages through his knapsack, revealing a loaf of bread, a slice of cheese and a sausage.

What is he doing?

Is he... offering it to me?

Is he being kind?

"Please, have some. Please take this as further payment for my stay."

I... I do not know what possesses me to accept these gifts. It is simple, and there seems to be nothing wrong with this offering.

Doubt.

Doubt hits me once more, like a hammer to bone.

I have always been afraid. Even around the vampire, I am still afraid.

But doubt will come and strike me at times.

Is the world truly that wicked?

Are the wolves really as close to the door as I imagine them to be?

And how much more wicked can he be than I?

I am the one who is tainted.

The evil lurks within *my* blood.

The blood that feeds the vampire.

Perhaps... perhaps there is no ulterior motive behind this man?

Could it just be me?

I stand in silence, pondering these gifts. I look at the man, meeting his eyes. I see no hate. No malicious intent. Only... concern.

I cannot believe myself as the words leave my lips. "Would... would you like something... to eat?"

He smiles. "I would enjoy that very much."

I retreat to the table, taking a plate and some cups. "I... I have no spirits... to offer you. Only milk and water."

"Either will suffice for the likes of me," the man says with a chuckle.

To my own surprise, I find myself smiling back.

He has a... calming presence.

It is as if he can feel my fears, the tension that grips itself onto my being... but chooses not to abuse it.

Perhaps I misjudged him.

I take out a knife to slice the meat.

Perhaps he has no ill intent. I could let him stay for the night.

The blade's edge slips into the sausage.

Could I, for once, feel safe around an outsider?

I cut the slices too thin.

Could I manage being watched by a set of eyes?

A sting in my thumb as crimson drips down toward my wrist.

"Oh!" I gasp, startled more by the sight of sliced skin than any pain I ought to feel.

"Ma'am?"

I look at the wound.

Blood.

Blood on my hand.

Blood in the air.

Its scent stirs something in me.

I ought to be nauseated. Frightened, even.

But no. I am awakened.

I gently writhe my legs against each other. Pressing my knees together, I try to keep my lust at bay. My uncut hand grasps onto my dress, clenching the fabric so to take my mind off the blood.

But I fail.

The light has been turned.

My body knows what the sight of blood brings.

The promise of pleasure soon to be fulfilled.

"Ma'am? You're hurt! You're bleeding," the man says. "Here, let me help you."

His eyes meet mine, now wider. The small irises appear to drown within a sea of white.

Wide eyes.

Powerful eyes.

Looking at me.

Looking.

At.

Me!

Looking.

Looking!

No!

No, no!

No, no, no!

I cannot.

I am not.

Not safe.

Not alone.

Eyes are on me.

I need help.

I need them.

I... I need my vampire.

I need their touch.

I need—

"Here, take this," the man says, holding a cloth for me to take. "Press this on the wound."

Stop the bleeding?

Stop it?

Take away the lure that brings the vampire to me?

Above, a creaking of wood.

The bed!

I jump. Not out of fear or concern, but out of want.

The want to be touched.

The want to be fed upon.

I—Lord, save me—cannot go without it.

And this man wishes to stop it?

I look at him.

I see his eyes.

Eyes on me.

Eyes!

On!

Me!

Any goodwill I might have is lost in his insult.

How *dare* he insinuate I do not wish to bleed.

I am a wicked woman.

My evil is in the blood.

That blood is the only thing that gives me security.

Gives me pleasure.

And he would take that away?

Rob me of it?

I inhale, then speak: "Get out."

"I beg your pardon?"

"Get out!" I snap. "Out! Out! Out, out, out, out!"

The man hesitates. Does he intend to overpower me? To force me to recant and let him stay?

With a blind fury, I reach into my pocket and take the coin he'd paid me, throwing it at him as I howl like a wild animal.

He stares at me, then at the coin, aghast at my outburst.

For a moment, he shuffles his right foot.

He's contemplating approaching me.

He's coming for me.

He'll overpower me!

Do I try to find a weapon to defend myself?

Will he take it and inflict harm on me?

Will he... kill me?

The man stares at me with those eyes. Those terrible eyes. Yet... there is something in them. Sadness? Pity? Remorse for what he's done to me?

Whatever the case may be, he relents to my demand, shuffling toward the door, his knapsack thrown over his shoulder. He does not take his eyes off me.

No!

Stop looking at me!

"Out!" I roar.

Shaking his head, he exits, turning back once more with a confused look. I pay it no mind, slamming the door shut and pushing the beam in place to lock it.

I reclaim my solitude. And perhaps I have spared him from the horror that is about to unfold.

The horrors I crave.

Tears stream down my cheeks. My legs tremble as I fight to stay aloft. I gasp for air. I wish to howl in terror, but I cannot muster the strength to voice my pain.

This terror.

The absolute horror of it all.

Hell is real... and it is the eyes and the laughter of others.

Only here do I feel safe.

Alone. No, not alone. With my vampire.

The boards creak. The vampire has awoken from their slumber. I stand there, my hands pressed against the door, thanking the Almighty with all my heart that the visitor took his leave.

The door upstairs creaks as it opens.

My heart stops racing.

Slowly, a weight rolls over the steps down to the ground floor.

In eager anticipation, I rub my thighs against each other.

The vampire slithers towards me, their shadow engulfing me in darkness. Just and God-fearing women would have screamed and fled from this unholy apparition. But I? I feel... calmer. Serene. They bring me comfort. They soothe my worries and make me feel at home. With the vampire—while I don't feel safe, I feel calmer.. The lack of human eyes can be credited for this.

Slowly, I turn around. While secure in their presence, my breathing increases and my heart is ready to leap from my bosom.

The vampire stands before me. Their thick, massive body, as if made from pure muscle, needing neither arms nor legs to stand. Their mouth, its many teeth just behind the layer of grayish skin, salivating at the sight of me. By their head, little dots whose function I am ignorant of. I have at times considered that they could be eyes, but they do not resemble those of people. My companion. My lover. They are like the bloodsuckers, the leeches from the bog, yet massive in size, intelligent... and capable of erotic desire. A humongous worm-like being that has bedded me. Made me theirs.

"Huuuhhrd?" they speak in a drawn-out groan.

I shake my head.

"Hhuuhheehhllp?" they ask, straining to form the word.

Again, I shake my head.

Their body shivers. Their teeth move rhythmically, taking in the smell of their next meal.

They move in closer.

I say nothing. Words are no longer needed. We've always said more with our actions than our words. We know what we want.

The vampire needs to feed. And my own appetites need to be satiated.

With my thumb, I begin to pry open my dress.

The vampire, this bloodsucker, moves closer. Their head gravitates towards the wound on my hand.

The straps slip from my shoulders, baring my breasts.

The vampire begins to suckle on my blood.

The dress falls to my ankles, revealing my legs and ass.

Their body begins to pulsate, writhing as they feed.

I press my hand against their mouth. Their skin, ribbed and smooth, forever coated in a fluid that sticks to me.

The vampire moves its worm-like body away from my hand. They know their spittle stops my blood from hardening and wounds from healing. It is moments like this where I feel they see more to me than just food and carnal pleasure.

That, or they find suckling blood from above my breast a better place to feed.

Closer to my heart.

Closer to the source.

I wince as a circle of razors punctures my skin.

They suckle on me. Their body writhes as my blood seeps into their mouth.

My legs tremble.

My toes clench.

My... my cunt—

I... I must—

I—

"Ooooh, Christ preserve me," I moan and gasp.

As always, within the first few moments when my vampire feeds on me, I come.

Being punctured—penetrated in such a way, violent in its purpose yet gentle in its intent, it makes me climax each time. Like a harlot, a whore of Satan's minion, I come from being fed upon.

And they have only just begun.

Their body moves. The lower half, that is.

The rear slithers between my legs, then up, onto my rear and clasping onto my buttocks. They briefly tease me, letting their second mouth slither over my small bum, towards the little scars made in a perfect circle into the flesh.

I shiver, still reeling from the orgasmic delight my bloodsucking lover granted me with their feasting. Feeling the small blades pierce my skin and enter, I nearly jump in the air, overextending the muscles in my legs as I lean on the balls of my feet.

The vampire comes closer. Both mouths are sucking my blood at a gentle pace. Forceful enough for their hunger to be sated. Gentle enough that I won't lose consciousness. They are not subtle with their desire, grinding their body against me.

Their first mouth retreats from my chest. Blood runs down my breast, a droplet dangling from my nipple.

Their other mouth releases my rear, coiling their body around my leg as it inches towards my womanhood. Their bizarrely textured skin grazes against my hair below. Their many teeth explore my folds, but they don't bite or draw further blood.

A pity, really.

Then, finding the bud of my rose, their rear mouth slides over my flesh. A jolt of terror shoots through me. I know what those teeth are capable of. In one motion, they could maim me. Yet, to be at their mercy, to have to place all my faith and trust in that they will not hurt me is almost a greater aphrodisiac than any spirits or potions could be. I am more frightened by the gaze of others than I am of my lover biting down and undoing me, by rosebud.

It is during times like these I am aware how different I am. How my thoughts and desires are nothing like those of others.

But I cannot change them.

I cannot change *me*.

I push my hips forward against their mouth, urging them to continue, to tease and engulf my pussy with their maw. With my hands, I take hold of their body. I have never laid eyes on a man's sex in my life, so I try to imagine taking hold of a lover's phallus in such a manner. I push their skin back, then push it toward me. Does the vampire enjoy this? I cannot say. But if they didn't, I would know.

Their dangerous but enthralling act drives me toward luscious madness. All my fears vanish, although I am more vulnerable now than had I been with a man. With one hand I squeeze and stoke the smaller ends of their body while they suckle on me. With my other hand, I pinch my nipple until its sting shoots lightning through my chest.

More.

I want more.

Teeth, blood, and spittle are no longer enough.

That thrill of being robbed of my womanhood with a mere bite is no longer enough.

I need more.

I.

Need.

More.

And as if the Lord has heard my prayers, the vampire complies.

Their body squirms. Then, with a violent hacking, they pull away from my cunt and spew a mixture of spittle, their body's outer fluids... and my own blood onto my stomach.

Dripping down my leg.

A small stream, gliding over my cunt.

It... it is fascinating.

Arousing.

The inhumanity of it all.

Their almost demonic appearance.

I have tried.

But my desires.

My hunger.

My uncontrollable urges.

I cannot.

I *will* not.

Oh, Lord, preserve me... *I need them.*

Grasping onto my vampire, their soft worm-like body coating my arms in their fluid, I pull them close to me. I relinquish the strength in my legs and let the world claim us, lying myself down onto the cold stone floor and pulling the dark gray worm onto my body. Placing my heels into their hide, their thick muscles pulsating as my fresh blood nourishes them, I push them down.

Further.

Further down.

Just where their sex aligns with mine.

I cannot confirm what it is they have. There is no cock. There is no cunt. What is there is an area, a soft and fluid-soaked area that twitches and pulsates even further the more I touch it. And what I've found to give them—and myself—the greatest pleasure is when we align with each other.

Placing their massive body atop of mine, I shuffle down until I feel their area against my pussy. Body against body. Sex against cunt. Then, with more strength than I normally could muster, I grasp my hands into their hide. They contort their front end, curving downwards as they drool fluid and blood onto my face and chest. Black dots sit in a row, but I cannot see them as eyes. No one is watching me as my lover lies on my body.

They wish to take me.

I want them to.

I tilt my head back and moan, telling them to proceed as I dig my fingers into their ribbed hide and push them upward.

They take my invitation.

The weird worm, the bloodsucker of the night, fucks me. Grinding their sex against mine, they shiver with each pulsation.

I have never been bedded by a man. On some level, I remain virginal, ignorant to how this act would be done between two children of God.

But lying with my vampire, no doubt a spawn of Satan, I cannot imagine anything that could be better.

Their weight on me. That massive girth, trembling now they've been fed, presses down with all their might, gyrating and pushing into my cunt as it practically smothers me with their desire.

I bleed. I fight to breathe. I lay trapped beneath them.

I am happy.

I am safe.

I am wanted.

Only here do I feel unafraid. Only here, lying beneath the bloodsucking worm of the night, do I feel loved.

So enthralled by their grinding and the pleasure I receive from the act, I practically jump when they suddenly speak.

"Ghhhhooouuuddd?" they ask.

I nod my head. "Yes! Very!"

"Fhhhuuukk?" the vampire mutters.

"Yes... yes, my darling. Fuck me," I gasp.

They increase their speed. I lean back, my legs in the air as I clench my toes, thunderbolts of delight coursing through me. There may be evil in it, but there is also a heavenly fire that now courses through my blood.

The pressure.

The softness.

The caressing of my rosebud and my folds.

Their warmth.

My sin... and how being sinful is better than being afraid.

A tear rolls from my eye.

"Ppppaaaayyyaaan?" my love grunts.

"No! No, darling!" I gasp. "I'm—"

"Whhhuuuuuuuddddd?" they say, pausing.

"I'm a wicked woman. Sinful," I mutter. Then, like a cat clawing at its prey, I dig my fingers and toes into my lover's body. "Make me feel good. Fuck me, understand? Fuck me!"

They look at me, perhaps pondering my sudden outburst. But as commanded, they resume their grinding, their pace faster than before.

I am bound for the pit.

But this, this sensation? It is worth all damnation.

"Oh! Fuck!" I groan loudly.

I do not speak often.

In my solitude, I often retreat into silence.

Not now, though.

I moan.

I grunt.

I gasp, like a harlot of the street.

Slut of the worm.

I cannot be quiet.

Not when I feel *this*.

This good.

This heavenly.

This enraptured by our debauchery.

My lover begins to shake, writhing violently while my embrace keeps them in place.

They are close.

Soon, they'll come.

And knowing this, feeling this, I too race towards orgasmic delight once more.

We quiver in rhythm.

We writhe, a dance of flesh, lust, and fluid on the cold stone floor.

They hiss.

I groan.

They salivate, dripping more fluid and my blood.

I clench.

They shudder.

"I—I—"

"Ggrrrhhhhh!!"

And then, we stop.

We spasm, as if struck by lightning.

Like an animal, I howl, my climax taking control of my body.

My thoughts are no longer mine.

My body is no longer mine.

I belong to this pleasure, moaning and gasping as I writhe under the massive body of my lover.

My sweat mingles with their sticky fluids.

The juices from my cunt coat their area.

They too writhe and gargle, their teeth on both ends twitching as they climax atop my small thin frame. A thick mucus, a substance I haven't identified yet, pours from its area and onto my cunt.

We lie there in our reverie. Me, my arms around them. They, their elongated body curled around me.

The floor is cold, and with the fire now truly dead, the chill from the storm outside brings a cool air into my... *our* home.

But I feel none of it. I am warmed by my lover, the bloodsucker. Slut-fucker. The damned by God, vampire.

Their lust... Their love.

For now, all that I fear has ceased to exist.

All that I need is here.

What brings them to me, that wickedness that taints my lineage? Because I welcome it. It has brought me joy. Only at times like this, I thank the Lord for giving me that part. That part that can only be found within me. That part that is in the blood.

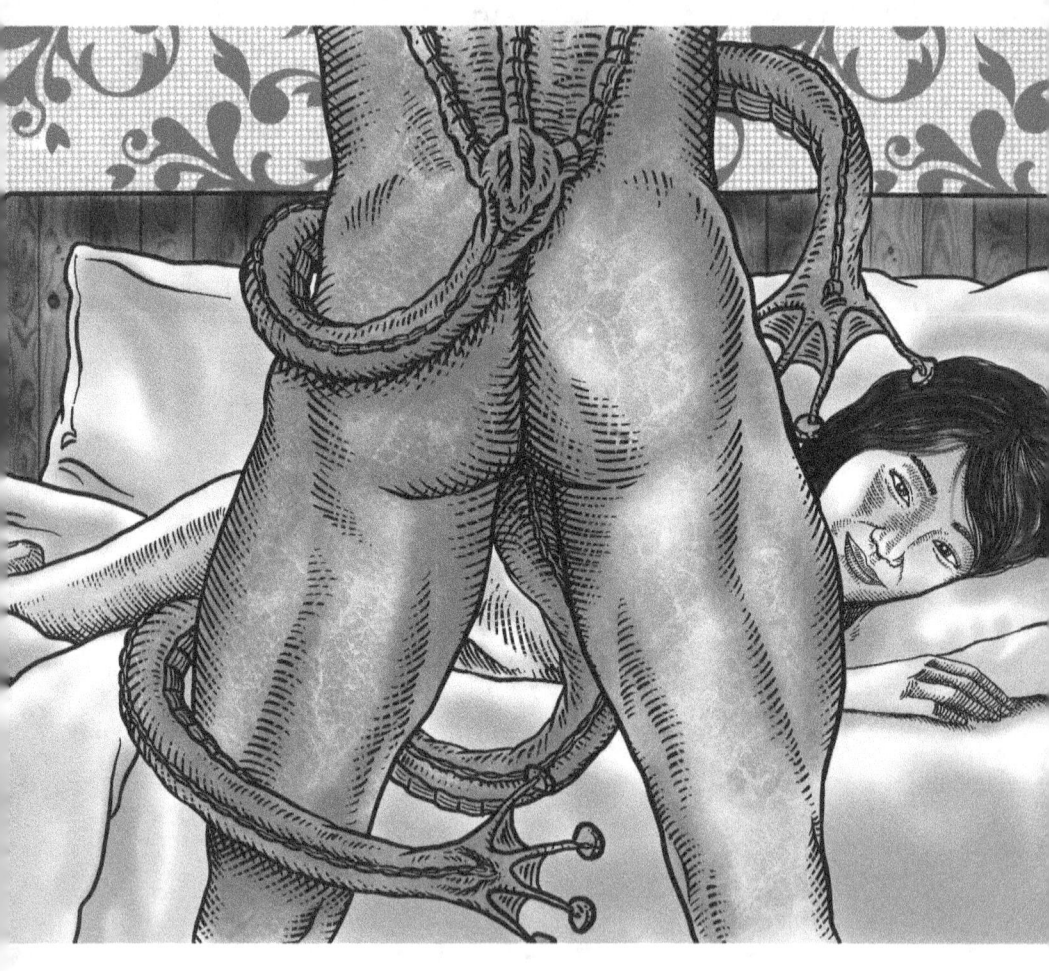

DEVOUT CONSUMMATION

SAM CRAIN

Milla and Adam fell asleep masturbating to thoughts of each other when they couldn't make love in person, as a pact between them. Sometimes they even did it while in bed together, Adam always maintaining that it freed their fantasies, kept them loose and liberated, Milla never finding evidence that he was wrong.

Adam's nape tasted salty, and he buried his face in her chest before standing abruptly and yanking down her tank top in the same motion. He caressed her breasts and traced a finger down her spine, teasing, 'til he reached the cleft of her ass, where he teased her again and she groaned aloud.

"Not enough, not nearly," she breathed into his ear, and he chuckled deep in his chest and turned her toward the wall, stripped to the waist, and slipped her house-pants down. Milla was bare beneath and he was hard. She reached behind her, as if she needed to check. She'd seen his eyes dark with lust and the omnipresent question: did she love him? It made him look absurdly young, even as the lust made him old, so that he was as perfectly balanced between them as one of the Fey. She thought this clearly as he thrust into her—

The problem was, Adam was dead, killed in a car accident months ago. She was meant to have been in the car with him, going to a dinner party, but she'd been violently ill. He'd kissed her anyway as he left, and she still felt that kiss as fever thrummed through her while a police officer told her the love of her life had been thrown through a windshield. The fantasizing kept him close for precious shards of time—and she let herself believe that, wherever he was, he was doing it too.

But every morning, she had to wake up to the fact that he was dead. He no longer lay beside her, and this had become the ultimate long-distance relationship. That which she'd most feared had come to pass. She'd built up her courage once to ask him: *What if you die?* She'd braced for him to make fun. He often did, to disarm his own fear, refusing to be crippled by it.

But he'd not laughed nor turned the question back on her (*what if* you *died*). He was older than Milla and recognized statistical fairness. His eyes, dark with the desire that never left the two of them, met hers gravely as he said, "I would find you again. Whatever it took." The intensity of it made her breath catch as he gripped her hand hard enough to hurt. "Do you believe me?"

"Of course I do," she'd said, the last syllable lost in the kiss she gave him, thrusting her tongue deep into his mouth as though certainty lay there under his tongue.

She *had* believed him, but the months had eroded her childlike faith into a desperate hope lodged like a pebble in her shoe she wouldn't take out. Just like she still believed he might walk in one day and ask why there wasn't enough supper for him.

Milla put her briki over its burner and remembered buying it with Adam in a Norwegian-American antique shop up in rural Washington. The proprietress of the shop had thought it was for gravy. She'd been so happy to find it there, of all places, on that half-sunny day. "It's for coffee," she said now, just as she had then.

She had clients and started her work clock on the dot. It was long past the point where her clients were sympathetic. The first six months, sure, but she'd reached Time to Move On territory and carefully guarded how she hadn't—as if it were a secret to anyone who knew her.

Her best friend Carly had texted twice since yesterday:

Go get 'em today, girl, and *Stop ignoring me. I'm coming by Friday, so be dressed up to go out.*

Milla sighed and texted back: *Not ignoring you. Just buried under paperwork,* and turned the phone off, remembering their last in-person conversation.

"You need to get back out there."

"Oh, come on, Carly. I'm not twenty anymore, or even thirty."

"You're not dead yet, either." Carly had met her eyes then. Even two months earlier, she would have flushed and apologized, but they'd crossed the Grief Rubicon. "What harm could it do, getting laid?"

"Besides possible gonorrhea?"

"Funny," Carly said, even though it wasn't.

"I don't want to." She wanted to sound like an *adult* but worried she came across as whiny.

Carly inhaled through her nose like a mother seeking patience, so she probably *had* whined. "You may need to. It's not like you're gonna join a knitting circle or a convent, right?"

"I don't think those are my only options," Milla said. "I've been thinking about getting a couple cats."

Carly shrugged her shoulders up to her ears. "As long as you're happy. *Actually* happy."

But what was *actually happy* without Adam?

Milla was grateful for a work-from-home day. And it wasn't dinner, but lunch. She really did have a lot of paperwork to catch up on. Invoices, receipts, the odd form to comply with government oversight. With no appointments for the afternoon, she'd resolved to cook, pretending it was for Adam. It wasn't codependent, she stubbornly maintained, to enjoy cooking for other people. Even if one of those people was dead.

"Eating is one of the primary social acts," Adam had said.

"Like sex?" she'd asked, and he'd given her a look, not like she was wrong, but only obvious. She could live with that.

"When I'm home alone, I don't always bother," Adam said. He cooked perfectly well and sometimes more ambitiously than Milla did, but in her opinion, he

was too bound by recipes, which always surprised her. A man as alternative as he is? Clinging to recipes was a contradiction. But then, it bespoke his lack of faith. Adam needed things proved, but dealing with him took a lot of faith.

This rather bitter thought matched the grated turmeric she'd added to the rice, complemented by the earthy warmth of thinly sliced ginger, both roots measured only by eye.

The rice simmered. There was chicken to have with it. She could garnish it with chopped cilantro if it hadn't gone off yet, and a squeeze of lemon. There was always lemon in the house.

With Adam, there'd always been a starter, too, but Milla had fallen out of the habit. She racked her brain and the fridge. Well, a salad would do, if she took the time to slice a little apple and green onion over it—the green onion could also go over the chicken, now that she thought of it—and made up an oil-and-vinegar dressing. None of this olive-oil-and-a-dash-of-soy-sauce she did when resigned to being alone.

The table was set. She even, *yes, damn her,* put out a second setting. To see if it made her feel more or less lonely. A little experiment, you could call it.

The salad bowl chimed hollowly as the tongs hit its edge. The salad was all right, though the apple she'd sliced was mealier than she'd expected, a better candidate for a Dutch baby.

It only really would've mattered if Adam were *actually* here. The thought stole into her head without her intending it, and she studied the worn woodgrain of the dining table to keep from crying and over-salting her salad leaves. Trying not to look at the plate and cutlery she'd laid out on the other side of the table.

More lonely after all.

The rice cooker went and Milla returned to the kitchen for the main course.

"Still refusing to cook from recipes, then?"

Adam's voice made her clench her hands around the serving plate rather than drop it like someone in a movie might. That saved their lunch.

Adam sat behind his place setting. It was daylight, so she could believe it was real. She only *really* let herself hallucinate in the dark, when she reached for a warm body that wasn't there.

Something dripped, like rain down a windowpane. He wore a loose silk shirt with flowing sleeves that came past his wrists. His hands were an angry red, from what she could see, but she didn't question it, not then.

"You're late," she said, setting the steaming chicken and rice down and *really* looking at him. "Are you eating, then?"

Adam laughed, a little huff of breath more than sound. So distant, yet so achingly familiar. "No questions, just food?" he said. "I was gone so much longer than I meant to be. Forgive me?"

"First things first," Milla said. "I made it for you."

"You'll have to help me, then. It's...hard for me to eat these days."

Milla cut the chicken very small and dished up a modest serving of rice. Swapping the fork for a spoon, she offered him a mouthful.

"You always knew it'd come to this," Adam said as he accepted the bite and chewed. Almost immediately, he winced. *Feeding him*, he meant, because they had expected to grow old together.

"Adam?"

"It's the ginger and turmeric—they burn."

Milla thought first and suddenly of vampires and garlic but shook it off. If his mouth was like the rest of him, he was chewing on an open wound. No wonder it hurt. "Just the chicken, then?"

Adam shook his head. A little blood trickled from his hairline to his neck, like a tear in the wrong place. "Give me both. I want them."

The thrill this gave Milla was a darker red than the blood—wine-dark, edging toward black. It raised the hair on her arms and made her wet as she gathered another bite onto the spoon.

"Thank you." He could barely manage the words by the time he'd emptied his plate.

"You're welcome."

He looked at her, hard, and his eyes were just about the same. Dark with desire for her—she couldn't just be imagining that—with that question in the back: did she really love him still? She put a hand over his, squeezing gently, mindful of the raw, bleeding flesh.

"We keep our promises, don't we?" Adam said, visibly relaxing.

"We do." His wedding ring was dug into the appropriate finger, skin or none.

"You remember what you promised me?" He was thumbing *her* ring now, which had never left her hand either.

"I remember everything, Adam." They'd written their own vows, of course. She'd promised to feed him, as long as he was hers to feed. He'd promised to hold her, as long as she was his to hold. But what fairytale were they living in now? She needed to know so that she could act as required of her.

"I had to make a new pact to come back to you. It cost me my skin, as you see."

"What keeps you from bleeding to death?"

"The curse. The pact came with it. I expect the gods found it funny."

"Which gods?"

"Take your pick, really. I asked them all, and they didn't sign their work."

Adam stood, wincing, undid black drawstring pants so that they puddled around slippered feet. Everything was structurally sound, but he had no visible skin at all, as though they—the god or *gods* he'd mentioned—had flayed him. His fascia and viscera pulsed visibly, blood chasing itself through arteries and veins. Milla had never seen anything so heartrendingly lovely. Her hand went unconsciously to her mouth and her breath caught to see his cock and testicles so utterly naked.

Still hers. Oh god(s), still *hers*.

"Can I?" she asked, stepping around the table. "Can *you*?"

"We can. But maybe we...shouldn't. Skin is...replaceable."

Replaceable. He could be whole again. Yet Milla could not help but reach out and stroke him between his legs as he stood before her. She was gentle, but the strength of his reaction was like an arrow loosed from a longbow. He moaned but didn't pull away, hardening under her searching fingertips.

Hammurabi's Code scrolled across her mind's eye as if on a crawl: eye for an eye, tooth for a tooth—and a life for a life.

She could do that for him.

Friday, she'd dressed with care—club wear, which she rarely donned but kept in a corner of her closet, testament to the motto, *"be prepared"*. She didn't look forty-one in her mirror, and it wasn't only wishful thinking telling her so. The cavernous grief that'd previously dug through her face had filled in, and her hair was thick and shining. She'd do, if she left before Carly arrived. Her text: *Sorry, called into a work thing tonight.* Adam knew not to answer the door.

Flirting failed to hook any of the men she tried, even without her wedding ring on. She rubbed the wee callus it left on her palm, about to pack it in for the night when a woman caught her eye and held it, smiling. She was talking to a couple of others in a lull between songs, if such throbbing electronica could be said to have songs.

"I pick metal bands and wine the same way," the woman said, grinning with what was either flirtation or self-consciousness. "The name and the art on the front."

"And what if you can't read the label?" Milla asked, diverted.

"I take a chance. I'm Bethany."

Not for long. The music kicked up again, so Milla sidled close to say into her ear, "You want to try your luck back at my place?"

"You've got metal and wine?" Bethany shook mahogany hair out of eyes the silver of driving rain.

Milla shrugged and winked. "Take a chance."

Bethany laughed and took Milla's hand readily without even knowing her name.

Getting back to her place was so easy that Milla felt almost drunk on it. And there *was* a little spark between them, dancing between their joined hands. Ironically, Milla *looked* like she was doing exactly what Carly had been nagging her to do month after month. Bethany got blackout drunk faster than Milla expected, and she was pleased she didn't need the chloroform in the drawer of the coffee table.

She'd raised her brows at Adam, who emerged naked as soon as Bethany was out cold.

Now what?

Get her down to the basement, *quick.*

"You may not want to watch," Adam said. His teeth were longer, sharper, so that his words slurred a little. He severed Bethany's jugular while Milla looked on, letting the blood run out into the trough. He bit at Bethany, tearing the skin away in a long, imperfect sheet. Each tug hurt him badly, Milla saw, but he didn't stop until Bethany's flesh was nearly as bare as his own.

"Help me, please." Tears of agony ran down his face as he tried to lift the fresh skin. Milla steeled herself and wrapped it around him, thinking it would hang like a beach towel, but as it touched him, it stuck and smoothed out.

One more surprise awaited them: Adam had breasts now, and his cock was *under* this new skin, pressed down tight and unreachable. "Can you feel that?" Milla asked, stroking the slight bulge it made.

"No, I can't." He laughed hard. "More tricks, is it?" he asked, looking up at nothing. The laughter raised the hair on Milla's arms and she searched his eyes. *They* hadn't changed. Had they?

They hadn't, and in her relief, she reached for him and they made love on the concrete basement floor, avoiding the plastic tarps. Adam's breasts were responsive, and he moaned in Milla's ear as she touched them before probing downward for his clitoris.

It was no terrible thing, she thought in their bed in the gray before dawn, to have this different body. They were both bi, so it didn't have to *mean* anything earth-shattering about them.

Other than us being murderers, of course. Adam's eyes opened in the dim light as if he'd heard the thought. "We've got to leave town, you know?" Milla said. "Before people start looking for her."

So, they ran. They buried Bethany's corpse with quicklime, Milla never more grateful she'd refused Carly's offer to move into the city and "*rejoin the land of the*

living". Her nearest neighbor was nearly four miles away. It had been her and Adam's haven, but it was too risky to stay with Adam now wearing Bethany's face. People who knew her would ask questions.

Milla had savings—enlarged, ironically, by Adam's life insurance policy—so quitting her job was no hardship. On the contrary, she was delighted to be having sex again, and such a variety of it. They were happy in an apartment in another state, and Milla thought of Adam privately as a revenant; it was the closest term she could think of.

But really, he was Adam. They read together, took long walks, cooked each other meals in the tiny yet serviceable kitchen, and made passionate love multiple times a day, Milla always checking Adam's eyes. She'd never been happier there, where no one knew them except to say "*hi*" in passing. And no one had come looking for Bethany or found her real body. She'd texted Carly: *Met someone. Gone on a long vacation.*

"You remember how we met?" Adam asked as they lay in bed late one Sunday.

"That godawful slam poetry session. I'd been trying all evening not to laugh, and then I saw you roll your eyes at the ceiling and I lost control."

"And then you dragged me to that hardcore show the next night."

"For some real poetry—and good drumming. What time d'you call this?" she teased with a glance at the clock. Breakfast at nearly one o'clock in the afternoon felt like the height of decadence. She was starving.

It went on like that, things sweet as summer cherries.

Until Adam's skin began to crack.

At first, she believed it was a sunburn, and she put aloe on it, but it peeled all the way down to reveal muscle.

"Oh, gods," Adam breathed as she probed this new raw place in his side. "We'll need to do it again."

Milla steeled herself, helping him out of the old skin, blotting his tears with feather-light pats of cloth that still made him grit his teeth. The skin lay in pieces at their feet and she sought Adam's cock with her hands. It hardened even as he swallowed a scream, and Milla wanted him—the *real* him—with such urgency she forgot to be gentle and pressed him back into the wall of their bedroom, guiding his cock into her in the same motion.

Adam cried out, but it wasn't, "Stop," it was, "Yes, oh, Milla, *yes.*" She held his eyes with hers as they climaxed together, caught him as he slumped against the wall.

"I love you," she said. "We'll find you another." *Feed you, as long as you are mine to feed*, so she'd said. She pushed aside the thought that the sex they'd had just now put to shame all the sex in the Bethany-body. She'd find a man this time, and all would be well.

A man was easy to find in the dive bar of a college town a ways off, perfect from his overly gelled hair to his cold eyes. "No means yes, yes means anal," he'd said on his third Milwaukee Best since she'd arrived. He peered around, hoping for laughter but got only a single awkward titter from the back. *Yes, he'd do nicely*, once she hooked him.

"Language, young man," she'd said, with all she could muster of her forty-one years.

"You're into it. I can tell." Those cold eyes couldn't mask his insecurity, his desperation to be wanted even when he himself didn't want.

"Maybe," she said. She made herself look at the skin alone, lithe and tanned, all but unblemished. Oh, to be twenty with a fake ID and think all women belonged to you. "Come back to mine and prove it to me," she said, letting her murmur stir the tiny hairs on his neck.

"Sure," he said. "Yes, means anal, right?"

She let her smile widen and thought of Red Riding Hood and the Wolf as she led him upstairs to her hotel room. He was drunk, but not drunk enough that it interfered with his equipment. She could see it pressed against the button-fly of his jeans and hurriedly poured him a slug of drugged Jack Daniels. "Man enough for a real drink first?" she challenged.

"I'll need it, old bag like you," he said in kind, tossing it back—and was unconscious before he could touch her. She wrapped him in the blankets off her bed and Adam, on cue, brought a bellhop cart. They got out the back way without being seen.

In the bathroom of an out-of-business gas station off the highway that made Milla think of cannibals selling human barbecue, they did the deed, careful to bring the blankets with them until a truck stop in the next state.

In a Motel 6 that night, they sealed the ritual with Adam now as lithe as the frat boy, and Milla searched his eyes yet again. Still the same, thank the gods.

"*This* one can last us," Adam told her, and she let herself believe it, falling asleep in his arms. *As long as you are mine to hold.*

She dreamed.

A flayed beast, all fascia and ichor, whose flesh went from brown to green to brown as blood poured from its fangs. Its ears resembled a bat's. Its eyes were not her husband's—she awoke with a gasp.

They'd found another apartment in another place, this one with a lake-view patio, and dared to believe that could be the end of it, walking around the lake in all weathers.

Of course, it wasn't. In spite of a rigorous moisturizing regimen and religious use of a hat and sunblock if outside during the day, the frat boy's skin began to flake away like old paint.

"Once more," Milla said, nauseated as she washed away the dying skin, then aroused at the sight of the flesh beneath. *The real Adam,* she thought before she could stop herself.

But she felt rebellious and left her wedding ring on when she went hunting again, in a bookstore coffeeshop this time, not a club or a dive bar. She was sick to death of pretense, disgusted with herself for trying to see only the skin. It's not like that frat guy had been some great loss to the world, willing to stick his dick in a stranger's ass just for agreeing to a hookup.

("*Old bag.*")

But Bethany—what had she done wrong, other than be too trusting of someone with decent music taste in a club that had anything but? Milla thought these things as she sipped a long, dark Americano and looked up to see a man of middle age, brown-haired, his beard full but not long. He saw her notice him and got up. A large scar ran up his left shin to his knee. He wore shorts that did nothing to conceal either his vitality or this scar. As he sat down across from her, his eyes glittered a clear azure.

"Good to meet you, I'm Charles," he said, reaching across the table to shake her hand. He had a good grip. Three parallel scars ran over his right wrist, glowing faintly as he gripped her hand in his. He caught her staring. "You look like someone who knows about hard times. Are you widowed?" He glanced at her wedding ring with sympathy on his weathered face.

"I was," she said. "Widowed, I mean."

"Think about ending it at the time?"

"Yes," she said without quite meaning to. She was captivated by his scars, wanted to keep looking at them, even wanted to touch them, but meeting his eyes again, they were the wrong color. "What about you?"

"Thought about it, sure. After I ruined my leg, it seemed like life was over. Was supposed to go on this months-long hike with my wife, a long-deferred honeymoon. I'd kept promising her and putting it off. And when she heard how long I'd be in physio to walk again, she left me."

Milla's eyes flew open. "That's—"

"No. I deserved it. I made her wait until she just couldn't anymore. I can see that now. You want another of those?" He nodded to her Americano.

"I'd like that. Thanks."

It was...*nice*...having coffee in daylight with someone interesting, someone new. He'd go back with her and then—could Adam keep these scars? But Milla couldn't shake her nightmare, either. And she didn't want to kill Charles and take his skin, especially when, real truth, the sex with Adam was best when he was completely bare—and sex with anyone else could never hope to compare.

Milla got up.

"Hey, where are you going?" Charles called after her, holding a fresh coffee, but she pushed through the exit door and broke into a run.

Adam was waiting for her. His eyes lit to see her as they always did. He was swathed in a fluffy bathrobe to spare his flesh.

"I can't do it again," she said as she reached for the knot of his robe-belt. "I want *you*. Like this." She ran her tongue over his chest, tasting sweat made coppery by his blood.

"Oh, thank the gods," he said, and kissed her as though she could never hurt him, as though he wanted her to. She kissed him back, stroking him, dropped to her knees and clasped his ass in both hands as she took his hard, raw cock into her mouth.

"I love you," Adam breathed just before he screamed. She could just see his eyes, dark and soft.

I love you too, she thought as he filled her mouth. *I'm more of a monster than you are.*

ANGEL BEYOND THE FLAMES

C. CHARLES KNIGHT

She awoke with lies on her fingertips.

I'm fine, she tapped, answering yet another concerned text from her best friend. Another morning, another day for excuses. Early light slanted through the bedroom curtains in shades of gray, passing its unwanted touch over the jumbled pile of blankets pinning her legs to the mattress. The quilt her mother had given her on their wedding day, a cheap microfiber, and an Irish wool in plaid. The latter two impulse buys, retail therapy.

Abbey didn't have the energy to put the phone aside and, anyway, the dancing ellipsis told her she wasn't done defending herself yet.

Deb

He did it again, didn't he?

Yes.

Abbey

No, everything's fine. Really.

No, it isn't.

The next message came too quickly. Clear that Deb wasn't buying it. God-damn friends who know you so well.

Deb

> Let's get out of town. Just for a while. That little place up in Ithaca, you loved it there!

She did. But *he* would never let her go. Not without him. *How did I not see it coming?* A question she'd unfairly asked herself on a daily basis. The all too common story many smart, strong women shared. Like them, she'd fallen victim to a master manipulator, a man with the consummate charm of a sociopath.

"I dunno, Deb. We'll see," she typed; her friend would know as well as she did that "we'll see" usually meant "no".

The dots swam across the bottom of the screen, but this time Abbey pressed the power button to send the reply to the darkness. She didn't have the energy for the tug-of-war. Placing the phone facedown on the side table, she reluctantly got up and padded across the floor into the bathroom. Catching a glimpse of the bruise in the mirror, she turned away and sat with her eyes on the tile.

It wasn't always like this, was it? It wasn't. In fact, it had started almost like a romantic comedy. A meet-cute at a local deli led to a day of walking in the park, ice skating, dinner. Before she knew it, she'd fallen for him. Greg Ambrose. The handsome young man who had so much potential and a gentle smile. He knew all the right things to say. Worse, he knew how to make her laugh. That was what got to her the most. She'd been caught up in the whirlwind and, before she knew it, they were on their honeymoon in the Amalfi Coast. That first year was like a dream. But as dreams so often do, it turned to—

A knock at the door made her jump and sent a chill down her spine. She never used to be jumpy, but then, she'd never been... *Fuck, left the phone.* Could have checked the doorbell camera from right here. Maybe if she took her time they'd go away.

Another knock followed by the ringing of the doorbell.

No luck.

She stood and smoothed out her gown before sliding the robe over her aching arms. Reluctantly, she looked into the mirror to pull her hair over the darkened eye. The house was gray in the shadowed, pale hue of overcast light, which subdued everything and brought out the cold austerity of the décor. It wasn't her style, but Greg had insisted on a modern design that she only now appreciated as a reflection of his inner self. A sharp bravado that encased a frosty core. Far more important to display the illusion of power, confidence, and wealth than to live in comfort. Not much of her existed here in this place she called home; even her body, warm and animated, was little more than a ghost floating from room to room.

The doorbell rang again. *Jesus, I'm coming, I'm coming.* She tried to suppress the irritation and allowed a sigh to escape her lips before opening the door. The vision before her was perhaps the last thing she'd ever want on a day like this.

"Well, good morning, sleepy-head! The blessed day is not one to squander," said the mask speaking to her. Abbey had known many women like Mrs. Crandel, the self-important Bible-thumper who put on a saccharine face under which she lived out in the world. Thinly veiled judgment oozed out of her Southern mouth, from which there was almost always a faint scent of gin.

Awful early for the spirits, isn't it, Mrs. Crandel? Abbey tried to hide her contempt, and she was generally proud of herself for the skill. "Good morning, Mrs. Crandel, what can I do for you?"

Mrs. Crandel's face contorted briefly; perhaps the contempt wasn't as buried as Abbey had hoped. That was fine too. "Oh, well, I know you and Greg don't attend services—" *there's the judgment,* "—but we would *love* to have you both this Sunday. The Church is having a fundraiser to support that poor Carlisle girl who lost her family in that horrible plane crash a while back. Just terrible! Could you imagine a father doing all those awful things? It's a wonder the little dear survived at all."

It was always fascinating to her how "The Church" sounded capitalized when Mrs. Crandel said it. An emphasis, however subtle, that made it insufferable. Abbey knew about the Carlisle Tragedy; it had been all over the papers. Greg apparently had some loose connection with someone who had known Steve Carlisle well. They couldn't imagine what would have come over him, but there was no question he'd lost it after the crash. That poor little girl. "That sounds like a great thing, but I'm afraid we're out of town this weekend." *Another lie.* "I'm sorry." *And another.*

The shadow of a scowl passed over the uninvited guest's face just before the smile returned. "Oh, well, maybe next time then."

Abbey had already started slowly closing the door, hoping the hint would be taken. "Yes, maybe." *On a roll with the lies today.* "Good luck with everything. I've got to go now. It was nice of you to stop by." *There it is again.*

"Of course, dear, you have a blessed day. I will keep you in my prayers."

Great. The door clicked shut and Abbey turned to let her back fall against the cherry wood, part of the paneling digging into her shoulder blade. The judgement came from so many directions. From within, her own scrutiny plagued her, but the myriad of glances, however subtle, from other women were like daggers of appraisal.

Worse, it was primarily from women who had no insight into the relationship and who put on whatever feigned happiness they liked as they bounced their strollers along the sidewalks. The pity on their faces, as though her inability to gestate somehow diminished her worth. Fucking reductionist shit rampant in the patriarchal infection that'd done nothing but continue to spread under the guise of social progress. *What fucking progress? What a joke.* One step forward and twelve back; only the language had changed and, even then, had it really? Still, it made her angry how much it got to her. Women were supposed to want those things, weren't they?

But she didn't want them. She never had, so when the doctors assured her she was incapable of it, she pretended to be devastated. The perfect show. Oh, they ate it up, all those women who wore the masks, those faces that lied to the world about how grateful they were for their lives and the beautiful, perfect miracles they brought into the world. Under her own mask, it disgusted her. Abbey let out another slow sigh before she pushed herself forward and into the kitchen.

On the gray granite countertop, the coffee maker stared at her in somber reproach and stainless steel fuckery. But like any other situation where a thing held something she desired, she just smiled and fed it ingredients subserviently. As it percolated, the warm scent of arabica beans filled her with desire and hope. Some days, there was just not enough coffee in the world.

She retrieved her phone from the bedroom. The red badge over the messages app counted fifteen. *Jesus.* Her eyes fell back on the bed, an ache from the swollen socket, a part of her tempted to crawl back inside. Fighting against her will and desire for avoidance, she ran her fingers over the glass and the phone sparked to life.

The first five messages were from *him*. Greg. A tune she'd heard many times: *I'm sorry, just made me crazy, love you so much it boils over*, et cetera, et cetera. Bullshit she used to fall for and now couldn't reconcile with her staying.

No. That wasn't fair. She stayed because he'd taken control of all the finances and had done a remarkable job of isolating her from most of the world. She could have stayed with Deb, but she'd be out of a home and out in the world looking for a way to make it on her own. Not impossible, but he sure made it feel so. The bastard had a preternatural ability to flip those tiny, hidden switches in her insecurity.

His stream of bullshit ended with a little ray of light—he'd be going out of town for a business trip. *Freedom.* They'd talk when he got back in a week, make up for... blah, blah, blah. *Same old shit.* Abbey fell to the bed with a sigh of relief and stared up at the ceiling. She didn't allow herself to close her eyes, to be ravaged by the delicious taking of the sandman. Instead, she checked the few texts from Deb, all of which were gently nudging her to consider leaving town. To her own surprise, Abbey felt it might just be a good idea after all.

She thought about texting Greg and letting him know, but for whatever reason, Abbey put it off. Even on the seven-hour drive from Cradle Cross up to Ithaca, she let the music and the conversation and the lull of the humming tires fade him from her mind. It was the first time in as long as she could remember that he wasn't there in her head; it felt like an escape and, in a sense, it was. Besides, he would be busy with his business trip, probably chasing girls half his age and drinking—always drinking. He almost never called when he was out of town, and the chances of his finding out where she'd gone were low. He wouldn't approve, so why take the chance? *Fuck him.* She'd be home before he got back, and he'd be none the wiser.

The campground was in a hollow within a small valley covered in evergreens. *Glamping* was the term Deb used and gave her shit for never having heard it before while assuring there would be comforts like light, heat, and a real bed. It was well-maintained, and campfires burned around the common area as they pulled up in the late afternoon. The smoke rose desultorily, longing to touch the clear sky above as the sun began its gentle westerly decline. Their tents were secluded down a trail leading farther into the woods, perhaps fifty yards from the bar and seating areas. Because of the late booking, there were three tents between them with ample space around each to improve privacy. With Abbey's preference for immersion, Deb took the one nearer the top and agreed to meet up in an hour.

The tent was the size of an efficiency apartment, with thick canvas draped from a high peak over a platform of quality decking. The flaps were open over a sheer insect screen, allowing Abbey a glimpse inside. It was quiet and allowed a gentle ambient light to break the canvas and softly illuminate the minimalist appointment. Small camping lamps rested on either side of the table, but they were unneeded. A king-sized bed draped in a Diné-patterned comforter and accent pillows sat under a window, the flaps open to another screen and allowing a soft breeze to pass through. She placed her bags on the desk in the corner and took off her shoes before falling onto the bed. It was firm but comfortable. The air passed over her face with the sweet scent of pine, and all of her muscles relaxed as her eyes closed and sleep took her.

A pink hue had flooded the tent by the time Abbey woke. The setting sun left the sky painted in dithering shades of amber and crimson. Checking her phone, she'd slept a couple of hours with visions of a beautiful mystery—tall, dark, handsome, a cliché that had crossed her dreams before. Deb hadn't disturbed her, but, knowing her, she was probably at least two bourbons in and chatting up some guy at the bar.

Abbey sat up and dragged her bag over to the floor. She selected a white linen dress, which always made her feel light. She'd never seen herself as particularly beautiful, but when she slipped the dress on she couldn't help but feel faintly desirable.

Breaking over the small hill, the gravel crunching under her flats, the bar came into view. It was a large, covered structure with no walls, allowing for a clear image of everything going on inside. Sure enough, there was Deb, conspicuously leaning over from her chair at the bar toward a well-built man probably ten years older than her. Her movements and posture were rife with telltale signs of flirtation Abbey had seen hundreds of times. For what it was worth, it didn't appear to be unwelcomed. The two were having an animated conversation when she walked up and placed a hand on her friend's shoulder.

"Abs!" Deb said while laughing through a Cheshire grin and sipping an obnoxiously large mixed drink through a novelty straw. "Good of you to join us, sleepyhead! Oh, Tom, this is my best friend Abbey. Abbey, Tom."

She was giddy. How many drinks had she had already? It wouldn't be the first time she'd have to babysit her friend after a few too many, but she was hoping Deb would ease back so she wouldn't have to. This was supposed to be a relaxing trip. No sooner had the thought entered her head, she felt bad about it. She offered her hand and engaged in the expected pleasantries, but what she really wanted to do was be alone sitting by the fire. She would. Later. Best to get the lay of the land with this guy first, make sure he wasn't a clear threat.

As the hours yawned by, the bar gradually filled with visitors. Some lounged in corners while others sat around the firepit. The giggling—a combination of alcohol and saccharine games—continued incessantly, leaving Abbey sitting next to the courting couple, feigning amusement when Deb would occasionally turn and place a hand on her knee or shoulder. A gesture designed to make her feel a part, not forgotten, while also indicating how well it was going. Deb would sleep with this guy, no question. Another night solo.

She scanned the area, taking in the couples and hopefuls talking and laughing and drinking. How many of them were as lost as, or more so than, her? How many were just keeping up pretenses, the outward appearance of happiness? Could any of them actually *be* happy? Deb reached over to get her attention and gave *the look*. The one saying unquestionably that she may or may not be back later, *after*, and with that the two headed off into the night toward her tent.

Just beyond the eaves at the corner of the bar, the firepits blazed with well-stocked fuel, flames licking ever upward and then retreating like a hesitant lover. As they parted wildly, Abbey caught a flash of something striking. Soft features made pink by the glow of the fire, a gentle androgyny in their countenance with sweeping black eyebrows in a permanent invitation and dark eyes that demanded attention. But between the flickers, it was attention they offered, gaze locked with Abbey's.

It was piercing in a way that stripped Abbey bare, leaving her exposed, vulnerable. The hairs on the back of her neck stood and a swell of heat and ice converged violently inside her. All certainty became lost somewhere in the storm when those eyes flashed. But it was more than the glossy reflection of the fire; it was something from within that told the story of infinity. Impossibly old; wise in ways apart from this world. Atavistic. Red and yellow twisted in the total black of those pupils, alternating as venomous serpents do, and yet the siren's song was intoxicating; unyielding as the absolute terror of gravity.

Abbey's impulse was to turn away, but she seemed unable, too fixated on this angel beyond the flames. The angel's lips turned up provocatively at the corners as they moved, and as Abbey's eyes adjusted, their lines were revealed to her. Somehow beyond binary labels, yet clearly having the body she always wished she'd owned. *Sexy, desirable.* The only words that her mind could find in an otherwise dark void of... of what? Surely not *lust*. She couldn't remember the last time she had wanted perfunctory sex, much less held such a drive as lust, but whatever she felt in the moment was certainly akin. She tried to put it out of her mind, making the various futile arguments that she was married and, moreover, not into women. Then again, this being wasn't precisely that.

Abbey felt flushed beyond the drink she'd consumed. She needed to get away before she couldn't stop herself from falling into the beckoning abyss. But before she could summon her body to get up, a man approached and took the seat Deb had so recently occupied. One of his friends sat next to him. He wasn't her type, even if she were in the market, but it was clear the dance was about to begin.

"Stan!" the man said a little too loudly. *Drunk*. "I'm Stan. I saw you sitting alone and couldn't imagine anything more tragic." His words would have been cheesy and unwelcomed even if they hadn't been slurred.

She worked to keep her voice polite but firm, hoping not to inadvertently elicit an unwanted reaction. "Nice to meet you, Stan. I have to go meet my friend."

"Whoa, whoa, whoa, now..." the drunk man said, placing his hands on her shoulders and preventing her from walking away. Abbey's body tensed. Too many times had she been here, with others, with Greg. "Just one drink, that's all. Come on." Hot liquor on his breath, sweaty palms on her shoulders.

She fought back the tremble in her voice. "No, thank you, it's been a long day and I need to go." Panic set in as he stood, followed by his friend, both of whom were now facing her and barring her way.

"It's so early, and you're too beautiful to leave without letting me get to know you a little," said Stan.

Abbey didn't like the look in his eyes, or the smile on his friend's face. She glanced hopefully around the bar. No staff in sight and no one near enough to get attention or help, at least not before this escalated. The darkness loomed behind the two men, a dangerously short trip from the bar to the veil of the treeline. She didn't have her phone or her keys or anything meaningful to use in defense. "Please. Please let me go. I need to check on my friend."

"Let you go? Whoa, now, nobody's keeping you here. I just wanted to buy you a drink. Don't be a bitch about it, huh?"

Before Abbey could do anything, a presence drifted against her shoulder and, suddenly, a dark figure stood between her and the men, breaking Stan's grip on Abbey. A tall, feminine figure with a strength somehow palpable. The angel from beyond the flames. The voice was otherworldly, with a conviction conveying fearlessness.

"I believe she already answered you. Walk away."

Stan's drunken face darkened further, and he took a breath to give what was certain to be a witty retort and thinly veiled threat, but the angel tipped forward toward him, and his face twisted with confusion, then fear. Stan and his friend, mouths agape, eyes wide, slowly backed away, then turned to scuttle off.

The angel turned slowly to face Abbey. She wasn't sure if she'd actually seen it or not, but her eyes told her she'd caught the briefest flash of spidery black veins retreating and fading from around those beautiful eyes. No trace of such a thing was there now—it must've been the rush of adrenaline playing tricks with the light. All that remained were the lovely features she'd seen from a distance, somehow increased in perfection with proximity. The alabaster of their skin, like a sculpture, softened and came to life, contrasting the volcanic darkness of their hair and eyes. Piercing was the word that came to mind, fierce but soulful irises hinting at a depth beyond time, asking to take her and reveal the wonders of worlds unknown—into a Caravaggian darkness. So taken by the angel's beauty, Abbey's voice caught in her throat; her heart-rate shifted from the rhythm of fright to a warm, deep, intoxicated thrum.

She wanted to say something clever, something cool, but all she could manage was, "Thank you."

The angel smiled. It was soft and disarming. "The audacity of boys masquerading as men."

"Not sure I've ever met one who wasn't."

The angel shifted their head with an approving grace. "Drink?"

Fuck, yes! "That would be lovely." Abbey couldn't deny she was taken by this creature, but she wondered if it was the novelty of the situation, her confusion, or some indescribable magnetism over which this person held power. Whatever the case, it was nice to feel safe and be seen for once. Perhaps the most powerful thing of all. "I hope those guys sleep it off and get out of here. Wouldn't want to run into them again."

They took seats at the bar, and without turning their head, the angel said, "I wouldn't worry about them. They won't be bothering anyone."

There was a confidence to the words that brought terrible comfort. Safety was an illusion not to be trusted—one of life's repeated lessons—and the soft hand grows hard when it suits its mood. Still, Abbey let some shard of naivete severe what she knew at some primitive level and allowed herself to wonder at whatever it'd been that had scared off those men; it was a remarkable reaction given the relative size differences and their three-sheets bravado. Whether by the drink or the intoxicating essence of this angel—or some twisted chirality of the two—fear and attraction became indistinguishable. Whatever self-consciousness that otherwise dominated her when Abbey met someone new, particularly someone with such awful perfection and quiet ferity, dissipated and gave way to an odd contentment. It was as though they'd shared some deep, dark secrets over a lifetime of experience.

"I'm Abbey," she said and offered her hand.

The angel took the offering with a gentle grace and pulled her forward and into their body. They softly kissed her cheek and whispered, "Pleased to meet you, Abbey. I'm Anaye."

The warm words passed over the cooling spot where their lips had so recently departed and ghosted across her ear, sending a cascade of tingles down her spin and over the nape of her neck. Warmth from her core radiated to arousal, causing her inner thighs to unconsciously shift and squeeze together in hungry friction. Feelings she thought lost to the misery of the recent past, buried in the deep soil of trauma, clawed their way up to the sweet release of air. Whether she dared to allow it to grow was not something she felt was in her control, gradually sweeping her away on the rapids of abandon, and that was all right.

It was good, wasn't it? Proof she was still in there, still vital, still breathing. Still had the capacity for desire. It was intoxicating. Who was this stranger, this otherworldly savior and breaker of inhibitions? Was it more exciting for the lack of knowledge, for the novelty of anonymity? It didn't matter. Not now. Abbey would have time to overthink later, as she always did, but uncharacteristically she'd defer it to reflection and, for once, live in the moment.

They talked. Truly talked for what must have been hours. The bar had cleared out and closed up, leaving only the lonely firepit they had moved to perhaps minutes or ages ago. It all swirled together, and Anaye's hand tenderly placed on her thigh, index finger making little spiraling vortices within the dimple below the convex of the muscle, left Abbey divided in her attention and her respiration heavy. This creature, a beautiful and dangerous angel, saw her beyond the surface, penetrating into the depths of her soul. A level of intimacy thought lost long ago, impossible, but here now beyond doubt.

Before Abbey could think better of it, or care what her adulterous and abusive husband would think, they were in the tent as though transported on a rift. The dim camp lights that washed the room in a sepia warmth as the gentle breeze brought subtle scents of pine to vie with the depth of Anaye's body. The angel's hands slowly hovered over her skin as to reach the very threshold of perception. Up and over her hips, where the white linen dress bunched at her waist. An electric gaze locked between them in unbreakable truth.

Abbey reciprocated the exploration but with less subtlety, her body succumbing to a ravening where such restraint was impossible. Something unhinged, deeply primal and aggressive she had no idea lived within her; wild and dangerous and frightening. A place where she would be lost forever.

The creature's body was firm but soft, inviting the desire to taste it. Before she could take the leap, Anaye's lips were already on her own in a deep kiss. The hunger grew, and Abbey moved to put the weight of her body on the angel, but the creature's strength was greater, and they were suddenly on top of her, the weight of their body pressing Abbey into the bed. The angel ran their hand from her neck, over her breast, down the side of her body until it reached her hip where it squeezed. Something primal activated inside, and Abbey's body uncontrollably shuddered. Anaye's onyx eyes flashed with frightening but welcome desire as their hand released the grip and moved between her legs. Abbey arched back, and she could feel the pleased breath of the angel on her lips before she whispered, "Is this all right?"

Abbey had no breath to speak but nodded her head in a way that unquestionably conveyed an emphatic *yes* and begged for no further questions. Anaye smiled as they ran their fingers over the soft material, a thin barrier Abbey desperately wanted removed. As if the message were conveyed, Anaye guided a finger around the edge of her panties and pulled them aside before running it between her lips, spreading a soft wetness over the hooded bliss beneath.

Her entire body filled with flame as the creature's finger repeated the tiny, slow circles teased on her thigh only hours before. Anaye's lips began exploring her neck and over the slope of her clavicle, inching down, and with their other hand pulling the dress down from her shoulder to expose her breast where the journey continued. Time lost all meaning in the impatient savor as the creature's mouth finally found its destination. Her hips rocked as the warmth of their tongue outlined her parameter before sliding between. The angel's finger moved inside her, causing her back to arch with pleasure as it curled upward to apply a firm pressure within. Their free hand grasped her hip to hold her under their control as their tongue found the hooded core of her desire.

The experience was explosive and drained her of her energy. Abbey's reciprocation, while surely enthusiastic, could not be recalled when she awoke to the mid-morning sun streaming in through the open window flap. She signed deeply and smiled as she reached over to find a cold side of the bed.

The angel was gone.

She vaguely recalled a discussion before she'd passed out. Something about Anaye needing to leave before dawn, which Abbey had reluctantly accepted. The faint memory of asking if she'd see them again felt desperate and foolish, but the creature said it would be so.

Abbey rolled onto her back and stared at the peak of the tent, the amber hue of the sun reaching from behind as the shadows of trees danced gracefully across the canvas.

She reached blindly for her phone on the side table and pulled it over her face. A text from Deb waited.

Deb

Meet you in the bar for breakfast. Be ready to spill.

Of course Deb knows. She had a preternatural sense of these things. Or had she *heard* them? Just how loud had things gotten last night? So caught in the moment and disinhibition, she'd made no effort to be quiet, so maybe Deb had overheard it all. Or worse—maybe she had come by to check in and saw it.

Fuck.

What's done is done.

And, besides, she surprised herself to find she had no regrets whatsoever. Everything about the past however-many-hours were new and altogether out of character for her. Was this an early midlife crisis or some kind of awakening? Either way, it felt good.

Deb was sipping a mimosa at a table near the bar. Abbey couldn't imagine drinking anything but water right now. Playful recrimination danced on her friend's face; there was no avoiding it with her. Her supportiveness and excitement made Abbey uncomfortable, although she couldn't say what response would have been better. They agreed to leave it as a whim, an indiscretion never to be spoken of again, but, naturally, Deb would give those knowing looks for the rest of their natural lives.

They spent the day following the narrow trails fanning out from the campsite, a long and winding series of paths that took them along streams, weeping rock faces, and a few stunning waterfalls cascading in the sun. Her body felt released, free of the oppressive confines of that home and the cavern of a bedroom in which she spent far too many hours.

Deb, although entirely unasked, paddled on about her conquest as they walked. The air was warm and sweet under the shade of branches overhanging the well-maintained path. Abbey's mind drifted to a dreamworld where she abandoned that previous life and started anew here. Out in nature and away from bruised flesh and aching bones. Away from his hands promising love the morning after they'd rained down brutality.

If only he would disappear and, in his vanishing, liberate her from her prison.

If only.

Something stirred within Abbey—a strange feeling in the pit of her abdomen. An emptiness filled with something else. What was it? She was tired; maybe that's all it was. She searched the recesses of her mind to determine if the night brought remorse for her actions, if perhaps the weight of it was catching up. But no. It wasn't that. Everything in her said she'd done nothing wrong. After all, how many other women had Greg taken without a care for her? She had ample proof. The bastard didn't even try to hide it. What was it then?

Abbey left Deb to continue her flirtations in favor of an earlier bedtime. The angel hadn't made an appearance tonight, but that was all right. Perhaps for the best. What did she think would come of it, anyway? Some things were best left to perfect moments in time, tiny infinities residing only in the fondness of memory and untarnished by reality.

The small trail lights typically illuminating the walkway to her tent were sleeping, leaving only the pale moonlight to cast uneven grays between the trees and over the underbrush. Her feet crunched against the gravel as she made cautious progress and arrived at her equally dark quarters, a deep void beyond the pyramidal opening.

That feeling again, in her gut like a knot. The faint scent of an aftershave she knew too well swam in her mind. *Impossible*. She stepped through the screen and fumbled her way to the side table to light the portable lamp.

The harsh white light temporarily saturated her vision, preventing her from fully appreciating the figure sitting in the chair across the room within the folds of shadow. The voice came before her acuity returned, and there was no question.

"I trusted you. I gave you everything. I leave for an important trip, and how do you repay me? Run off without asking. No word. Nothing. What am I supposed to do with that, Abbey? Tell me."

Greg's voice was even, a quality of cold indifference always present just before things went wrong. Her body tensed and the knot in her gut twisted violently. The faded bruise over her eye stung as though refreshing itself in anticipation or intrusive re-experiencing. *How did he find me?* Her eyes briefly falling on her phone lying on the side table gave her the answer. Of course he would track her.

He got up slowly, standing straight with menace and predation. She couldn't help but glance at his hands. His eyes were frosty with detached rage. The corner of his mouth turned up in a sickening sneer, and before she knew it, he was on her. Fast. *So fast*. He vaulted over the bed between them and seized her about the arms, pinning her in place. Paralyzed with fright under the crushing weight of his hands, she barely registered the pain flaring from her muscles. His breath was hot and tinged with bourbon; his tolerance prevented the spirits from dulling his strength.

He was saying things, awful things, she knew that, but her mind was roiling too violently to process the words. She could feel it coming: the dissociating. That protective place her mind took her in these times, just as the ferocity began. One of his large paws released its grip and she could feel the shifting in his weight signifying the striking posture. Then there came a whooshing sound, as though the air had been sucked from the tent, and she was certain the fist had taken flight.

But no.

Abbey opened her eyes to a flash of flame and Greg, torn from his feet, whipped over the bed and onto the floor. The fire died around Anaye's dark figure where they were facing their target, leaving only the outline of their back and the shimmering coal of their long hair hanging desultorily to their waist. The creature's posture suggested preparation, those once provocative lines now akin to a beast preparing for the kill. A sight reminiscent of the night they first met, when Anaye's body stood once before between Abbey and danger.

Abbey had no words. There was an insincere compulsion to say *no*, to stop the angel from what came next. But Abbey didn't want to stop it. Instead, she watched as Anaye flew through the air with frightening speed and fell upon the crumpled form of the man who'd hurt her for years.

It was violent and horrible and terrifyingly beautiful. The angel's body moved around and over Greg, turning to the lamplight where Abbey could see the long black veins running like spidery rivulets from their darkened eyes, their sclera filled with the black of their irises, leaving the sockets in total voids. Their lips were likewise Stygian pitch and pulled wide into an unnatural rictus grin. The long fingers, once offering so much pleasure, now angry with sharpened talons that ripped into Greg's ribcage. The separation was quick and with an ease suggesting great strength as arteries burst with pressured turbulence into the air and across the canvas and bed. A hot, metallic scent filled the room as spatter flung in warm particulate over Abbey's face.

The creature bared its wide rows of razor-sharp teeth as one hand shoved into the chest cavity with a sickening squish to remove the rapidly beating heart. A savage series of bloody geysers shot in all directions as the organ separated from its branches and the body of Greg kicked and seized against the grip of death. The thing that was once Abbey's perfect angel held the muscle and watched the last twitch fade before ravenously consuming it with horrible speed. The creature looked up, eyes locking on Abbey's as dark arterial blood ran from its mouth in thick streams and chunks, a pool still sitting in its upturned palm and trailing in coagulating slow motion down its alabaster arm.

It was in that moment that Abbey's head swam nauseatingly as though her cerebrospinal fluid were swirling down a drain, and she fell like a ragdoll to the wooden floor.

Darkness took her limp body.

She passed out.

As her eyes opened, the glare was too much to take. Abbey bolted up, her mind having picked up from the images just before shutting down. She looked around and slowly realized she was somewhere else. The hospital room was quiet aside from the soft beeps of a small machine monitoring her vitals. Deb came quickly from the chair in the corner and began shushing her and saying, "It's all right, it's all right."

As it turned out, they'd found in her tent, comfortably in bed but unresponsive. She'd been in a sort of coma for nearly two weeks, but there were no signs of trauma or pathology. There was no mention of a bloodbath found in the room, and Deb confusedly assured her the only thing they'd found in those lodgings had been her.

Had it been a dream? It was far too real. Too visceral. But if it had been real, what happened to all the evidence?

She composed herself and hesitantly asked if there'd been any word from Greg. No, there hadn't. He wasn't answering his phone, but voicemails had been left for him. Probably out partying as usual or not giving a shit—also as usual.

But Abbey knew the truth. The creature, her angel beyond the flames, had saved her. Not only from the attack, but from the prison of the true monster who'd held her captive. Where was Anaye now? Would she ever see them again? When Deb broke the news to her, that's when Abbey was sure she would.

"It's crazy, I know. But there's no doubt. They ran tests... Abs, you're pregnant."

She knew. Somehow, even the day after the encounter, she knew. That feeling deep inside. A physical impossibility overridden by something beyond this world. Anaye certainly didn't have the earthly equipment typical of such a result but had nevertheless imparted something of themselves in the act that burrowed into her womb and sparked the process of gestation.

She was free now. Greg would never hurt her again, the angel saw to that. She'd keep her secrets, just these few, but the lies could stop now. There'd be no more deception to explain away bruises or make excuses. Not for him or anyone like him. Never again. No. The lies now would serve another master—her and her alone. Falling from her fingers and her lips to *protect* rather than to hide.

Lie or half-truth or secret, it came down to how she chose to see things. Abbey had learned the hard way how mental gymnastics offered a way of shifting a perspective. Was there a distinction between a secret and a lie? She told herself there was. And, anyway, she'd be the one pulling those strings and crafting the narrative. Choosing to believe the fictions she'd weave to lead this new life. It would be necessary for this baby, this child of the flame. Thinking on her life and all that had changed and all that would change more from there, it was all so bizarre but also beautiful. An intersection of miracles.

At least, that's how she chose to see it.

Inheritance

David O'Mahony

Rowan set the wicker basket down at the mouth of the cave and knelt, blowing air from his lips with a rasping sigh. The apples and cherries were just the wrong side of ripe, the tang hitting the back of his throat; but then nothing had grown right in the orchards that year. Accompanying the slowly rotting fruit was a hunk of dry, mouldering bread and a stone jug of milk left in the sun for no more than two days. At least *they* were meant to be in the ritual.

He'd almost scratched himself bloody by rubbing the nail of his left index finger on his right hand, though as much because sleep had eluded him for the better part of two days and nights as anything else. Two days without a drink—if he was getting jitters already, maybe he needed to find a new habit.

Rowan turned his itching finger to his scalp, picking under his chestnut hair. Maybe he should've showered, but it had been such a whirlwind since getting the call from his mother and having to race back home, leaving New York behind him for their vast estate in northern Maine, endless acres of farmland and orchards hidden safely within even more acres of pristine ancient woodland.

We need you back. You're the only surviving male Fitzroy. It's almost Samhain and the ritual must be done. Just don't be afraid.

It was the weirdest message he'd ever got from his mother, Miranda, and that was saying something.

INHERITANCE

Nothing about the place was like he remembered, and he'd only been gone six months. The evergreens lining the avenue to the house were browning and bald in patches, and the swathes of winter berries they'd planted—sole and juniper for gins, hawthorns and rosehips they sold to ritual magicians—were diminished, sickly things. Even the sign over the gate, saying simply *Fitzroy*, was tarnished. So much for being descended from kings.

But if it meant getting his inheritance, he wasn't going to argue. His parents had always been interested in the grim, the dark, the weird and fantastical, but this they'd kept to themselves. Or if they'd talked about it, Rowan had spent his life not listening. And anyway, what harm would one night underground really do?

"Are you sure I have to do this?"

"Yes," his mother Miranda said firmly. The white-haired servant Cotton whispered something in her ear that Rowan didn't catch. "Well, you can always say no," she added quietly. "But I don't know the last time that happened. The famine, I think. And do you really want to be the one that costs us everything?"

If his fool older brother Andrew hadn't gone missing in Norway, it would be him standing in front of the cave, trying to tempt the thing out. Rowan's twenty-first birthday was supposed to see him doing lines off as many men and women as he could cram into his hotel suite, not warding off the cold while waiting for, well, whatever the hell it was that lived in the cave. How weird that he knew they'd talked about it all his life, yet somehow had never known about the cave and could remember no details.

The path down from the house to the low mountains was bare, the thorns in the hedgerow dead before their time and spindly trees that should still have held the defiance of autumn reduced to nothing but skeletons against the pale blue of the sky.

After the drive to the house, he shouldn't have been surprised. Everything had been off since his father died. He'd had a good life, built the family business beyond his ancestors' wildest dreams, and died well. But everything had been a struggle since, even if for Rowan it mostly just meant less money in his account every month.

He spent his life on travel and parties and women; he'd never been ready to grow up.

It's just one night, he told himself. *Just one, probably completely fucked up, night. Still, what a story, yeah?* By morning it would be over and he could go back to being himself, just with access to his parents' millions. He'd done worse for less.

Provided the thing in the cave was happy with him. Provided he did a good job.

"Every eldest man in the family has done it for six hundred years," his mother said when he arrived.

Fuck you for dying, Andrew, and leaving me to clean up your shit.

From within the bowels of the earth came the long, slow scraping of sharp objects on immovable stone. At the heart of the pitch black, a deep orange light called itself into being, crawling toward him and steadily growing as it cast flickers on the walls. Somebody'd dug this place out a long time ago, Rowan realised as he shifted to stop gravel digging into his kneecap.

A stale wave of air hit him square in the face, making his eyes water and throat splutter. It was dry, ancient sweat and goatskin, with undertones of meat left to rot in teeth and the iron of blood. He knew that smell. It had been in the house the night his father died.

"Don't say anything," his mother whispered, prodding him sharply in the back. "Keep it together."

The orange light flashed, blinding him for a second until the dead stink almost bowled him over from right in front of him.

The creature loomed over him, at least eight feet high and just as wide. A great, shaggy goat's head reinforced with bone looked him up and down with penetrating green eyes, the puff of breath from its nostrils blowing the hair back from his forehead. As it turned, a sodden mantle of ancient leaves and mud rustled and shook as long, braided insects slithered out of it and onto the ground at its bony, gnarled feet. In a hand with fingers like jagged branches, it held a staff of fused femurs capped with a lantern of orange stone.

Rowan froze, every muscle straining, and his breath so shallow it almost didn't exist. What the hell was this? He was hallucinating, surely. Maybe there'd been some sulphur leak in the cave, or weird mushroom spores. It couldn't be real. And yet a quiet, insistent voice much like his father's told him, very sternly, that it absolutely was.

It craned down and sniffed at the offerings in the basket, grunting and huffing as it picked them up and secreted them within its cloak along with the milk. Then it leaned over and sniffed Rowan, who reared back as much as he could while Miranda and Cotton held him in place. The creature let out a sort of deep, throaty chuckle like the one Rowan's father would have made. A ragged nail felt across his jugular before grasping him firmly, but not too hard around the throat, lifting him from the ground as Miranda and Cotton shuffled behind him.

"Relax, relax," Miranda said, though Rowan couldn't tell if she meant him or the creature, which had let him go yet still dwarfed his full six feet.

It snapped fierce jaws at his mother, and Rowan could hear their boots click backward on the broken shale.

Rowan had his fists balled, ready to fight, even as part of him breathed heavily—eagerly, even—at the complete loss of control he'd just had. Why had nobody ever tried that with him before? Had he been too rich, too brash? His skin tingled where the creature had held him, and as he stood peering up into the shaggy head and the ragged strips of meat and vegetation caught in its razor teeth, it let a slender, gentle finger brush against his crotch, as if waiting for him to show an interest.

The delicate, teasing touch had him hard before he realised it. *What the fuck*, he thought, looking back at his mother as the creature withdrew into the opening to wait for him.

"You just need to spend the night, that's all," Miranda said, nodding at the creature like they were old, if vague, acquaintances.

"That's all?"

"That's all."

"And Dad did this?"

"He did. Every Samhain, no matter what else was going on in the world."

"And what if I change my mind?"

"Then you change your mind."

I kinda want to see how this plays out, though.

Jesus—where did *that* thought come from?

"Okay. Okay, see you in the morning."

Closing his eyes, he stepped forward, and the cave entrance closed behind him.

"You can open your eyes now."

The woman's voice was rich and earthy. He took a tentative breath, then a long and clear one as he found the air free of the stale sweat stink.

As he opened his eyes, a woman with skin the colour and marbling of polished limestone was emerging from the shell of the goat-creature, absorbing its bones into her as she reduced to his own height, though they still protruded as horns from beneath her quartz hair. The mantle of leaves thinned into a robe as thin as gossamer but the colour of new growth. The basket and milk had been placed on a small carved shelf next to a pile of sheepskins. The walls along the floor were lined with old bronze trays and bowls that had been polished until they reflected the light of the lantern, giving more than enough to see by. "I've had many names, but a long time ago somebody called me Gem, so that will do."

Rowan's heart hammered and his throat ran dry as she flicked a tongue of trailing ivy from her mouth and let it dance over his forehead, cheek, down toward his collarbone. At some point his shirt had come off, but he couldn't see it anywhere.

"So you're the one," Gem said, a rippling of stone shards running across her breasts and belly and standing out like a hedgehog's spines, but whether they were defensive or something else, he couldn't say.

"You're not as big as your father," she said, with a rough, shuddery sort of laugh as her eyes fixed on the bulge under his trousers. *Why did I wear the loose ones?* "But you'll certainly do. If you're interested, of course."

She plucked an apple from the basket, crunching down on it before screwing up her face in disappointment. "They were sweeter last time."

"It's, uh, not been the best year on the farm, or so I'm told." His father had died just under two years before, and his brother had gone missing twelve months after that. He wondered if he actually *had* ended up doing lines off somebody's chest and was now having a stroke, his dying brain making connections that didn't exist.

Her lips flowed into a soft, mysterious smile. "Bonds must be renewed. There was a time when all kings mated with the earth for the sake of a good harvest—so few remember that."

"Bonds? Huh? No, wait, what the fuck are you *doing* down here, anyway?" His voice dropped to a whisper. "Is it my mother? Do... do you need me to get you out?"

"Oh no," she said, gliding across the stone toward him on feet of purest ivory. The cave had to be fifteen feet high with a floor smoothed by time, and it stretched off into the far distance. The only light came from Gem's lantern. "I'm happy in the earth. I *am* the earth."

Wait, had she said mate with the—?

"Now you're getting the picture, Rowan." She threw her robe on the ground and stood, hands on hips, waiting for him to look at her. Instead, he gaped like a fool at her copper nipples hardening as she let her eyes wander over his crotch and chest.

"How do you know my name?"

Smiling, she drifted closer. "I know everything about you. There isn't a spot on this world that doesn't touch rock one way or the other." The side of one finger traced softly up along his cock. Stepping back, she shifted into a raven-haired petite woman with wide, strong shoulders—Adelaide, the first woman he'd ever slept with. Grinning at his recognition, Gem shook her head and flowed up and out until she was a taller, muscular blonde man all brawn and no subtlety with a hard-on to match—Mark, the first person he'd ever jerked off in front of.

Just as quickly, Gem was back to limestone skin and quartz hair, her hand sliding down between her legs as she traced along her pussy lips.

"*Everything*," she said. "Now show me that beautiful cock."

He'd unzipped almost before he knew it, groaning at the sudden freeness of his erection as much as at the touch of her smooth, cool hand as she pulled him toward her by his shaft. Her fingers roamed it deftly, pressing and sliding in equal measure. She trailed a thumb over the head of his penis, daring him to look down before pushing her vine-tongue into his mouth.

A dozen tiny shards of bone and rock thrust into him as she pressed herself against his stomach, his cries echoing over the bare rock of the cave. He would have sworn her body was made of stone until she was against him, and he clutched her ass hard to him, relishing the pulse of her muscles as she bit down on his neck and shoulder with rows of tiny teeth. The shards in his chest sucked at him firmly as she held him against the wall so tightly he could barely breathe—and didn't want to.

When she finally propped a leg against the wall and took him inside her, it was all he could to stop from cumming, the heat and wetness of her pussy so electric and intense he wanted to burst. She grabbed the base of his cock, holding it hard until he moaned and began to buckle against her. "Oh God," he whispered.

"Say it again," she breathed in his ear as she rode him. "Say it again."

"Oh God, oh God, oh God…"

"Now give me your seed. Put it in me." She fucked him hard against the rock. "Give it to me *now*."

The shards on her body stabbed deep into him as she came with an unfettered growl and he followed, pulsing into her harder than he'd ever done before. Then she thrust herself back, letting him moan and slump to the ground as he slid out of her.

He was bathed in sweat and breathing ragged, though she seemed unfazed. A long, red insect trailed out of her nose, jaw, neck, along her breasts, and dropped to the floor where it wriggled into the dark out of view. She began to glow a soft green around her edges, like mushrooms he'd seen once in Brazil.

"Is… is that it?" he said eventually, getting his breathing a little under control. *Why is my cock still so fucking hard?*

"You can go if you like. The seed is"—she rolled her shoulders—"perfectly adequate." She crouched down, breathing warm, sweet amber into his ear. "But I've seen right down into you and we've barely scratched the surface, haven't we?" She kissed his cheek tenderly and he cupped a hand to her breast, kissing her fiercely as she pulled him to his feet and toward the pile of sheepskins.

She looked down at his penis, still hard despite everything, still slick from her pussy. Biting her lip, she cupped his balls gently and squeezed until he gasped. Smiling, she ran her hand up and down the shaft gently with her other hand. Her eyes were a startling green, the irises rotating slowly like a kaleidoscope as she pulled the head of his cock against her stomach. "Don't cum just yet," she whispered, her tongue snaking out along his collarbone and cupping the back of his head, teasing around his throat until he gasped. "Don't you dare cum until I'm done with you."

She stroked him harder and faster against her stomach, then knelt without letting him take his eyes off her and sucked on him greedily, then furiously, until he came without warning, crying out as she caught his balls hard and pain shot down the shaft of his penis and all across his belly.

Her skin glowed a deep, contented green as she stood, smirking around the edges of her lips as he fought the urge to drop his hands onto his thighs and lean over to gulp in air. His muscles screamed as if he'd been running uphill on a midsummer's day without a drink, and his chest was a tattered mess of tiny pinpricks and cuts.

"Do you want to stop?"

"Can I?"

"Always. But the longer you last, the greater the reward—for everybody."

His hands were already on her ass, lifting her up as she wrapped legs as powerful as iron around him and slid down onto him without hesitation.

Even though he felt the life draining out of him with every thrust as they fucked on the floor, against the wall, or her on top, he couldn't keep his hands off her, no matter how many cuts he took from the shards in her chest or from her teeth as they ran free across him. As she wrapped her tongue around his throat, he begged her for more and every one of her orgasms made her shine brighter, made her throw her head back and let a thousand unknowable things ripple under her skin, which was soft as silk and unyielding as the mountain around them.

Eventually he collapsed back, breathing heavily as if his chest were caught in a vice, and stared at the ceiling as pulses of orange light from the lantern and green from Gem herself played across the rock.

Propping himself up on an elbow, heart hammering like a double bass pedal against his ribcage, he reached for the stoneware jug. His throat burned and head swam with thirst—just a drop of the aged milk, he said to himself, just a little drop to take the edge off.

Pressing the jug to his lips and tilting it, he gasped in surprise to find it a heady wine with the tartness of blackberries, and surprised himself even more by knocking the whole thing back in one gulp.

She laughed, an echoing hollow sound like a bag of small stones being shaken lightly. "As if I would allow a guest to drink sour milk," she said.

"Is that what I am, then? A guest?"

"Would you prefer to be a prisoner?"

She pushed him onto the sheepskins and he slumped willingly while she pinned him with her hips, her vine-tongue lolling down along her breasts and across his chest before she grabbed his wrists and held them up over his head. Her hair shone as pulses of green ran down from her scalp. Smiling deftly, her tongue rolling back into her mouth, she kissed him roughly.

Tumbling away from him before he could push himself inside, Gem laughed again and slipped over the stone deeper into the cave. "Come on," she said, picking up her staff of fused bone. "There's something you need to see."

Rolling onto one side and pushing himself weakly to his feet, Rowan swore that he caught his reflection in one of the bronzes against the wall. But it must've been some sort of trick—or maybe the wine had been a lot stronger than he'd expected. What if it had been more than two days since his last drink? What if he'd been here for a week, maybe longer? That ragged thing of skin and bone couldn't possibly be him, those protruding ribs couldn't possibly be his, the gauntness of body and face so unlike the robust, distinguished look he'd spent so many years honing in gyms.

But as she drifted off down the smooth stone corridor, the reflection went with her, almost of its own accord, and a few seconds later Rowan followed, even a moment out of her presence biting deep into his soul.

Dark gathered in as Gem and the lamp marched on, impossibly fast until they shrank almost to a pinprick of tussling green and orange light.

"Aren't you coming?" she said at his shoulder, making him jump. "It's not far," she said at his other side, and in the dark a soft, slippery sound rolling over rock ran up through his feet and shuddered at the base of his skull, forcing him to screw his eyes shut against a shock of agony.

When he opened them, he was in a broad cavern that swept up into the silent dark. Trails had been worn in the stone beneath him, polished smooth by a hundred thousand feet or something worse. The lamp staff had been thrust into a well-worn hole, throwing fingers of light menacingly in all directions as it rattled off the deep fissured rock.

"See anything you like?" And she giggled as she caught his chin softly and tilted his head up and around.

"No... no... what the *fuck*."

She laughed again, the shaking of rocks.

From a hundred niches hacked from the stone by brute force stared bloody, decaying faces, stretched and warped over crude rock mannequin heads, and each of them blinking desperately in the night as they tried to force words from lips that could no longer answer.

Redheaded men, bald men, clean-shaven men, bearded barbarian men almost rotted away to nothing, the moustaches of a century before and longer, the only thing in common being a certain haughtiness of the brow, a peculiar hollow by the chin like a dimple the same as Rowan's own.

"What the *fuck*."

"Indeed, dearest. What the fuck."

Catching him roughly, the delicate fingers digging ragged yellow nails into his skin, she kicked behind his knee until he slumped. The wall of undead faces tried to smile and laugh and whisper sweet nothings as he screamed, his pain and cries pushing back the slow march of time that threatened to eat them all.

"Look up."

"No," Rowan said weakly, head lolling against his chest. The shadows from her green glow danced across his sunken ribs.

"Look *up*."

In front of him, blinking rapidly and almost heaving with excitement, was the slashed face of his brother.

"Andrew? That's my—"

"No. That's *my* Andrew."

"But he was in Norway."

She shrugged, like a willow tree straining softly in the breeze. "If that's what they tell you. And yet here he is, having failed to do what he set out to do."

With fingers stretching too long for her frame, she brushed a face in the niche next to Andrew. The eyebrows still bushy despite streaks of green gore and blood, it was a face Rowan had only ever seen in yellowing old family photographs: his father's older brother, Harlan. Hadn't he gone missing during the war? His father never spoke of him, almost as if he were an embarrassment.

But what if it wasn't an embarrassment? What if Dad didn't talk about it because he was glad he was the one who'd ended up down here?

Still, Harlan's lips rolled and puckered silently. He wasn't trying to speak, Rowan realised, he was trying to *suck* something.

"What the fuck is this?"

"Well, a girl has to keep her options open, doesn't she? And there have been so many suitors over the years, and so many of them have been a dire disappointment—so many seeds just failing to take. Imagine promising the earth to itself and not being able to deliver? Still, waste not, want not. It gets so lonely in the dark."

She leaned over and kissed Harlan softly, then Andrew, then three more ruined men Rowan recognised from photos but whose names escaped him.

"All of them were firm men, good men, but they were all missing that spark. Yes, I think that's the word you'd use. They simply didn't... want it enough."

Rowan thought dimly of being told about family members dying young or abroad, as if there was some grim nobility in it. But why had so many lined up with some sort of catastrophe: Outbreaks among the livestock, fields of wheat turning to dust in drought, odd wasting sicknesses. Almost as if the land had rejected them.

As if the land—

She nodded, as if plucking his thoughts from the air. "I told you. The longer you last, the greater the reward. For you and your kin." She laughed her laugh of shaking stones.

Each of the faces wept blood at attention from Gem, all of their pale eyes falling on Rowan at once as their lips flowed in unison.

"What do they want?"

"A show."

"... A what?"

She smiled, the lips stretching until they burst into long, sweeping bones that trailed over her shoulders as her face cracked and erupted into the great, shaggy goat thing, legs popping until she towered over him, her skin erupting and bursting until it became the mantle of leaves and mud she'd been wearing at the cave entrance.

"Now, are you saying you don't want me one more time?"

She hiked up the mantle, exposing swollen pussy lips that trembled and pulsed.

He was on his knees before the thought was fully formed. *Oh God*, he thought. *Once more, please.*

A splash of water made him yelp and sit up in the same movement before his body shivered and recoiled from the morning cold.

"You're in one piece, then."

His mother's lips were pursed tight as her eyes looked him up and down.

Am I naked? Fuck, I think I'm naked.

Flailing a hand around, he was glad to find the greasy, filthy remnants of his trousers still protected some modesty, even if the rest of him was exposed to the open air.

"Well, she sure as shit did a number on you. You're practically skin and bone." She leaned back, lightly folding her arms and tapping her fingers. "Your father was the same, you know."

"He was...? You knew?"

"Knew? Oh Rowan, who do you think helped him burn off all those urges she gave him? You'll be the same, you'll see. But it's for the best overall."

"I have to go back," he said suddenly as Cotton scooped a callused farmer's hand under his arm and hauled him upright. "I need to go back, Mom."

She laughed. "Back *where*?" She swept her jaw behind Rowan, who turned to find he was facing a solid mass of brambles and sheer rock.

"Where the hell is it? Where the hell is it, Mum?"

"You don't need it anymore. Or maybe she doesn't need it. Not for another year or so, anyway."

Pain stabbed him in the gut like an assassin, and tears forced their way out of his dry eyes. "What am I going to do?" he said to everybody and nobody at once. "What am I going to do?"

Cotton rested a hand on Rowan's back and gently guided him toward the path back to the house.

"Don't worry," said his mother. "We'll find you somebody who can keep up with your... needs. I even have a suit I can give them to get you in the mood."

But if Rowan was listening, he didn't show it. Numb feet shuffled forward as his eyes stared into nothingness.

As he made it onto the path proper and turned toward home, the dead thorns in the hedgerow unfurled in the chill as green shoots pushed their way to the surface.

SOLOMON'S SONG
LARITA JANAE

"I grew up hearing stories of spirits. The Boo Hag was my favorite. How she would ride her victims, feeding off their breath in the night. I never believe it. Not until the night she rode me."

South Carolina was the last place Solomon wanted to be, but here he was again. His grandmother's death called him home, pulling him across several states with the magnetism that only ancestry could create.

He was her favorite grandson, despite their distance and the years between them. She left him everything; which wasn't much, but it meant the world to her. Her little house in the woods, and all its contents, were now his. It was exactly how he remembered it: worn down with time and love but somehow still standing—in a stubborn way, like her. It smelled of damp wood, jasmine, and black soap. Stories, told and untold, echoed within every room; lingering, sticking to everything like dust. Her voice lived on in every squeak of the floorboards. Her soul stitched with care into each quilt that told stories of their own.

After her body had been passed over and by, songs were sung, and she was returned to the earth. Solomon lay in her wooden bed with one of her books about

Gullah-Geechee folklore resting on his broad, tattooed chest. He thumbed through its yellowing pages, waiting for sleep.

Then a chapter about the Boo Hag caught his attention.

He smiled, a dimple forming on his left cheek, remembering how his granny used to scare him with these stories—a mischievous twinkle in her eyes.

Like she knew something no one else did.

Back then, as a little black boy full of imagination, he believed. These tales weren't just *stories*. The woods surrounding the house were a living, breathing entity, teeming with magical creatures that roamed just out of sight. Watching. Waiting. Some good, while others... not so much.

After moving away, he fell in line with a world that told him these teachings were wrong, *evil*. That his grandmother, with her love and respect for nature and spirits, was the villain. He forgot his roots, lost his accent, but he never forgot her or the last thing she said before he left:

"Don't let the Boo Hag ride ya."

He closed himself off. Became the kind of man who kept his voice low, his fingers busy, and his fist heavy. Women loved the way he moved through life like the world didn't own him. It didn't. Men didn't meet his eyes for too long unless they had a problem—or wanted one.

Suddenly, three knocks echoed through the house. Solomon dropped the book and looked at his phone. It was 12 a.m. Far too late for visitors—especially way out here.

He walked into the living room. A blanket of cold air seeped under the door, chilling his feet.

"Who is it?" he called.

No answer.

He was about to go back to bed when the knocks came again. Irritated, he swung the door open.

Moonlight poured in, and there stood a beautiful older woman with hair as white as snow. Her dark skin gleamed light blue in the twilight. She wore a simple cotton nightdress, a floral shawl draped around her shoulders, and held a bundle of wildflowers. Her feet were bare.

"I came to pay my respects," she said, her voice warm and smooth. Like the first cup of coffee in the morning. "It's a shame what happened to her. Ya'll never live very long."

"*Ya'll?*"

She held the flowers out to him. Something about her was off, but he didn't want to be rude. As he reached for them, his hand brushed hers.

Her skin—was as cold as ice.

She smiled, toothy and wide. "You're so warm and *soft,*" she said, eyes glowing red.

He jumped back, dropping the flowers, and slammed the door shut. His heart pounded. Thoughts raced.

He crouched, looking through the gap under the door.

No feet.

He stepped to the window, pulled the curtain aside, and sighed in relief. There was no one there.

Solomon opened the door.

Nothing.

No flowers. No old woman.

The only thing left of her was a cold chill that hung in the doorway on that humid summer night. And a putrid smell.

He shut the door, checked the locks, and returned to bed, shaking his head. Second-guessing what he'd seen.

Still spooked, he took the book and threw it.

"You're letting these stupid stories get to you again," Solomon muttered, settling back beneath the covers.

Eventually, he fell asleep.

Sometime during the darkest hour, the blue bottles rattled on the tree, the floor groaned, and a long shadow loomed over his limp body.

That night, he dreamed:

He danced by a fire burning bright against the night sky to a drumbeat that played with the rhythm of his heart. He was tangled in a slow, seductive dance with a gorgeous woman. Her body pressed into his. His hands gliding over her smooth, brown skin, maneuvering over her curves. She smelled floral and something wild. Her hair, soft and untamed. He inhaled, taking in her essence. The heat from the fire licked his skin.

Solomon awoke, covered in sweat and aroused. The sheets were tangled around his hips. He freed himself and ran a hand over his length. It throbbed, sending a wave of heat through him.

He briefly thought about relieving himself, but his grandmother's presence settled around him like she were still there. Watching.

It didn't feel right to do that here, in her bed.

He groaned, stretched his long body until his joints popped, then got up. Brushed his teeth, dressed, and laced up his shoes.

Decided that a walk would do him some good.

The morning air, heavy with dew, welcomed him. The woods were misty, glowing silver amongst the lush green landscape.

This was his favorite time of day. When the world was quiet.

He stopped at the blue bottle trees, remembering how he used to peer through the glass, looking for trapped spirits. He squinted in, watching the light dance within blue glass.

"All the bad ones get trapped in here."

Suddenly he felt like a boy again, sneaking out early into places his grandmother had always warned him about.

"Not all trees are your friends."

But he was grown now.

And she wasn't here.

So he could do what he pleased.

He wandered where he had been told not to. Nature welcomed him with open arms, enveloping him in beauty. He took in the sights and sounds around him with a renewed sense of curiosity—when the faint sound of a drumbeat broke through.

A breeze rolling through the trees seemed to guide him in the right direction.

He followed it, listening closely as the sound grew louder, pulsing with his heartbeat.

Through a thicket of bushes and trees—he saw her.

And everything around her blurred.

A woman in white, surrounded by plants, swayed like a fragrant flower in the wind. A small house—similar to his grandmother's but different—stood in the background.

Generally, he was the type to mind his own business, but something about her called to him.

Using the trees as cover, Solomon moved in closer.

Her long dress clung to her in all the right places. Watering can in hand as she tended to her plants.

The sway of her hips drew him closer.

She was mesmerizing. Her bronze skin shimmered in the light. Long, kinky black hair decorated with gold beads that hung down her back like a storm cloud, dancing just above the dip of her lower back. Her body, full and curvaceous, made his mouth water.

He felt warm—like he was standing too close to a fire.

She looked around at her plants, then turned to leave, but stopped.

"If you're gonna stare at me like that," she said, her voice warm and sultry, sending chill bumps across his skin, "you could say something."

She turned, smirking, eyes locked in his direction—like she could see him through the trees.

Solomon froze.

His cover blown, he stepped out, embarrassed.

"Uh... hi," he stammered. "I'm..."

She laughed, smiling so brightly her cheekbones lifted high, her eyes disappeared. The sweet sound of her laughter was like music.

"I know you," she said. "You're Solomon, right?"

He blinked, startled. And slightly turned on.

"Yeah... How'd you know?" He stammered.

She sauntered up to him, slow and easy, until they were only a few feet apart.

"I knew your grandma. My condolences," she said, her eyes searching his.

He nodded, internally fighting to find his words.

She dusted dirt off her small, well-manicured hand onto her dress, then held it out.

"I'm Asha,"

As soon as she said it, her name danced around in his head, playing like a song he'd never forget. When their hands touched, a jolt of electricity shot through him, lighting up every nerve-ending.

Without thinking, Solomon brought her hand to his lips and kissed it gently, savoring her scent for a moment.

Asha snatched back her hand, cheeks flushed.

"Oh god—I'm sorry!" Solomon said quickly, mortified.

What in the hell was that?

"First you're hiding behind trees and now you're kissing my hand?" she teased. "You're weird, Solomon."

He deflated.

"I like it," she added, eyes sparkling like raw honey in the sunlight.

He chuckled, but before he could respond, a sharp burning smell filled the air.

Asha's eyes widened.

"My damn cornbread!" she yelped, dropped the watering can, grabbed the bottom of her dress, and ran for the door. "It was nice to meet you!" she shouted over her shoulder.

Solomon stood there, smile on his face, watching her ass bounce with every step.

After the screen door slammed shut, he turned and headed home.

Thoughts of Asha filled every corner of his mind.

By the time he got home, the sun was high, but the heat didn't touch him. Solomon's body felt cold and off-kilter. Like maybe he was getting sick but it just hadn't hit him yet.

He was utterly exhausted.

Inside, he brewed coffee on the stove.

As he waited, he moved through the house, exploring places he wasn't allowed to before.

Now he couldn't get a whoopin'.

He headed straight for her "workroom", as she lovingly called it. It was a little room in the back of the house dedicated to her spiritual work. Bundles of dried herbs tied with string hung from the ceiling. Old books and jars filled with grave-yard dirt, herbs, and other powders lined the shelves. Candles, some melted and some new, sat in the window. One held the shape of her thumbprint.

He ran his finger over it, suddenly desperate to feel her touch and hear her voice again. The ache of her absence felt heavy in his chest.

He turned to leave but paused.

A piece of paper sticking out of the old wooden desk drawer caught his eye.

He opened it. The paper was attached to a worn, brown, leather-bound journal with a wax seal. He sat down and peeled it open, lump in his throat.

The first page read:

For Solomon

Seeing his name written in her handwriting felt like a kiss and a slap on the cheek all at once.

He took a deep breath, flipped the page, and began to read.

My sweet boy,

If you found this, then that means I'm gone. But don't you go on grieving too long. You got a life to live and things to do. Just because my body's gone don't mean I'm not still with you.

I'm in this house.

In the land.

I'm in you.

Don't forget who you is and remember what I taught you.

Throw out the salt.

Hang up the broom.

And whatever you do, don't let the boo hag ride you.

When you grow old and your time comes, I'll meet you in the sweet by and by.

I love you,

Grandma.

Solomon ran a shaky hand over his face. It came back wet with the tears that weren't supposed to be there. His heart hammered against his ribcage. Her words pulled something loose in him. Memories of her flooded his mind. Longing tugged at his heartstrings; guilt wrapped around his neck like a noose.

In his mind's eye, he pictured her out here all those years with nothing but stories and prayers to keep her company. His chest ached for the lost time he'd never get back. He held the journal close to his heart like it had the power to soothe him.

The sound of the blue bottles on the tree outside clinking caught his attention. His eyes closed, he listened. Then set the journal down.

And when he looked up...

A face looked back at him through the window.

It was a woman.

Not Asha.

Not the old woman from the night before.

Younger. Her features were sharp, her skin was the color of cinnamon. Her hair was locked, coiled like roots that framed her face. She looked feral, inhuman. Her hands gripped the frame like she was ready to pounce on him through the glass, eyes glowing red. A smile spread across her face, toothy and unnatural—

And then she vanished.

Solomon jumped up, looking through the window.

But she was gone.

He backed away slowly, confused, chest tight.

The sound of the floorboards creaking behind him made him turn around fast.

Nothing.

He shook his head, yawned, stretched. Wiped the rest of the tears from his face. Feeling silly for getting so emotional.

The scent of coffee drew him back to the kitchen. He poured a cup, settled his tired body into a chair, took a few sips—fighting to keep his eyes open. Caffeine was strong, but the pull of sleep was stronger.

He didn't read the rest of the journal.

He didn't throw out salt or hang up the broom.

He collapsed in bed like he had no bones. The sound of the blue bottles outside lulled him into a deep sleep.

His dream developed immediately. He was back by a fire that burned taller, brighter, and wilder. This time the drums played louder, more frantically, as if trying to awaken something ancient.

And there she was:

Asha.

They were naked, entangled in dance. Her supple skin gleamed with sweat. Her hips rolled, pressing her ass firmly against his groin. She wrapped his arms around her, guiding his hands over her bare body. Then she moved away, dancing on her own. He watched before reaching for her, his desire burning fiercer than the fire.

When his hands touched her again, they felt strange. Wet. He held them up to find they were covered in blood. When his gaze returned to Asha, what stood before him wasn't her.

It was a Boo Hag.

A creature of red muscle with hollow black eyes that peered deep within his soul.

A foul sulfur smell in the air.

She lunged, landing on his chest, feet and hands pressing down on his ribcage, pinning him to the ground. The fire exploding sent sparks into the air.

"Sing for me, Solomon," it hissed in many twisted voices at once.

It placed its mouth over his and began to suck.

The air left his lungs in one long, silent scream.

Solomon shot up, gasping.

It was so cold he could see his breath.

He sat up just in time to catch a glimpse of a shadow moving past the door. The floorboards squeaked under its weight. He jumped out of bed and ran after it, but found himself alone in the kitchen, looking around in a panic.

He leaned against a wall, trying to catch his breath, chest heaving. The house was quiet and everything looked normal.

But why was it so cold and what was that awful smell?

The blue bottles outside rattled as he poured himself a glass of water, gulped it down, and leaned against the counter.

"It was just a dream," he muttered, trying to ground himself.

As he headed back to the room, the wicker broom fell, landing at his feet.

"They're complicated but simple-minded creatures."

"The hell?" he snapped, jumping back.

"When they see brooms they have to count every bristle."

He picked it up, looked around, then put it back up on the wall.

"There," he muttered out loud. "Happy?"

The floor creaked as if answering him, sending a chill down his spine.

"I'm in this house. In the land. I'm in you."

A sudden whisper cut through the silence.

"Solomon!" it hissed.

He ran back into the bedroom and slammed the door shut.

Solomon stared at himself in the bathroom mirror, trying to control his breathing. He lightly slapped his cheek a few times, it then wiped a hand over his face.

"You're a grown-ass man," he whispered. "Get it together."

His chest rose and fell. His deep brown skin glazed with sweat, making the tattoos that covered his chest and curled around his arms shine like freshly spilled black ink. His body was chiseled from countless hours in the gym. Looked powerful.

He leaned in, his large, calloused hands gripping the sides of the sink.

"You're just tired. Ain't nothing here but your imagination," he muttered, looking at his face in the reflection.

When something caught his attention in the mirror.

Three long scratch marks trailed down the center of his chest.

Red, thin, and fresh.

He was also speckled with bruises.

He ran his fingers over them, wincing. The sting was sharp enough to bring tears to his eyes.

He glanced toward the bed.

Something looked *wrong*.

He shuffled over to find the quilt turned inside out. The fabric shredded, just like his chest. His brow furrowed, he held it up and examined it closely. How the hell had he done this in his sleep?

A heaviness settled around him.

The air became suffocating.

The quilt fell from his fingers. He examined the bed next and found the place where he had laid sunken in, deeply. The mattress molded to the shape of his body—like something heavy had weighed him down.

He was a big man.

But not *that* big.

Solomon backed away, returning to the mirror. Splashing cold water on his face, watching it drip from his beard.

"You're just tired," he whispered, shaking his head. "You need to chill."

But his body ached like he had been in a fight and had lost. The muscles in his shoulders and back were in knots. Normally he would take a hot shower but there wasn't one.

He looked over to the white clawfoot tub.

A bath. A hot bath would have to do.

He stripped down as the hot water collected in the tub. As he sank in, steam curled around him. The scent of lavender and lemon balm bodywash filled the air. The warm water clung to his skin.

He would just have to smell like an old woman today.

His phone lay on the floor playing some soothing lo-fi beats. Eyes closed, letting the music and the water soothe him until he was completely relaxed.

Last time he was in this tub, his granny had been washing him. Probably telling him he smelled like outside. Back then, he fit perfectly. Now his feet hung over the edge.

He probably looked goofy.

Weird.

Just like Asha said.

As if summoned, thoughts of her blossomed in his mind. The sound of her laugh. Her smile. The way her breasts rose and fell with every breath. The way the sun kissed her skin. How small and soft her hand felt in his.

He smiled.

The water and steam felt like fingers nails grazing his skin, teasing him.

He was hard in an instant.

This time, he didn't resist.

He tilted his head back, raising an eyebrow. "If you're here, Grandma... you might wanna sit this one out," he muttered to the ceiling.

He waited, but the house remained quiet.

No creaks from judgmental floorboards.

Solomon picked up his phone and attempted to find something to watch to *inspire* him, but videos just buffered. The signal out here was trash. He tossed the phone aside, closed his eyes, and let Asha take center stage in his mind.

As soon as his eyes closed, she appeared. She lay in front of him, playing with her large breasts, dark nipples erect. She lifted her dress, exposing her thighs. Then she opened her legs and spread her pussy lips to give him a good look. She bit her lip, staring him in the eyes as her fingers circled her swollen clit.

His hand drifted below the water, running along his length. He gripped it tightly, stroking himself once, and sighed.

In his mind, she slid two fingers inside herself. Her cheeks flushed, eyes rolled back, as she pumped her fingers in and out. Moaning softly.

He stroked himself faster.

His toes curled, body tensed—seconds before he came with a deep grunt.

He sat there for a moment, water going cold, trying to catch his breath. Somehow he still felt... unsatisfied.

He got out, dried off as the water drained from the tub, and dressed. As he pulled on a soft white t-shirt and sweats, his stomach growled.

Barefoot, he wandered back into the kitchen, pondering what to eat. He was looking into the cabinets when he saw a bag of cornmeal and a thought popped into his head.

Asha and her burned cornbread.

Maybe he could make her another to apologize for the awkward introduction.

After years of watching his grandma make cornbread in an old cast-iron skillet, he still remembered how. Some things you never forget—good music, good people, and good food. He tucked a dishrag into the front of his sweats like an apron.

"I'm officially turning into an old black woman," he muttered with a half-smile.

And got to it.

The cornbread came out perfectly imperfect. Golden brown on top and a little burnt on the edges. Solomon wrapped it in a clean kitchen towel and tucked it into a wicker basket he found in the cabinet. He tossed his makeshift apron to the side before checking himself over in the mirror.

He brushed his hair, beard, and made sure his skin wasn't ashy. And his breath didn't stink.

Then ventured out down the trail towards Asha's house, rehearsing what he would say in his head.

The walk there felt longer somehow.

The trees looked taller, stretching over him menacingly. Their moss-draped branches hung low, some like arms reaching for him, tugging on his clothes like they didn't want him to go. The cicadas' hum sounded dull, as if he were listening with fingers in his ears. A breeze blew through the foliage, pushing against him as if it were whispering words he couldn't understand.

Curses?

Warnings?

But still, he kept walking.

When the house came into view, he thought about turning back. His idea suddenly felt foolish—but the smell of something familiar pulled him closer.

Okra soup.

It smelled oddly identical to his grandmother's. His stomach growled loudly, the smell drawing him onto the porch.

He was already there. Too late to turn back now.

He took a deep breath and knocked. The door opened almost instantly.

Asha stood there in a bright pink dress with a bold floral design that hugged her waist.

"Evenin'," she said, smiling brightly.

His thoughts scrambled like TV static.

"I brought you some cornbread," Solomon said, holding up the basket. "Sorry about this morning."

She took the basket and stepped aside to let him in.

"Well, that was sweet of you," she said. "No need to apologize, though. I'm always burning something."

He stepped inside and was immediately struck by its beauty. It was a small space filled with personality. Abstract portraits and books lined neatly on the walls. Some books stacked in tilting towers leaned in the corners. Plants grew freely from pots like they paid the bills. It was cool and dark, like hiding under the shade of a tree on a hot summer day. The air smelled of honeysuckle and something unplaceable that stuck to the back of his throat.

"I was just about to make another batch. You read my mind." She motioned for him to sit at a table set for two.

Solomon raised an eyebrow. "You expecting someone?"

Asha shrugged. "Maybe I was hoping you'd come back."

He pretended not to be caught off-guard; he bit his lip and tried not to smile.

She placed two pots on the table—okra soup and white rice—then set the cornbread down. As she took the tops off the pots, steam curled into the air like long, gnarled fingers, filling the room with a scent so familiar it made his heart ache.

It was as if time folded in on itself.

He inhaled deeply.

It smelled just like the love he missed.

Asha sat down across from him. A lock of hair fell over her face as she spooned okra soup into his bowl. The first bite was intoxicating. He closed his eyes, savoring the taste and smell, chewing slowly.

Asha smirked, "I'll take that as a compliment."

He smiled. "It's just like my grandma used to make. Almost the same."

"It's funny how something as simple as tastes and smells can hold memories," she said, watching him closely.

He nodded, mouth full, his brain replaying old memories.

Asha felt older than she looked—not in a bad way. In a knowing way.

Solomon generally wasn't a talker, but tonight, conversation flowed as easily as the soup into the bowl. Minutes blurred into hours and the sky darkened.

Asha told him of her childhood, how she grew everything she ate, her favorite author, favorite artist. The paintings on the walls were all made by her talented hands. He sat back, stomach full, relishing the way she spoke of the things she loved with such excitement. She asked him about the city, his job, his childhood.

They talked until the creatures of the night started singing their songs, serenading them. Soon after, she rose from her seat and went around the house lighting candles, bathing them in warm amber light. Shadows stretched across the floor, dancing with the cadence of their voices. She pushed the pots aside and placed a few candles in the center of the table, then sat back down.

He studied her face in the flickering light—the gleam in her eyes, the curve of her lips, and the way her skin glowed with a golden undertone.

It felt like he was meant to be there. Like somehow, that moment was made just for the two of them. The world beyond her front door was wiped out of existence.

"So you're an electrician? That's a good job," Asha said, placing her chin in her palm. "Dangerous, too."

Their eyes met. He nodded, then looked away. Pouring them both glasses of cool water to distract himself.

"It can be," he said, offering her a glass. "If you're not careful."

"You must be good with your hands then," Asha teased.

She reached for the glass. Their hands touched.

A fire ignited in his chest.

"You have no idea," he said, looking deep into her eyes, smiling.

Asha blushed. "Wow. I walked right into that one." She took the glass, taking a sip.

"You did." He laughed.

The energy between them felt magnetic.

Something in the way she looked at him told him—yeah, she felt it too.

It was dark now. Crickets and pollywogs sang. The smell of rain hung thick in the air. A low rumble of thunder interrupted their conversation.

"Satan's beating his wife," Solomon said without thinking.

His granny used to say that all the time.

"Behind the door with a frying pan," Asha finished.

Solomon raised an eyebrow.

Asha stood, stretching. "Time to wash these dishes," she said in a sing-song voice that made him smile.

"Let me help," he offered, eager to stay as long as she would allow.

He grabbed the plates. She filled the sink with warm water and a couple squirts of dishwashing liquid. He plunged the dishes into the bubbles; the smell of lemon wafted up. They worked in silence, side by side, staring out the small window over the sink. She washed and he dried.

Being so close to her made goosebumps rise on his skin.

He glanced down once—just once—watching her scrub a pot with vigor. Her lips pursed, breasts jiggling softly with every motion. He cursed in his head and looked away. She passed the pot to him and her arm brushed his.

They both froze.

His breath caught in his throat and every hair on his body stood on end. He looked down at her. Her eyes burned into his, her lips parted.

He couldn't explain what came over him.

Before she had a chance to turn around, he stepped over, trapping her between him and the sink. He leaned down, putting his face into her hair, and inhaled. It was as soft as cotton. He brushed it out of the way. His lips found her neck, sending a light trail kisses across her soft skin. Asha sighed softly, pressing her body into his.

That was all he needed.

His swollen cock pulsated in response.

"What have you done to me, Asha?" he whispered softly into the curve of her neck. He bit her softly, wrapping an arm around her waist while the other explored her body. He squeezed her breast, slid his hand down her thigh, pulling her dress up until he felt skin.

She whimpered as his fingers found what they were searching for. She was warm, wet, and practically melted into his palm. He teased her clit slowly before sliding a finger in. She gasped, rolling her hips.

"I told you I was good with my hands," he murmured against her skin.

Thunder rumbled low as he fingered her, savoring the feeling of her and every sound she made.

Asha gripped his wrist and turned to face him. Their lips came together like two matching puzzle pieces, kissing hungrily. She slid her hands under his shirt, running her nails over his skin, moaning into his mouth. She pushed him, guiding him toward her bedroom.

Still tangled together, they stumbled out of the kitchen—his heel hit the edge of a chair, she knocked down a painting. They laughed, breathless, still entwined. They staggered farther back into the house.

As they entered her bedroom, he bumped hard against a door on his right. It cracked open.

Cccccreeeaaakkkkkk.

Thunder rumbled.

A foul, rotting stench wafted out.

He turned toward the cracked door, opening it the rest of the way. Flies swarmed out. He waved them off.

Lightning flashed outside, momentarily illuminating the room just long enough to see inside better.

Hanging from wire hangers—were skins.

Full-bodied human skins with a simple slit in the middle, just wide enough for something to step out of—or crawl into. They hung limp and slick, like grotesque costumes. Some dripping with blood, swaying slightly.

Something deep, dark, and stronger than fear kept him rooted in place, just staring.

His eyes lit up—like he'd been waiting for this his whole life.

As rain began to dance on the roof, he reached in, fingertips caressing an empty carcass gently. It was still warm.

They felt familiar.

"I told you not to be going out in them woods at night, Solomon."

"What are you?" he whispered.

"There's things out there older than the Bible. Older than your name."

"I'm the thing in the woods your grandmother warned you about," Asha said, her voice layered, like there was more than one person inside her speaking.

"Things that don't mean us no good."

He turned.

Her eyes were glowing red, matching the embers of desire burning within him.

"Aren't you afraid?" Asha asked, the skin around her mouth moving oddly, like it was coming loose.

"I should be," Solomon admitted, "But I'm not."

He stepped closer.

"I've been waiting for you for a long time," his voice rumbled like gravel.

He grabbed her hand, pulling her into him.

Thunder rumbled overhead as their mouths met and they backed up onto the bed. She straddled him, kissing like they'd craved each other for centuries. She ground a wet spot into the soft fabric of his sweats, eager to feel him inside her. Their lips broke for a moment as she tried to free herself from her dress.

Solomon didn't wait.

He simply ripped it, throwing it into the corner. His eyes roamed over her naked body before their lips met again.

"I want to see," Solomon breathed into her mouth, his voice heavy. "Show me."

Asha sat up, smiled mischievously, and slid off the bed with a dancer's grace.

Solomon took off his shirt, freed his cock, spit into his hand, and stroked himself slowly, watching her every move.

Her body swayed to the sound of the storm, then she vanished into the closet...

And an old woman came out.

The same one that knocked on his door the night before.

Staring at him with the same intensity.

He knew it wasn't right, but—he wanted to see what the dress was hiding.

"That was you?" he panted.

She nodded.

Her clothes fell to the floor.

Her gray hair glowing, breasts hung low, stretch marks looked like lightning splitting the sky. She walked over to a chair in the corner, sat down, and spread her legs.

He watched—transfixed—as she teased a nipple with one hand and circled her clit with the other.

"I've been watching you the whole time," she moaned, her wetness drooling off the chair. "I saw everything."

"Really?" he asked, breath heavy.

She nodded.

"Now, I'm watching you," he said.

He watched her juices pool on the floor—a waste.

His mouth watered.

He briefly considered asking if he could use some, but he didn't want to interrupt.

So he spat into his hand—imaging it was hers—and stroked himself harder.

They watched each other, their breathing in sync, matching the other's pace. The room pulsed with heat—*need*. Even with the space between them, it was like their bodies were touching. Fucking each other without physical contact. The chemistry between them was thick enough to gag on.

Asha rubbed her clit faster, squirming in the chair, hips lifting slightly. Her legs shook as she came. She moaned, grunting low, in three long, drawn-out breaths. Her cunt twitching with every sound. Her chest rose and fell as she caught her breath, then looked at him with a wicked grin.

He exhaled sharply, bit his lip, slowed his stroke.

Without a word, she stood and glided towards the closet—moisture trailing down her thighs, disappearing into the darkness again.

This time, what came out was the woman he had seen in the window. Wild hair in tight coils, eyes glowing, her body toned, sculpted curves, and effortless grace.

With a fuckable face.

She spun around slowly, letting him get a good look, then she crawled onto the bed—stopping at his moving hand.

She slapped it away.

"After seeing you that night, I couldn't help myself. Your skin is so soft," she whispered.

He felt the warmth of her breath with every word. She lowered herself, her lips grazing his skin, kissed around his shaft and tip before taking him into her mouth. Sucking him in a slow and methodical way that sent shockwaves through his body. Her tongue traced his length. She dipped her head lower each time.

"Shit," he moaned, gripping the sheets.

She took his hand, placing it on her head. She didn't have to say it. He could see it in her eyes.

He wove his fingers through her hair and tightened his grip, holding her in place—then took over. Forcing her mouth down onto him, thrusting his hips upward.

Over and over.

And she took it, eagerly, until she was swallowing him completely. Saliva trailed from her mouth, coating his cock and dripping down his balls.

When he felt like he was getting close, he tried to pull back. He wanted to cum but not now. He desperately wanted to enjoy this creature and all its manifestations; bask in its lies for as long as he could.

"S... stop. I'm gonna..." he said through clenched teeth.

She didn't.

She dug her nails into his thighs, holding him in place. Sucking him harder—devouring him. He tried to pull her hair to lift her off him—she moaned like his desperation was an answer to her prayers and bobbed her head faster.

He groaned, his voice filling the room, his body going stiff. Just as he was about to cum—

She pulled away as if she knew. Thick saliva ran down her face, swinging from her mouth to his cock. She didn't bother wiping it away.

"F... fuck," Solomon gasped, covered in sweat. The room was starting to spin. The storm picked up outside.

She laughed—deep and dark—bubbling up from somewhere deep in her stomach. The room dimmed. Shadows twisted. Candlelight flickered.

"That's exactly what I'm going to do," she growled, her eyes glowing fiercely.

Lightning struck as she vanished into the closet again.

Then stepped out as Asha.

She climbed on top of him, rocked her hips, she slid him inside her. They both gasped at the same time.

"Is that what you wanted to see?" Asha asked as she moved, clenching around him.

Solomon shook his head, gripping her hips, biting his bottom lip. He looked up at her, enchanted but aching—for what was *underneath*.

"Say it," Asha moaned, her voice thick like warm molasses. "Tell me what you want."

"I want to see *you*," he breathed, "The *real* you."

A smile spread across her face, revealing rows of sharp teeth as she rode him to the sound of the storm.

"You sure?" she cooed, teasing him, riding him faster.

"Yes."

"Beg."

"Please," he begged, his breath catching. "I... *need* it."

She changed her rhythm to a slow, deep grind, making small, tight, torturous circles on him, dragging out his pleasure. Her hands glided over her curves like she had just remembered she had them.

With one finger, she traced the delicate line of her neck, then pinched the skin at her collarbone—and peeled away the skin going down the front of her body until it lay open.

Solomon watched in silence, gently rubbing and squeezing her thighs in anticipation.

This was the striptease he'd craved.

She loosened the skin on her head, taking it off like a mask; it fell behind her, then she freed her shoulders. She wiggled her finger, then slipped her arms out, like she were slipping out of expensive silk gloves. The loose skin-suit hung around her waist in meaty folds.

What rode him was red, raw, and beautiful, in a poetic way that hurt to look at.

"Yes," he sighed, eyes rolling back.

Steam rose from her skinless, glistening body. Muscles and tendons shone red in the candlelight. Her blue veins throbbed, flowing over muscle like rivers.

Then she rose.

The wood floor creaked under her weight. She pulled the skin the rest of the way, as if she were stepping out of a pair of tight jeans. The limp skin dropped with a sickening wet thud.

Finally—she was free.

What stood before him was pure, *glorious*, and terrifying.

Nothing but muscle, bone, and ancient magic.

His.

In that moment, his body needed her like it needed *breath*.

She crawled on top of him until he was staring into her dark, hollow eye sockets. His hands moved on their own, caressing her face, her shoulders.

"You're the most beautiful thing I've ever seen," he whispered.

Then they kissed.

Wet, sticky, and full of passion.

His mouth muffled the sounds of thousands of tortured screams coming from inside her.

He rolled her over, grabbed her foot, pulled her to the edge, and slid off the bed. Standing over her, he kissed the soles of her feet, sucking on her toes, then kissed down her leg. He knelt, then buried his face in the space where her womanhood should've been. He licked and sucked the muscle and connective tissue while stroking himself. When his tongue found a hole, it thrilled him. He let go of himself and slid a finger into it.

She howled in response.

Her skinless talons gripped the top of his head. Her feet rested on his shoulders. He feasted upon her like she was his last meal until the wood floor dug into his knees.

He rose, licking the blood from his lips, his mouth and beard stained a deep shade of red. Blood dripped onto his chest. He licked his fingers clean, looking down at her laying there in all her *gory*. Her hollow eyes bored holes through him. Blood soaked into the beige sheets around her body like a demonic halo. He smiled, white teeth tinted red.

She reached for him.

Pulled him down.

And sat on top of him again. Somehow she was heavier now, pressing him into the mattress. Her hands pressing into his chest. She rocked her hips, teasing him with her moist body before gripping it in a skinless hand. She stroked him a few times before working him into her.

It squeezed in with a wet squelch.

His body writhed with pleasure.

And she rode him hard.

She was a viscera-gleaming goddess in the darkness as her hips slid back and forth. She placed a hand around his throat, squeezing as she moved. Bringing him closer to the edge with every rock of her hips, leaving a trail of fresh blood.

He moaned her name.

She leaned in, whispered his name into his mouth. Picking up speed, riding him so hard the wooden bed groaned with them.

"Jesus!" he cried, tears brimming as he gripped her waist.

The Boo Hag laughed. "He's not coming," she whispered. "You are."

And he did.

As if by command, his muscles locked, his back arched. It felt like his soul was being torn out. As he climaxed, he cried out in the dark.

He lay gasping in utter ecstasy, her body on top of his, still inside her.

The room spun.

The edges of reality frayed.

Even through the haze, he knew what she wanted. Crossing her threshold came with a cost.

His only reason for living was gone, and there was no need to prolong the inevitable. Besides, he was tired of caring about a life that didn't give a fuck about him. He'd get to be with his grandma again.

"Take it," He muttered. "You can have it all."

She leaned down. Her hand cradled the back of his head. Her mouth brushed his.

And she began to inhale, drawing his breath into her.

Slowly at first...

then deeper.

Deeper.

As his chest tightened, his vision blackened, he didn't fight. As his chest caved and he could feel his soul being sucked away.

He surrendered fully.

As the final breath left his lungs and passed through his lips, he wheezed out one word—

as beautiful and tragic as a song:

"Glory..."

"I'll meet you in the sweet by and by."

Solomon awoke with a shout, inhaling sharply. His phone buzzed across the nightstand. His chest was heavy, breathing labored. Sweat slicked his skin. A car zoomed past playing something loud that was more bass than music.

He was in *his* apartment. In *his* bed.

He sat up, head swimming.

Still alive. Still whole. Still breathing.

"It was just a dream," he told himself, looking around his dark room.

The phone buzzed again. The screen lit up.

"Ma"

His hand trembled as he answered the phone.

"Hey," he gasped in a voice that didn't sound like it belonged to him.

"Baby, I got some bad news. Mama... your granny passed." Her voice cracked.

"What?!"

Solomon's heart dropped, and so did the phone.

Déjà vu ran down his skin like ice water.

He had been here and done this before.

She was already dead.

Funeral over.

Stupid suit worn.

Then a hum tore through the darkness.

Haunting, soft, and familiar.

He knew the song:

"I'll meet you in the sweet by and by."

He turned his head slow. It was coming from the bathroom.

The door creaked open and a light flicked on by itself. The water started running.

He lived alone.

No one was supposed there.

But the humming continued.

He threw the blanket aside and stumbled toward the sound on shaking legs. He turned off the water. The mirror had fogged over.

Something moved beyond the condensation.

He reached out and wiped the glass—revealing a face.

His grandmother's face was as clear in the reflection as if he were looking through her eyes.

She didn't blink. Didn't smile.

She shook her head with a sad look on her face.

"I told you not to let her ride you," she said.

Then she was gone.

He was left staring at his own reflection.

Then from his room came a voice, soft and velvety:

"Bae, you okay?"

He backed away from the sink and turned toward the doorway.

She was in his bed.

Asha lay beneath the covers, watching him, the side of her face resting on the pillow, her dark hair spilled around her. One hand tucked under her chin. Like she belonged there. Her posture was too perfect, like she hadn't been sleeping at all.

She looked too peaceful.

More like she was pretending, posing. Her eyes sparkled in the dark, glowing red. She smiled. Wide and full of teeth.

And Solomon...

Smiled back.

YOU GO INTO THE WOODS TO DIE
ARLO Z. GRAVES

You go into the woods to die, they say. The Huldra of Blackberry Canyon lives there. You only go into her woods if you're looking for trouble. She hates men, they say, especially hunters.

The bell on the door of Jimmy's Rods and Tackle chimes as I enter; the familiar smell of sawdust and paint from the color-mixing machine greets me. Tchotchkes dangle on a rack beside the door. Postcards, key chains, painted figurines ordered from out of the country. From them, the Huldra of Blackberry Canyon watches me, eyes yellow as a coyote's, teeth gleaming wet and needle sharp. Her back's open like a rotted tree stump, but her front is supple and nude. Our sexy local cryptid.

She's just a legend, of course. A tourist attraction. I took her to heart anyway.

I wonder if Liam Crawford took her to heart too.

"Oh, hi, Miles," the old cashier, Willits, presses his bristly lips together when he sees me. "Paint pickup?"

I step up to the counter. I square my shoulders but lower my eyes from his. "Deer tags."

"Hm." Willits sniffs the air through his nose like a bloodhound. He goes to the back counter to the computer. "Know how to handle a piece?"

"You mean a gun? Yeah. Yeah, I know how to handle a gun. Dad taught me. We used to shoot in the yard."

"Hm."

He slides his glasses up his nose and squints at the boxy, grey computer monitor. "Deer hunting." He says it more as an accusation than a question.

"Yeah," I say.

"Hm."

The back of my neck grows hot and my palms sweat. It's not that I want to go deer hunting, but it's time. I've been out of college and back in Blackberry Canyon for a year. It's past time.

Satisfied with whatever the computer tells him, Willits hands me the tags. "Didn't even know you did hunter safety," he says.

"I did." I turn to go.

"Look out for the Huldra," says Willits. I can hear the smile in his voice, the upward pull of his lips.

My shoulders droop as I step back out into the quaint street of Blackberry Canyon. High clouds cast a steely glare over the once logging community. Tourists stroll the rickety wood sidewalks.

"Sure," I say. "Sure."

You go into the Huldra woods to die, and I suppose it's true.

Weighted under my pack, Remington 700 in a sling, I leave my car in the little lot beside the Moss Gulch trailhead and step into the shadows of the pines. "PACK IT IN PACK IT OUT" reads a sign. A twinge of guilt pokes in my guts and I lower my eyes.

What can I say about Blackberry Canyon National Forest? The deep shadows turn the heavy fern foliage a misty blue. Branches crawl with spectral lichen. Tiny, fragile orchids peek from the moss, speckled fairy treasures. No wonder the pocket of Scandinavian immigrants see mythical women here. You don't have to try.

The Huldra. She is beauty and demise. She may look like a woman, but she is other. If you see her from the back, she is hollow as a burned-out stump, a false entity, a ruse. Or so the stories go.

My teeth grind as I walk. The straps of my pack cut into my shoulders; the rifle weighs more than I thought it would.

I, too, am a burned-out stump. I, too, am a ruse.

The setting sun turns the high clouds pink. The Huldra woods falls into a lavender darkness. I set up camp and build a little fire. I turn a can of stew around in my hands but don't pop the lid. Is that what I'm going to do? Eat cold canned chili?

Opening my pack, I dig down and unearth Barbie. She's one of the old ones, from the '90s. A strip of her hair changes color in warm water, or at least it used to. A crinkly foil mermaid tail covers her lower half like a sleeping bag and her sparkly smile beams at me. My older sister, Darcy, cried and tore up the house when '90s Barbie went missing. But I never gave her back. I hid her between my mattress and box spring and took her out late at night to marvel at her. Her hair, so lush; her eyes, fixed in plastic bliss. The curve of her waist and pert, unreasonable breasts.

When Darcy got '90s Barbie in her Easter basket, I couldn't look away.

"Will I grow up to be like her?" I'd asked Mom as we drove to services.

Mom's brow snagged and her mouth grimaced. "Of course not, Miles."

I stand and place '90s Barbie across the fire against a tree. Shouldering the Remington, I adjust the parallax and find Barbie through the scope. Her smiling face, her blank expression.

They never found Liam Crawford's body. He went into the Huldra Woods and never came out. We were in the same grade going through Blackberry Canyon's junior high and high schools, and I remember his auburn hair and watchful brown eyes. Liam sat with me at lunch sometimes, but we rarely spoke. I remember one day he came to school with a purple eye and blood on his nose.

I wanted to ask him what happened, who did it, but I said nothing.

And then Liam went into the Huldra Woods and never came out.

A tragedy, read the papers. *We mourn you, Liam.* But did we? Did Blackberry Canyon mourn?

Will Blackberry Canyon mourn me?

A branch snaps in the darkness beyond my little fire. I snap too, back to the moment, back to myself. A zing of apprehension crawls up my spine as my ears interpret the shuffle of forest duff as footsteps.

I lower the rifle and rest my forehead against the edge of the barrel.

Is this what I want?

Setting the rifle down, I pop the canned chili and find the fork in my pack. I chew the cold, meat-adjacent lumps as tears trickle off my chin. Might as well.

A voice yelps in the woods and I fumble the can. My heart lodges in my throat. Moments later, a yelp calls back from a different direction. Foxes. I listen as they warble and then scamper away.

I spoon gelled beans into my mouth. The crickets fall to silence, the hair stands up on my arms. I try to chew another blob of chili but my tongue has dried like a parched riverbed.

Will mountain lions come for me? Will bears?

I place the can beside the rifle and retrieve a bottle of oxytocin, leftovers from my wisdom teeth surgery. Opening the lid, I pour ten tablets into my palm and count them. One, two, three...

God, you're such a coward, Miles. You've never once gone after what you want. Not once. Except for '90s Barbie.

A coward I may be, but I can't go back to Blackberry Canyon one more time. I can't be Miles Paget one more fucking day. I reach for my water bottle.

Glowing eyes meet mine across the fire. Terror grips me by the throat and pins me down.

It's a deer, I tell myself. It's a coyote, a fox, a...

It stands up. Taller, taller, the eyes look down at me from seven feet up.

A high, thready scream tears from my throat and I shove myself backwards. I forget my rifle, I forget the pills. Self-preservation overrides everything else and I scramble into the darkness.

Footfalls bound after me. A hand twists into the collar of my flannel jacket. It lifts me off my feet.

I choke on air, my mouth so dry. I thrash, weak and floundering in the claws. I am thrown to the ground. The creature falls over me, snarling, hissing. The claws arc back and pause, a heartbeat away from shredding the life from my pathetic body.

Fear wins, and I black out.

My own campfire swims into focus. My mouth is sticky and my arms tingle. I blink my eyes to clear them. Nothing hurts; I must have fainted.

I'm upright, but something holds me from behind, my weight limp in my jacket, like I'm hanging from a coatrack. My eyes drift down. At my feet I see the Remington 700 and the can of chili knocked on its side, chunks oozing out. Beans squirm like grubs as my eyes blur. Scattered oxytocin pepper the duff. I count them: one, two, three, four... are there only four?

My eyes are heavy, but I still taste the residue of terror in the back of my throat. I was eating cold chili, I heard a sound, I had the oxy, I...

I saw eyes.

My heart throbs in my ears, my breath sounds amplified. I scan for missing pills. I don't dare look up.

I feel her. I can feel the space she occupies across the fire from me. Vast, an ocean of wilderness, and yet contained. Bare feet, pale and clawed, step into the glow of the fire. Long, slender legs, a narrow waist like '90s Barbie. Her face—my gaze finally reaches her face seven feet up.

She regards me, eyes flickering in the campfire light, hair a tangle of copper blackberry vines. She inspects me and then stoops, claws hovering over Barbie. She twists her body enough I can see the hollow in her back, crusted with bark, crawling with insects.

She never touches Barbie. Crouched at the base of a tree, the Huldra looks up at me as I hang. Her long tail swishes over the duff, the end tufted in reddish hair. Her breasts sway as she moves. She is nude and mossy, sinuous and soft. Only the eyes bring terror. And the teeth. Her jaw opens on some unnatural hinge, revealing every razor tooth inside.

My body shakes with adrenaline, yet floods with relief. Impossibly, the choice is out of my hands now. I no longer have to give up. I need only surrender.

The Huldra stands and approaches. She brings the dark night with her and the smell of wet leaves. She leans closer and sniffs. Her mouth pulls into a snarl and I close my eyes, awaiting the bite, the tear, the hot blood. It doesn't come.

When I open my eyes, I find the Huldra of Blackberry Canyon regarding me still. Her cat like ears perk and lower, her expression pensive and sad.

"Hunter," whispers her voice. Her voice is the song of crickets. "Trespasser." She leans closer and sniffs again. Her claws reach for my jacket and rest against the buttons. Her head tilts.

From here, hanging on a tree like a felled deer, she fills my eyes, terrible, infinite, and yet, like Darby's Barbie doll, I *want*.

I yearn for something I cannot have.

The Huldra's lip lifts over her sharp teeth. Her nostrils flare. She leans in, face a whisper from mine. "Name," she says.

"Miles," I stammer. "Miles Paget."

Her brows furrow. She moves closer still. The glow of her eyes swallows me. "I can take it from you."

"My... my name?"

"Yes. I can take it away."

I say nothing. I don't know what she means.

"All men who hunt my woods must die," whispers the Huldra. A claw straightens and presses into the center of my breastbone. "Will you let him die?"

Sweat beads on my face and back. The fire crackles, higher and higher. To the side, '90s Barbie watches, face blank with bliss. The Huldra moves around me. I feel her warmth, I smell campfire smoke and gunpowder in her hair. I feel the gravity of the hollowness inside her.

What is her offer? All I know is, I cannot refuse. I *want* it.

I count the oxy on the forest floor. One, two, three...

"Yes," I say. "Yes..."

Her claws peel the clothes from my body. Naked, unsupported, I settle to the forest floor.

The Huldra stalks around me, crouched over, claws long and stained with fungus. Her wild hair forms a curtain around me. "What is the name?"

"Miles," I whisper again. "Miles Paget."

"Miles Paget," the words sibilant on her full, moist lips, between her jagged teeth. She cups her hands as if holding the name and brings them to her mouth. She drinks from them until Miles Pages is no more.

I feel the name slip into her and away from me. Its hold on me rips free, like roots pulled from the soil. They come loose with a jolt, and I fall forward on my elbows, pale, naked, and nameless.

The Huldra crouches lower. Her claws smell of soil and mushrooms as they cup my jaw. "All men who hunt my woods must die."

"Yes." My eyes drift closed.

The soft tips of her fingers press my bottom lip, her claws click on my teeth.

"I can take him away," she says.

"Yes." I taste her fingers, vegetal, a hint of summer berries. "Yes. God, yes."

"There is no god here." The Huldra's hand slides under my back, lifting me up, pulling me closer. Her long thighs frame mine. "There is only me and you. Are you ready?"

I nod. Her body heat floats through me like the creeping sap inside the trees. "Yes. Please, yes."

Her mouth closes over mine, her breath fills my lungs. I taste spring pollen and autumn leaves. I taste the rivers and the mud. Her tongue curls into the roof of my mouth. '90s Barbie watches.

We slip closer; she pulls me into her, warm flesh and sinew, a body both eldritch and mortal, distant and close. She is the forest but she is also a gentle touch against my hopelessness and arousal.

I want her. My body wants her. This shell I wear yearns for something deeper, and yet I, the nameless one, still cower. My hand trembles in the dirt, feels the pills melting into the soil. One, two, three...

YOU GO INTO THE WOODS TO DIE

She looks down and settles into the leaves with me, head tilted, waiting for me to act. My hands grasp her waist. I crawl to her, I kiss her belly and kiss lower. The Huldra's legs surround me and pull me closer as I taste deeply of her, a salty wetness. Her voice growls through the fallen leaves. She tastes me back.

The horror of finding a tongue in my mouth passes quickly. It licks my teeth and slips down my throat like milk chocolate. I let it plant whatever seeds it wishes.

The Huldra's breath moans. Her claws sink into the meat of my back. My spine arches and I whimper. Then, the pain dissolves. The claws burrow, depositing lichen and spores, connecting me to the creeping mold beneath the forest floor.

Finished with what small boons I can offer, she lifts me from her. "Let me give you more," she says. "Let me give you better."

The Huldra holds my body like a ragdoll. Her tongue licks the curling hairs from my chest, her lips cup my nipples. I shiver in her hands, wet clay, nameless and shapeless. She kisses down my belly, breath warm and damp as a muggy summer night. She takes me in her mouth and looks through my eyes, down to the weeping child in me, that child still asking: *will I grow up to be like her?*

She bites. It crunches and I howl. Blind agony pushes me to my back in the soil.

The Huldra sits up, straddling my writhing form, red drooling from her chin. I melt like the oxy melts, leaving skin slime and pumping hot red blood. Behind the Huldra, the fire crackles and pops.

Her hand covers the wound and my body stills. A cool comfort spreads from her palm as mycelium tendrils knit the torn skin. Lying over me, she cradles my head in one hand and pushes two fingers into me. I wince and weep, but give beneath her. She changes me at her whim, reshapes my meat and bones, my pain and pleasure.

God, the *pleasure*. It burns at her fingertips and spreads through my belly, my lungs, my throat until I cry, skin aglow with unseen fireflies. We kiss again, my own blood coppery in my mouth, and she steals my voice. I give it to her.

Beside my forgotten Remington rifled and a spilled can of cold chili, I give myself to the Huldra of Blackberry Canyon. And she gives me myself in return.

I wake in the ashes of the campfire in a gray new morning. I lie on my back, watching the maple and pine sway overhead. A deep exhaustion weighs me to the earth, a warm satisfaction. The long, clawed hands that rake through my hair are those of a stranger. I turn them over and sit up.

I watch my own belly rise and fall with my breath, my new and fungal fingers shake. Fresh blood dries on my thighs from the wound she left there. I touch it, my skin pimples in a chill. It is already healing. I bring my clawed hands to my chest. My soft new breasts quiver with my heartbeat.

Beside me, a young woman gathers my strewn camping supplies. She turns to me, nude and slender and human, quite human now. Bits of leaves and sticks cling to her long auburn hair. Her brown eyes smile.

I sit on my knees, my tail curls around them. "I know you," I say.

We sat together once. We had human names once. We shared a comfortable silence.

"Yes." She stands. "One day, you will know you, too."

The woman dresses in my discarded pants and flannel. Shouldering my pack, she lifts the rifle into her arms. She checks to see if it is loaded.

She spends a moment looking me over, then smiles, pleased. "All men who hunt my woods must die," she says, and walks toward my car, toward the town of Blackberry Canyon.

I sit for a time and then stand. I lean against a pine, fragile and shivering. I am weak now, new as a dragonfly crawling from a pond. But I will become powerful. Oh, yes. I inhale the slow, moist mana of the forest. *Oh yes.*

I smooth my palms over my hips, my breasts. I slide them around my waist and into my hollow tree back. This is not my body, not the body I came here in. Yet it is more mine than it has ever been.

'90s Barbie still sits against the tree across the firepit.

I watch the woman with auburn hair until she vanishes into the morning mist. It is me, imprisoned in the forest now. I am the Huldra of Blackberry Canyon.

I am free.

HEADLESS
ASTRA CROMPTON

Clouds obscure the moon, rendering the moor a black smear beneath a bruised sky. Aisling prays the night is dark enough for her to reach the road before being found out. If her luck holds, her parents won't discover her empty bed and the apology on her pillow until well after breakfast. That's if Tilly doesn't lose her nerve and spoil her flight. If Aisling can only reach the crossroads, then the offerings in her pockets will spirit her far away from a dreaded marriage and a future full of squealing brats and too much drink.

She will not allow herself to become her mother.

With a fistful of skirt, Aisling hurries across the field despite the heather snatching eagerly at her petticoats. Her ankle turns in a rabbit hole, and she goes down hard. She scrambles up before the pain can fully bloom, knees shocked cold with the mud, and breath hitching ragged in her lungs. In the fall, she's lost her bearings and turns aimless as a weathervane in a weak wind.

There! The sundered oak marks the boundary. The crossroads can't be much further. The night is already bitterly cold—she can't manage her skirts and cloak both—when a drizzling sleet begins pattering down. She pulls her hood up over her loose hair, bows her head against the elements, and pushes on past the hedgerow—

—and swiftly tumbles into the ditch at the side of the high road. She lies in the icy sluice at its bottom for a moment, sky spinning and water seeping through her woolen layers. *This is better*, she reminds herself, *than marrying Seamus Byrne.*

Exhausted, Aisling claws at the sodden bank to haul herself back onto the shoulder of the road and fishes in her pockets for the offerings: a twisted bit of twine soaked in buttermilk for three days and three nights on the waxing moon; a silver coin to pay the crossing; a lump of wax, fashioned into a grinning skull. With an Arcadian prayer through chattering teeth, she breaks her fingernails in the effort of burying the offerings in the frozen mud.

Then she waits, and hopes, and prays for the night to take her away.

At first, she thinks the tremor might just be in her own leaden limbs, but it gathers upon the distant and empty road, soon accompanied by the thunder of hooves. Surely only phantoms arising from a desperate want.

But when sudden flame steams through the dark toward her at a reckless pace no human driver would dare—her hopes flare brittle-bright in answer.

Six black horses gallop nearer, fire streaming from their nostrils, sparks flying from their flashing hooves. To their harness a black hearse carriage is chained, piled high with coffins. And on the box seat—grinning head held aloft in one corpse hand and reins seized fiercely in the other—is the Dullahan.

Terror fills Aisling. The instinct to run surges life back into her frozen feet. It takes all her courage to hold her ground as the horses lurch to a stop upon her offerings. The headless coachman twists a wrist to turn that grinning, leering skull upon Aisling. In the flickering fire surging from the horses' nostrils, the head is cadaverous with shadow. She flinches, focusing on the too-sharp teeth; to look a Dullahan in the eye is to be stricken blind.

"You would dare stop a sacred hunt for souls?" A voice seeps out of the head, cracked as wind through a broken pane, sharp and keening. Higher than Aisling imagined it might be. She squeezes her eyes shut to deny the urge to look at that hellish face more closely. Mastering her morbid curiosity, she peers instead at the long, fluttering black cloak that covers the coachman from collar to boots. A delicate foot arches on the box seat's brace. The hand around the reins, colour of stale sourdough, is small and well-formed. "Will you not speak?" the Dullahan demands.

"Begging your pardon," Aisling stammers out, bobbing a hasty curtsey, "but if you're hunting for souls, I offer mine."

The carriage's equipage creaks as the coachman shifts to regard her more fully. The outstretched arm lowers the grinning skull to meet her at eye-level. Aisling stares intently at her muddy boots and twists her fingers in the edge of her cloak, heart pounding. *Freedom,* she tells herself fiercely. *This ghoul can give me freedom.*

"Look at me, girl," comes the command. "I'll not blind you."

Slowly, Aisling lifts her gaze. The corpse-hand clutches a fistful of fiery red hair, as long and tangled as Aisling's own chestnut curls. The grin is as sharp and terrible as before, the chin pointed, the cheekbones hollowed out by hunger and death. The blazing eyes are full of hellfire, brightly framed by long, golden lashes. Aisling sways, dizzy.

Not a coachman at all. A coach*woman.*

"Why do you offer up your life so easily?" the coachwoman demands in that cut-glass voice.

"Because it's gone and sold already," Aisling confesses. "My parents, they've chosen a man for me, from the village. It's a life I don't want—can't abide—but my folks won't see reason. The wedding's tomorrow, and I'd rather be dead than have that man touch me in consummation."

"*That* man?" After a whistling breath, the Dullahan asks, "Or *any* man?"

"Oh, any and all! They're all the same! I won't have no man's babies! I'd sooner die—"

"So you've said." The Dullahan pulls back her flaming head, wrist twisting to regard her on an angle. "But do you really understand what you're asking, girl? Only the dead can ride in my coffins. You've a chance now, while I still don't know your name, to take a different road. Make a different life for yourself."

"I couldn't go far enough to ever be safe. And what means of making money is there for a girl who won't be touched by men? No, I won't starve, homeless. This path is certain. Quick."

"Oh, it may not be quick. And it won't be painless." The headless coach-woman shifts her hold on the reins to quiet the restless horses. "If you give me your name, I'll take all from you. Strip you down to quivering bone. Pull the life from you, pulse by pulse, until you're restless dead. Like my horses. You'd be damned for eternity, forced to wander and roam... as I do."

Aisling bites her lip. Those blazing eyes challenge her courage. The icy wind whips the flaming locks skywards like a torch. She had thought this would be a quick escape, but no. She's trading one hell for another. And yet... The ghoulish light in that pallid skin has its own sort of beauty. An untouchable finality. Aisling makes a fateful choice.

"I would rather an eternity of undeath than a mortal lifetime as a wife and a mother."

The Dullahan lets out a sharp sigh and hops down from the box seat. Beneath the black cloak that swirls around her like smoke, she is lithe, agile. She plops her decapitated head back upon the stump of her neck almost carelessly so she can use both hands to open the back doors of the hearse. Despite all the coffins lashed to the carriage roof, this space is empty and eerily cavernous.

"In you pop, so we can conduct our business. Or are you too full of fear?"

This close, the coachwoman smells musty as a tomb. A slight motion along her jaw proves to be a maggot squirming. The hollows around her blazing eyes reveal the shape of the skull underneath in a way that's almost... intimate. Like if Aisling could run her thumb along that ridge, she'd know the ghoul as well as she knows her own bones.

But the entrance to the hearse yawns like an eager grave. If she gets in there, Aisling knows, no living soul will emerge. Heart in her throat with dread, she gathers her sodden skirts and climbs into the hearse on hands and knees.

A medical stink fills the shadows, but it barely masks the putrefaction of rotting flesh. Her stomach tightens into a fierce fist, and she's glad she hadn't managed to eat any supper. The hearse's doors close behind her with a terminal *click*. A shroud of silence cocoons her; she can no longer hear the stamping of the horses or the pattering of the sleet. Just the distant creak of the carriage harness like a hangman's rope, slowly swinging.

But Aisling is not alone in the darkness. She collapses onto her rump and turns to find the Dullahan looming over her. The black cloak against the lightless interior of the hearse makes her rotting face appear to float, headless in the dark. That ghoulish light beams from somewhere deep inside her, making her terrible smile leer like a jack-o-lantern, her blazing eyes seem to flame like the horses' nostrils.

Her corpse-pale hands unclasp the cloak at her throat, and its coiling shadows fall away to reveal a spare body clothed in a tattered black dress, old-fashioned, but once smartly cut. Then she reaches out to touch Aisling's cheek. Her bony fingers are cold as the rain outside, but they send an unbidden shiver down Aisling's neck. Unaccountably, her nipples have grown hard enough to chafe against the boning of her stays.

"Aren't you a pretty one," the Dullahan croons, leaning closer. There's no air left that doesn't smell of the grave, so Aisling forces herself to take slow, courageous breaths.

The coachwoman's icy hands unbutton the collar of Aisling's high-necked dress, caressing her unblemished skin with longing. Perhaps remembering the days when her own head was so firmly attached. Without warning, she pulls Aisling to her, sharp teeth scraping along her rabbiting pulse, tongue trailing a cold, wet line from jaw to collarbone. Sending a devilish shiver sinking to her pelvis, the Dullahan whispers against her whetted skin, "I think I'll enjoy taking your name."

Aisling bites her lip and prepares for pain. For a knife to slice her throat. For her soul to be burned from her bones.

Instead, those icy hands continue to unbutton her dress, unhurried, almost reverent.

"What are you—"

"You don't want your clothes to get tattered, do you?" the Dullahan answers, mouth still suckling at her throat in a way that sends new waves of fear and excitement to gather deep in Aisling. "You'll be stuck wearing these forever, so we might as well keep them as pristine as we can. Besides, you'll want something between you and the splinters of the hearse."

Aisling allows the dress to be peeled from her soaked skin, all broken out in gooseflesh. Her stays and petticoat—despite the six inches of mud along the hem—appear already ghostly in the gloom. The coachwoman pulls back to regard her, adjusting the angle of her drooping head with one hand and pushing Aisling's sodden hem up with the other. As her bony fingers pass the stained stockings and reach naked thigh, Aisling gasps, alarmed more at her own pleasure than at the cold.

The fingers trail higher, slow and inexorable as death, up the delicate skin of Aisling's inner thigh. She can't help but shiver, eyelids fluttering.

The coachwoman's cold hand settles over Aisling's mound with an unexpected belonging. Her palm cups Aisling's heat, a perfect fit. She gives a coaxing squeeze, and Aisling gasps again. Encouraged, the Dullahan's grip firms, massaging in ways Aisling longs for. Her pulse descends to take up its beat between her legs, and she finds her thighs relaxing open of their own accord.

"As I thought," whispers the headless coachwoman. Not a hint of shame in that whisper—but then, she's already dead, and Aisling soon will be, too. So, what does it matter if she gives in to this pleasure? She's passed beyond saving—and passing eager.

Two skeletal fingers follow the wetness between Aisling's labia and press in, slow but deep. The ice of her doesn't melt despite Aisling's growing heat, and for some reason, that makes Aisling angry. How dare this creature stoke such a fire in her and not be burned by it!

Without thinking, Aisling reaches for that tattered black dress, tearing at its antiquated pins, seeking a way beneath taffeta and velvet, keen for more of that cold, unyielding flesh. A rumble of thunderous laughter fills the hearse as the Dullahan allows her garments to be stripped away, that luminous inner fire causing her lean, hard body to glow against the black.

"Oh yes," she keens, "I'll enjoy taking your name!" Her hand moves more forcefully now, three fingers spreading Aisling wide as her thighs loll apart. The coachwoman straddles Aisling's thigh, grinding her dead flesh against her warmth as if she could coax some heat back into her nethers. Her corpse-blue nipple dangles above Aisling's mouth like forbidden fruit. Aisling lunges for it, grasping the breast with her hand, biting at that cold nipple, suckling as if she could draw milk from it.

Then the coachwoman pulls her head from her severed neck and lowers her grinning mouth to Aisling's chest. Though her breasts are still confined by her stays, the decapitated head kisses at her sternum before moving down beneath her gathered petticoats. Above her pumping fingers, the Dullahan's sharp mouth settles against her mound. Her long, cold tongue folds around Aisling's nub and begins to lap and pull.

A spark of lightning lances up Aisling's belly. This—*this* is new. "Devil take me," she moans against the Dullahan's hovering breast before fiercely clutching at her ribs and drawing the second breast into her mouth instead.

Her loins are filling with fire. A storm brews deep in Aisling's core, a storm she's held back for years, a storm that sent her running from the altar. It boils through her now, rending her breath from her lungs, pumping all the blood from her heart. Filling every nerve with searing heat until she is sure she'll die.

Only, the Dullahan's head pulls away from her clitoris; Aisling lets out a desperate whine, hips bucking toward the still-working arm. She's dripping wet from her own hot fluids, her pulse thundering between her thighs like the horses' sparking hooves. She lets the coachwoman's hard nipple slip from her panting mouth to see her disembodied face mere inches from her own.

Staring into those blazing eyes, pleasure filling her to the brim so that she's writhing for more, even the maggots crawling through that dead flesh have become beautiful to her. She grabs the head from the Dullahan's raised hand and brings it to her mouth, kissing hungrily, moaning into those too-sharp teeth.

Freed from its burden, the second hand slips beneath her skirts and a bony thumb presses against her throbbing nub, stoking the fire in her to blazing hot in a few deft flicks. Aisling cries out, begging for release.

Against her lips, the Dullahan whispers, "Give me your name."

"Ah!" Aisling's head is swimming deliriously. She cracks her eyes open to see the Dullahan's burning gaze staring into her own, straight down to her withering soul. Sparks fill her vision. *This,* she knows, *this is how I'll go blind—from the pleasure of it.*

"Give me your name, and I'll give you release," the coachwoman promises.

"Aisling!" she howls. "I'm Aisling Kelly!"

The coachwoman's fingers dig deep, scraping against the depth of her as the second thumb rubs her to white-hot pleasure. The storm in Aisling breaks at long last, shuddering through her every muscle, every nerve, every limb. She cries out in ecstasy—their pact is sealed.

Icy hands withdraw. She falls limp beneath the crouching form of the Dullahan, letting the flaming hair splay across her heaving chest as tremors roll through her like receding thunder.

Inch by inch, the cold steals over her body, hardening her muscles, freezing the sweat that soaks her skin. She is chilled, through and through. Corpse-cold.

In the silence, the Dullahan dresses swiftly, though her clothes are a little more torn than when Aisling first saw them. Then she gently takes her head back from the cradle of Aisling's limp arms and perches it precariously upon her severed neck.

The headless coachwoman unlatches the carriage and pushes the doors open to the night. She grabs Aisling by the ankles, all her soiled petticoats bunching around her hips as her dead weight slides out of the hearse. With a whistling grunt, the Dullahan flops Aisling's cold body over her shoulder and hoists them both up onto the roof where the coffins are waiting.

The creak of wet wood squeals. The carriage jiggles as the fresh corpse is thumped into a pine box. The echoing of deft hammering: nails sealing the lid tight over the blinded face. Another soul claimed by the headless rider.

The coachwoman hops down, so spry and lithe, and rubs the resin from her dead fingers. "I've a long way to travel yet," she says, voice once more wind through cracked windows. "Get dressed."

Within the swallowing black of the open hearse, the shade of Aisling Kelly pushes herself stiffly to sitting. She lifts a hand to shove tangled curls back from her cheek. Her face is icy. She lifts her arm; a ghoulish light emanates from beneath her remembered skin.

Aisling pulls the discarded dress over her ghostly frame and struggles with buttons that keep slipping through her frigid fingers.

HEADLESS

The Dullahan extends a beckoning hand, rot staining her palm. Her flaming red hair is more tangled than ever. Maggots drop from her cheek onto the black velvet of the bosom Aisling had so recently suckled as if she were a starving babe. Is it just her imagination, or is there a pitiable sweetness in the razor edge of that smile now?

"You can ride back here... or up on the box seat with me." The sleet has softened to snow, but Aisling no longer feels the weather. The living world will never touch her again. "When we get to the next crossroads, you're free to roam as any ghost."

Aisling turns her own blazing eyes to meet the Dullahan's. "I ride with you," she says fiercely. "You've taken my name, haven't you? We belong to each other. Forever."

PREY
INDIGO LARKSPUR

Davina chews on her thumbnail as Chad drives down the dark forest road. *Road* is too strong a word. *Trail* is more like it. Unpaved, something four-wheelers used, not actual vehicles. Despite that, he's only half paying attention—or more accurately, whoever is on the other end of his text messaging seems more important than making sure the truck keeps on its current path rather than going over the steep drop-offs to the left or right. The thick trees on either side of them cover the path in shadows. Shadows that are only getting deeper as the sun starts to set.

Her anxiety is really starting to spike, and she wishes Chad would just give the road his full attention until they get to whatever clearing he's heading to.

She knows better than to say anything, though.

After two years together, Davina doesn't recognize herself anymore. She's shrunk in on herself. Made herself smaller so as not to set him off.

The two had met at college and been friends for a year before they started dating. Chad was always sweet and charming. Sure, there were a few women who'd complained about the way he'd treated them, but she took him at his word when he said they were trying to get back at him for not wanting to be in a steady relationship. He'd always been upfront with them: it was just fun. Nothing serious.

When he confessed his feelings for her, that he wanted to take her out, she was ecstatic. She started spending almost all of her free time with him. Then, without her realizing it, she was only ever spending time with him.

She got bad about responding to friends' text messages, turning down their offers to hang out or even to just grab coffee. On the rare occasions she did accept, she'd end up bailing on them when Chad decided at the last minute he wanted her attention.

Eight months into dating, she moved in with him. That was when some of his charm started to fade. At first it was small things, little critiques about how she cleaned or cooked. He'd snap at her for books left piled on the coffee table, but quickly apologized and blamed it on being tired.

Eventually it turned into nitpicking things about her appearance. Always talking about how pretty the blonde models or actors on TV were, saying purple hair was fine when you were a teen, but *"you're going to be a junior in college soon; no one is going to take you seriously with purple hair and a lip ring"*. Especially not his parents. How could he possibly introduce her to them? His father was the CEO of some big company, his mother was a prominent member of their country club and hosted charity events. Chad would be embarrassed if he tried to bring her around.

Then it was her name. Davina was fine enough, but her friends and family had always called her Davi, which was "too masculine" and people would assume she was a dyke. Nina was a more respectable name.

The one time Davina had spoken against him about this, pointing out that she was bisexual and *had* dated women, that he *knew* this, he just laughed, said all women do that in their teens and early college years, but she was with him and obviously it was out of her system now.

When she explained that being with him didn't make her any less bisexual, he got angry. If she was so into women, then why was she with him? Was it a joke? *Pity?* Then he took off for two days and didn't respond to texts or calls, leaving her to ruminate in her guilt.

That should have been the moment she left. Instead, she'd apologized when he finally called her back, begged him to come home, and agreed to start going by Nina.

Now, two years later, here she is: sitting in the passenger seat of his truck, her hair bleached blonde, one length, and past her shoulders. Her lip ring? Gone. Friends? Gone. Degree? Never got it, because once Chad graduated he needed her to support him while his career took off, and she became a shadow of who she'd once been.

He'd never hit her, but he'd broken her all the same.

She knows he cheats on her—it's probably another woman he's texting right now—but a part of her feels like, after everything she's given up for him, she has to stay. Otherwise, it was all for nothing. She *has* nothing.

Besides, things aren't always bad. He still has his moments where he's the guy she'd originally fallen for. Those small moments aren't enough, but she tells herself they are.

By the time Chad finally parks the truck, the sun has almost set.

"Hurry up and grab the tent, Nina. Set it up while I get a fire going."

"Are you sure we can camp here? This doesn't look like a campground. The clearing isn't very big and the trees are fairly close. Isn't that a fire hazard?"

"Are you really questioning me right now? I try to bring you out for a nice weekend getaway because you're always complaining I'm gone so much. I find a nice forested area where we can have some time, just the two of us, and you're bitching? Seriously? Fuck it. Get back in the truck; we'll just go back."

"No, I'm sorry. It's beautiful, really. You know I just get anxious. I'm sorry."

Chad looks at her for a bit before heading to the back of the truck for some wood he brought with for the first night.

"It's alright, babe. You're lucky I love you. I'm sure you'll find a way to make it up to me later." He gives her a wink and focuses on the wood again while she grabs the two-person tent. She takes it right up to the treeline so there's room for the firepit under the small opening in the trees.

He'll expect a blowjob as her way of "making it up to him". There was a point in Davina's life where she enjoyed giving oral to her partners. Male and female alike. Now, it's the same as setting up the tent. A chore. A task to be completed before she can move onto the next.

Sure enough, after the sun has set and the fire is going, Chad asks Nina to hand him another beer from the cooler beside her. As she hands it over, he grabs her wrist and rubs it against his crotch.

"See how good I am to you? Even after you hurt my feelings earlier, I still want you. Don't you want to thank me for taking time out of my schedule and bringing you out here?"

Without a word, she gets up and drops to her knees in front of his lawn chair, unbuttoning his jeans and pulling down his zipper. As she takes him out of his boxers, she can tell he must've had more to drink than she realized as he started the fire, because while he's semi-hard, she can't seem to get him fully erect.

As she's licking and sucking him, a prickling sensation crawls up Davina's spine, making her shoulders tense the way prey might when it can sense danger nearby. She tries to scan the woods as best she can from her position, but it's fully night now and with how dense the trees are around them, everything outside of the illumination of the fire is pitch black.

It's probably just a raccoon or some other animal. As they drove here, they really didn't pass any other cars, and she's fairly certain this isn't an official campsite. She wouldn't be surprised if this is actually some sort of national or private forest that's supposed to be off limits to the public, and that they'll get a hefty fine if they're caught.

Finally, without finishing, Chad stands up.

"Ugh. I'm too tired for this. You can make it up to me tomorrow."

He makes his way to the tent, but Davina tells him she's going to pick up a bit and make sure the fire goes out completely. He barely glances back before heading into the tent, stripping down and quickly passing out.

Davina, meanwhile, sips a beer she doesn't really like and stares into the forest. She still gets the impression she's being watched, but instead of scaring her, it makes her feel something else. Excitement. Desire. Things she hasn't felt for a while.

The Creature has watched them since they turned onto the trail that led this way. She always pays attention to those who enter her territory. It isn't often; some forest rangers once in a while, those she tends to let be, as long as they are caring for the forest properly. An illegal hunter—now, those tend to not be as lucky.

She can sense what type of person most humans are by reading their desires. The ones who mean harm to her forest or to others become her prey. The depravity she senses from them determines just how long she plays with her food before finally devouring them.

The man in this truck is definitely prey. He may not seem as depraved as some of her others have been, but something about him, the way the woman in the truck reacts to him, makes her want to drag out his suffering.

The interactions between the two as they set up camp only strengthen her desire to hunt him and drag out his fear. When the woman drops to her knees before him, The Creature sees her lack of interest in the actions, sees her mind wander. She sees her try to scan the forest, like a doe searching for danger without giving herself away.

After the man, Chad, goes into the tent, The Creature stays and continues to watch the woman. He called her Nina. It doesn't fit her; she wonders if the woman is aware of the slight grimace she makes whenever he says her name.

She's intrigued by this human woman. She's been around long enough to recognize the signs of a person entrapped by the snares of another. This little doe is broken, but The Creature can still sense some of the woman she is meant to be, who she probably was before this Chad dug his claws into her. A part is just waiting to be set free again, and The Creature is happy to help her with that.

The woman sits in her chair and scans the forest again. She can't possibly see The Creature. The Creature is the wood, the shadows; she is only seen if she wants to be seen. Yet, when the little doe's eyes stop, she seems to be looking in this very direction, seems to sense The Creature staring right back at her.

Then the little doe slides her hand into her pants, her arousal scenting the air. The Creature inhales deeply, taking in the aroma. She smells of blackberries, the essence sharpened by her arousal. It takes more self-control than The Creature would care to admit to not go to her and take her. Her shadows lengthen, stretching toward her little doe. She wants to spread the doe's legs and bind them in place, then wrap her wrists together over her head, while she uses more shadows still to slip inside that sweet cunt. She wants to bring her to the cusp of pleasure, make her little doe beg for release, just to deny it for a little longer. To make her surrender all the more intense.

She pulls her shadows back, denying herself just as she would this beautiful woman pleasuring herself before the fire. She won't do so for long, though.

Too soon, Nina has reached her climax. After cleaning up and ensuring the fire is completely out, she enters the tent with that man.

Nina cares about the wellbeing of the forest. A turn-on for The Creature, who loves her woods and the souls within it.

Once The Creature can tell Nina is asleep, she glides into their camp. She guides her shadows into the mesh window of the tent and into her sleeping bag. Her shadows trail slowly up the woman's legs; her eyes flutter open and meet The Creature's. This is enough for her to form a link and slip into her little doe's subconscious.

Davina wakes up in the forest. She's not in the clearing, Chad and the tent are gone, and she's surrounded by trees, but she's not afraid. When the naked woman steps from between two pines, shadows writhing around her, Davina knows for sure she's dreaming.

Despite the dark, moonlight illuminates the woman. She's clearly inhuman, but stunning. Her eyes are large and golden, slitted like a snake's; dark hair falls around her, leaves and branches intertwined with it, but it doesn't look unkempt. It looks like they are a part of her. Antlers, like a deer's, reach out from the top of her head, but where a deer's might be more rounded at the points, hers seem sharp enough to cut.

Her skin is reminiscent of the forest floor dappled in the bits of sunlight that break through the thick foliage—varying shades of greens and browns. It should be off-putting, but all Davina can think of is how the mounds of this woman's breasts would fit perfectly in her hands. How she'd like to take her dark nipples into her mouth and lavish them with her tongue, lick up the slope of her breast to the juncture where her neck meets her shoulder. Then bite and lick the spot.

As she's imagining this, Davina's eyes are drawn to the woman's slight smirk and the forked tongue that licks sensuously across her full lips.

"Oh my little doe, I knew when you finger-fucked yourself as I watched that I had to have you. Knew I could make you want me just as badly, but I had no idea it would be so *easy*."

The woman's voice is rich, with a slight cadence that makes Davina think of the wind rustling through the trees.

As she speaks, she moves forward until she stands directly in front of Davina. Her golden eyes stay locked to hers. Davina should respond, but she can't seem to find her voice.

The shadows around the woman reach toward Davina, caressing her cheek and neck.

Finally, she asks, "Who are you?"

The woman smiles. "I've been called many things by many people, but you can call me Arduinna. And you, my little doe, what is your name?"

"Davi. Or, well, Davina."

The woman let out a laugh; it startles Davina, but only because it's unexpected. Then she becomes self-conscious. Does her name sound so ridiculous after all?

Abruptly, the laughter stops. A shadow slips under her chin and forces her to meet Arduinna's eyes. "Don't do that. Don't look away. Forgive me. I was not laughing at you. Your name is beautiful. I was laughing because I unknowingly called you little doe, and your name itself is Little Deer."

Davina is still processing her words when Arduinna's tongue snakes out and licks her neck. The woman's eyes close, and she sighs as if she's just had a drink of water after wandering the desert for too long.

All thoughts leave Davina except for those wondering what that forked tongue would feel like on her clit or plunging into her wet core.

A low growl brings Davina's focus back to the woman before her. "Oh, Davi, you taste like nectar and your arousal smells just as sweet. I want to hunt you and then devour that sweet cunt once I catch you. Do you want that? Do you want me to lick you until you're screaming my name?"

Davina can hardly breathe and just nods her head.

"No, my little doe. I need to hear you say it. Tell me what you want."

It's hard for her to voice this. It's so personal, so embarrassing! But Arduinna's eyes never leave hers, and Davina knows no matter what she says, her companion will not laugh or ridicule. This goddess before her wants her just as bad.

This knowledge gives her the courage to speak.

"I want to run through the forest, knowing that you're chasing me, hunting me. And when you catch me, I want you to devour me."

"Alright, then. If you want me to stop at any time, no matter what, just tell me to stop. Understand?"

At first she only nods again, but after arching a brow, Davi replies. "Understood."

"Then run, little prey. *Run.*"

It has been centuries since she gave her name to anyone, even those few lovers she's had now and then, but it feels right to give it to her little doe. Especially when she sees it kindle that fire in her eyes. Yes, Davina's fire may have been banked, but it wasn't put out.

She will help fan those flames, and then she will make the one who had tried to extinguish them pay.

Arduinna slowly stalks after Davi. She doesn't want the game to end too quickly, and by the strengthening of Davina's arousal, the other woman doesn't want it to either.

Finally, when her prey stops behind a tree to catch her breath, Arduinna stops a little ways back too. Then she sends her shadows forward, and up her prey's legs until they reach the juncture between her thighs. The shadows rub Davi's clit through the fabric of her sleep shorts. Her doe's head tilts back on a moan.

More shadows bind the other woman's wrists together and bring them above her head. She can smell the quick spike of fear, quickly followed by the increase of her arousal.

Ahh, her little doe likes to be a little scared.

She comes around the front of the tree so she can see her prey's face, but keeps herself hidden. Under her silent instruction, a shadow covers Davi's eyes, two more spread her legs apart and bind her ankles and knees so she can't move or close them. Then Arduinna splits the shadow that is working her clit so the other half can run along her cunt at the same time. Two more to caress her nipples over her tank top, and a final one wraps around her throat. Gently, for now.

Davina's breaths become more rapid and shallow. Her sweet arousal is tinged with fear.

"Arduinna?"

Letting her voice come from everywhere and nowhere, The Creature asks, "Do you want me to stop? Say the word and I will."

Davi lets out a small whimper. "No, please. Don't stop,"

With a wicked smile on her face, Arduinna increased the pressure of the shadows. "Oh my little doe, you have no idea what you've gotten yourself into."

Davina shudders at Arduinna's words, but more from pleasure than from any fear. What little fear she *does* feel only adds to her pleasure. She never knew fear could be a turn on. Yet she also knows she is safe.

With her vision blocked and unable to move, the sensations at her clit are much more intense. Her nipples are hard and she wants her goddess's mouth on her. Everywhere.

"Ard…" a moan escapes her lips before she can say more.

"Yes, my little doe? Do you want to come?"

"Pl... please." Another moan. Davina tries to buck her hips forward to chase the friction she needs. She's so close, but soon there is another band around her waist, keeping her hips still.

She lets out a cry, half in agony, half in pleasure.

"Not yet, my little doe. I'm not done playing with you just yet."

Davina whimpers, "My Goddess, please. I need to come."

Arduinna moans. "Oh, my little doe. You beg so prettily. I'm so wet. While I've been playing with you with my shadows, my fingers have been buried in my own cunt. I'm thinking of all the ways I plan to devour you."

Davina almost comes from her words alone. She needs her mouth, her hands, *anything*.

"Taste how much I want you," Arduinna says as she slips two fingers into Davina's mouth, stroking her tongue, coating it in her arousal. It tastes like honey and jasmine. She sucks on her fingers, moaning as she cleans off every last bit, desperate for more.

Too soon, Arduinna pulls her fingers from her mouth. Trailing them down her neck, her nails lightly scratching but not breaking skin. Upon reaching her tank top, The Creature slides her nail down the center between her breasts—she must have sliced the fabric as she went, because Davi feels it being pulled away, her aching nipples caressed by a breeze.

Arduinna steps away, the shadows between her legs stop, and the ones that had been working her nipples don't return.

She can feel Arduinna staring at her, but she doesn't know if she is still close enough to touch, or if she's moved out of reach.

She tries to squirm but is still bound in place. Just when Davina is about to call out for the other woman, a forked tongue flicks over her right nipple and she jumps a bit at the unexpected sensation. Arduinna chuckles as she closes her mouth over the nipple next, her hand cupping her left breast and pinching slightly. While she plays with the left nipple, she sucks and bites the right. Flicking her forked tongue over the peak and then pulling as much of her breast into her mouth as she can, sucking hard once, before releasing both breasts again.

The experience is a sweet kind of torture for Davina. She's never been given such intense pleasure by any of her lovers, and it has been almost two since she's felt even a hint. She feels like she might die from it, but she can think of worse ways to go.

Then there is a flick at her nipple again, this time the left. Arduinna repeats her administrations to the left breast. "Can't have her feeling left out," she says around Davi's nipple.

When she pulls away the second time, she speaks. By the sound of her voice, Davina knows she is just as affected by her own administrations as her. "Davi, my good little doe. My perfect prey, tell me what you want."

"You. *Please*. I need you. Your mouth."

She licks up her neck and bites on her earlobe before whispering, "Where? You have to tell me where you want my mouth."

"My pussy, please. I want to feel your tongue on my clit. Feel it inside me…"

"As you wish." With one last bite to her neck, the other woman drops to her knees in front of her, bringing her hands down to Davi's hips. Arduinna sucks on her through her shorts. Davi's hips try to buck forward again. She whimpers and moans as she is teased. Close, but not close enough.

Then the shadows shift, pulling her forward, away from the tree, her knees over Arduinna's shoulders, but she must have done something with the shadows to prevent her from closing her thighs together. Her arms are brought down to her sides, the blood rushing to them, and bound to the tree. Her shoulders are pressed into the bark and bound by shadows again.

"Fuck, Davina. Your cunt is weeping for me. It's gorgeous."

Then her mouth is on her, sucking at her pussy. The flat of that tongue pushes into her slightly. Davi tries to press her hips into her mouth more. Arduinna moans into her core. Then, as she licks at her folds, teasing her entrance; she brings her thumb to her clit and presses.

"Fuck!" Tears stream down Davi's face from the intensity of the pleasure and the lack of any release.

"Are you alright, Davina? Why are you crying?"

She can hear the concern in Arduinna's voice, knowing if she asked her to put a stop to this all right now, she would. It makes her bold.

"I'm okay. I just want you so badly. I want you to make me come."

Arduinna moans. Davina may be the one bound, yet she still has so much control. She likes it.

The shadows drop from around her eyes, the tendrils around her neck squeeze a little more as Arduinna speaks again. "Look at me, Davi, look at what you do to me."

As she looks, Arduinna sits back on the grass and spreads her legs. She brings her hand down through the dark curls between her thighs, then dips her two middle fingers inside herself. With a moan, she arches into her hand. Davina moans too.

Gods, her little doe is stunning.

Arduinna tightens the shadow around her neck a bit more, not enough to cut off air, but enough to notice. Davi gasps and moans. Whimpering Arduinna's name.

Arduinna slides her fingers out and up to her clit, circling it, teasing it.

"Gods, pet. I'm picturing you riding my face, suffocating me while you chase your release and I finger-fuck myself. Me licking your cunt and your perfect little asshole at the same time."

Davi's eyes go a little wide. The blush creeping across her cheeks spurs Arduinna on.

"Oh, my good girl wants such naughty things. I can see it. You want me to tongue-fuck that tight little asshole. You don't know which you want more. My tongue in your cunt or your ass, but don't worry, little doe. You can have both. You have no idea the things I can do with this tongue. But you will. I'll show you."

Davi's breathing quickens, her arousal dripping from her beautiful pussy.

Arduinna is close to her release and knows her pet is too. She crawls back over to her and, with no warning, slides her tongue inside Davi's sweet cunt, massaging in and out of her core with her forked tines while the flat of her tongue further back rubs her clit.

She continues to finger herself as she gives Davi oral until they are both coming together.

When they both finish riding out the waves of their orgasms, she uses the shadows to bring Davi gently to the ground on a bed of moss, then positions herself between the human's legs again, lapping at the come dripping from her doe's center and sliding her own slick covered fingers between Davi's ass cheeks and pressing slightly into her puckered entrance.

As the other woman sucks in a breath, Arduinna looks up at her from between her legs and smiles. "You didn't think we were done yet, did you?"

"Wake up! I'm starving." Chad nudges Davina as he crawls out of the tent.

Davina lays there for a moment longer, confused for a moment about where she is. Hadn't she fallen asleep in the forest?

She looks down at herself. Her clothes are there, unblemished and whole.

"It was just a dream, a very *vivid* dream if the ache between my thighs and wet panties are anything to go by," she mumbles to herself, feeling inexplicably sad that Arduinna was simply a figment of her subconscious.

With a sigh, she grabs a hoodie and crawls out of the tent to prepare breakfast for her and Chad.

After they eat, Chad decides they should go for a hike. "Gotta make sure you burn off that extra bacon you ate this morning. If you keep that up. You're not gonna be able to fit into the dress for the charity event Mom is throwing next month."

"I hardly think four slices of bacon now and again is going to be a big deal," Davina grumbles. It may have just been a dream, but having Arduinna, a stranger, treat her with more kindness and respect than she's received from her own boyfriend in years, makes the echo of who she used to be start to rise to the surface again.

"Geez, Nina, it was a joke. Chill. You always take things so seriously." Chad rolls his eyes. "Come on, are we going for a hike or not?"

Davina thinks about arguing more, but it's pointless. She changes into her leggings and puts on her tennis shoes, following him into the forest.

She has to admit, it *is* beautiful here, and the deeper into the trees they go, following mostly game trails, the more of last night's dream replays in her head. A flush fills her face and it isn't from the exertion of trying to keep up with Chad's longer strides.

Lost in thoughts of her dream lover, Davina doesn't notice that they've made it back to camp, or that Chad has halted.

"What—" Before she can ask much more, she hears a feminine voice.

"Oh, thank goodness! My car broke down a few miles from here, and to make matters worse, I locked myself out and my phone in it. I started walking and noticed your camp."

Looking from behind Chad's back, Davina sees a woman who is a little taller than her, with olive skin, deep brown hair that looks almost black, and beautiful golden eyes.

She gasps. She knows those eyes, even if they don't have the slits; she'd recognize them anywhere. But how is that possible? It had been a dream, hadn't it?

Relax, my little doe, you'll give us away, and I'd like to play with my prey a little more first.

Arduinna's voice comes across as a whisper in Davina's mind. Startling her and also making her aware that Chad's talking.

"Lucky for you! Take a seat and have lunch with us. You must be hungry." As he speaks, he pulls out a bottle of water and hands it to the stranger. "A beautiful woman like you shouldn't be walking in these woods alone. There're a lot of dangerous creatures around."

The woman's smile is more a showing of teeth, but Chad doesn't notice. "You have no idea. I'm absolutely famished."

A chill runs down Davina's spine. Chad seems oblivious to the predator in their midst. No, he's too busy checking Arduinna out to notice. Even if he hadn't been, he wouldn't ever think a woman could be a danger to him.

Davina could say something. Warn him. Yet she keeps her mouth shut. *She's in no danger. She isn't The Creature's prey today and Chad won't have the enjoyable experience she had last night.*

If the human male wasn't so distracted by her own human appearance, he would have noticed the looks between her and his girlfriend. May have questioned why she was traveling on such a secluded road or how she came upon their camp if she was trying to reach town.

But all he can think about is how he can get his girlfriend away long enough to fuck her.

She looks forward to toying with him—to making him suffer for the things he has undoubtedly put Davina through. She knows it is unlikely the other woman will want anything to do with her after she kills Chad. Humans always seem to be averse to the killing of another human. No matter if they deserve it or not.

Normally, The Creature wouldn't care, but she realizes that she will be sad to scare her doe away. Yet, she will do it and be glad to know that Davina is free of him.

Davina gets Arduinna some food while Chad runs to his truck to retrieve his phone.

"Thank you, little doe," Arduinna says, her hand caressing Davi's as she takes the food from her.

Whispering, Davi asks, "Was it real? Last night."

Again, she responds without words, directly into her mind.

*Yes. And no. You never left your tent. We never touched in this physical realm. Yet, both of our spirits, the essences of us, the part of us that makes us, **us**, were together in that place between waking and dreams. It isn't diminished or lessened because our physical bodies weren't there.*

Davina is processing this when Arduinna continues, *But make no mistake, my Davina, I very much look forward to playing with you in this physical realm too.*

As she says these words, Davina feels her shadows wrap around her throat and lightly squeeze.

Chad returns then, staring at his phone with a puzzled look. "Huh. It's weird. I had service before we set off for our hike, but it's not picking any up now. Why don't you hang with us until it comes back?"

As the day wears on, Chad drinks, not noticing that the two women only drink one drink to every one of his three. Or the unnatural shadows that flow from the stranger to crawl up his girlfriend's legs and rub her clit through her pants. The little whimpers that escape from Davina or the satisfied grin that crosses Arduinna's face.

No, all he notices are the sound of his own voice and the cleavage that Arduinna's tank top reveals.

As night falls and the fire lights their small circle, Arduinna calls Davina over to her and pulls her into her lap. She's taken the second chair and Davi had been sitting on a fallen log.

"Wh—what are you doing?" Her heart races as Arduinna brings a hand to her neck and starts to pull her face close.

"I thought it was obvious. I'm sure Chad doesn't mind. Do you, Chad? You want to watch us play together, don't you?"

Chad stares at them. Clearly torn.

Davi knows what he must be thinking. He's asked her so many times for a threesome. Whining, "*What good is it to date a bi woman if she won't fuck other women with me?*" Yet, she also suspects he's jealous that Ard is showing her attention and not him.

This is confirmed as soon as he opens his mouth.

"I don't know. What's in it for me? Blue-balls? Or do I get to play?"

The grin on Arduinna's face is all predator as she says, "Oh, don't worry. I plan on playing with you too."

Again, Davina is amazed that Chad doesn't sense the danger from this woman. He clearly is only thinking with his dick.

Arduinna pulls her attention back to her, bringing her lips a hair's breadth from hers. *I am going to kill him, little doe. He is not a good man. Even if I hadn't sensed it and his terrible thoughts the moment he drove into my woods, I would for the way I have heard him speak to you. For the way I have seen him try to diminish your fire. I want you, body and soul, Davina, but I will not take what is not freely given. If you wish to leave, do so now. I will not think ill of you.*

Arduinna keeps her eyes locked on Davina as she speaks this into her mind. She is grateful Chad is drunk; he's oblivious.

"You'd just let me leave?" she whispers.

If you're asking if I would kill you because you chose to leave, you wound me. I told you to if you wished.

Davina knows there is something wrong with her. Arduinna's declaration that she'd kill Chad, based solely on the way he's treated her, doesn't scare her. It *excites* her. Makes her feel cherished.

She crashes her mouth into Arduinna's. "I'm yours, body and soul," she gasps between kisses.

At that declaration, Arduinna lifts her and places her in the chair, kneeling on the ground before her. She removes Davi's shirt, then pulls down her underwear and leggings at the same time. Bringing her mouth back to Davi's for another fierce kiss, before trailing her hand down and squeezing her breasts, then dipping her hand lower, until she comes to her clit. She slowly rubs and Davi arches into her hand and moans.

"Fuck, that's hot. Now you get naked too, Arduinna," Chad says while he unzips his shorts and pulls his dick out, gripping himself and grunting.

Davina starts to pull away; she had forgotten for a moment he was there, but suddenly she is so disgusted with him.

Don't look at him, little doe. Just look at me. Feel me, she says as she slips first one finger into her wet pussy and then a second.

"Hmmm, you're so wet already."

"Well, that's a first. Usually she takes forever. Now, when are you going to stop wasting your time with her? She's such a mouse. I thought you said I'd get to play too."

The Creature's eyes flash in anger. "I've found that if it takes someone a while to become aroused, it's usually a failing of their partner. And don't worry. I plan on playing with you quite a bit."

Chad's alcohol fogged mind seems to skip over the insult and only latch onto the latter part of her statement. "Then come over and play already."

Arduinna massages her fingers inside Davi a few more times, but as she expects, after playing with her so much throughout the day, it isn't long before her pet is coming on her hand. When her release finally subsides, she slowly pulls her fingers out and brings them to her own mouth, licking them clean. She tastes even more delicious in the physical plane.

"Last chance, Davina. If you don't want to see what I do to him. Leave now."

She'd been shocked when Davina had kissed her and said that her body and soul were Arduinna's; it was more than she could have hoped for, but she had to give her just one more chance to run.

"I'm staying."

As she rises to her feet, she lets the glamour drop and the creature she is emerges. Because to do what she is about to do, she cannot be Arduinna, but The Creature.

"Then be a good girl and watch, and know it's all for you."

As she turns toward Chad, his drunken eyes slowly widen and he tries to stand up, knocking his chair over, his dick now limp and hanging out of the opening of his pants like a sad little worm crawling out of the earth after a rainstorm.

"What the fuck? What are you?!"

"I am many things, but right now, for you, I am Retribution."

The Creature's shadows prop his chair back upright and force him into it. Binding him so he cannot move.

"What's the matter, Chad? I thought you wanted to play?" *She rakes her claws down his chest, leaving deep gouges in their wake as she asks this. He screams and she smiles, her sharp teeth gleaming in the firelight.*

"Nina! Fucking do something!" *Chad sobs, trying to tear himself free.*

"Her name is Davina, you worthless pile of flesh." *She pries his mouth open while her shadow fetches the Bowie knife Chad used earlier to cut branches from trees. She places it in the fire and while it's heating, she grabs his tongue, piercing through the tip of it with the claws of her thumb and index finger.*

More shadows wrap around his head to hold it still. When the knife is finally heated to a red-hot glow, she brings it to her hand and slices through his tongue, cauterizing it as it cuts it off.

She takes the severed flesh and swallows it whole.

"That's for every time you injured her with your words and called her by a name she despised."

She then takes one of his eyes. She has more plans that she wants him to see, but he only needs one eye for that.

"For every time you looked at another woman." *She eats that, too.*

Snot runs down his face and if he was pleading for mercy, well, who could say. Even if he'd had a tongue to form the words, it would have done him no good.

The shadows lift him, because she refuses to get on her knees for this man. No, the only one who she will get on her knees for is her little doe. Once his groin is level with her face, she wraps her hand around its base and her fork tongue flicks out and encircles it, pulling it toward her mouth. He whimpers as she comes closer to the unimpressive member. She pauses and stares at him for a moment—before she slowly bites him in half. He screams and passes out. She wraps her shadows around him where her hand had been, making a tourniquet of sorts. She doesn't want him to bleed out too quickly.

She slaps him until he comes to again.

"That's for every time you fucked another woman and every time you forced her to pleasure you without making sure she had pleasure in turn."

The Creature turns back to Davina then, who's been quiet this whole time. She worried she'd see fear in the woman's eyes, but is surprised to find none. Instead, she sees lust, and something more. Gratitude?

Davina throws herself into The Creature's arms. Arduinna cups the woman's ass and lifts Davi until she wraps her legs around her waist. Davi twines her hands into The Creature's hair and kisses her.

Carrying her to a grassy spot still lit by the fire, she lays Davina on her back. As she does so, her shadows pull Chad so he is facing them and can see them with his one good eye.

"Now Chad, with the last of your time left on this earth, I'm going to make you watch while I pleasure the woman you unfathomably believed you were better than. I want you to watch while I make her come over and over again. I want you to realize in your last moments that every orgasm you thought you gave her was fake as you hear what her real orgasms sound like."

Then The Creature proceeds to do just that. Doing all the things she'd done to her little doe the night before so she can experience them in her physical form. After an hour and several orgasms on both women's part, she releases her shadows from around his shaft and lets him bleed out.

At some point in the night, Davina and Arduinna went into the tent together and made love. Out in the grass, in front of a dying Chad, that had been more primal, and it was definitely The Creature she'd been fucking, but The Creature was a part of Arduinna and she enjoys both sides of the forest goddess.

They eventually fell asleep, tangled in each other, and it was the best sleep Davi had gotten in years.

Now, she can feel the sun beating in on the tent, making it too warm to sleep comfortably. She is alone and worries for a moment, but when she opens the tent, Arduinna is sitting outside. Chad's body is gone, but she isn't going to ask where it is. She doesn't care.

"Good morning, little doe."

"You're still here."

"Of course I am. Where else would I be?"

In the light of day, Davi suddenly feels shy. "I... I don't know. I guess I figured you'd have gone now that you did what you set out to do."

Arduinna is quiet for a moment, studying her. "Do you want me to go?"

"No!" Maybe she'd said that too quickly. Sounded too desperate, but she doesn't want her to leave.

Arduinna doesn't seem put off by it. She just smiles. "Then what *do* you want?"

"You. I want to be with you."

"I cannot leave this forest, Davina. It is my home, and I am bound to it. I would never ask you to give up your life in the real world."

"What life? I let Chad become my whole life. Here, in these woods, with you, is the most alive I've ever felt. Even before Chad, something was always missing. This place. It feels like home."

Arduinna stands and holds out her hand. "Very well. Then home it will be, for as long as you want it to be."

Hand in hand, The Creature leads her doe into the trees that will become her home. To a place where Davi can become a predator in her own right if that is her wish, or simply live out her days basking in the all-consuming love of her monstrous goddess.

SWAMP PEARLS
KELSEY CHRISTINE
MCCONNELL

The Lady of the Swamp has lived in these dark, murky waters for decades—maybe even longer. Whispers about her are passed around town, but no one really believes the stories. Anyone who could prove that she's here is long gone, their bones tangled up in muddy mangrove roots, flesh hanging bloody between her sharp teeth.

She doesn't have a name, not beyond what the local ghost stories have dubbed her. But she does have her passions: sucking the heads off rattlesnakes, rending men limb from limb, and pretty things. She likes car keys, plucks them from the pockets of most of her meals and hangs them shiny and tinkling from the low bowing tree branches. An overflowing collection of necklaces and bangles clashes around her throat and wrists. She's got a stash of buttons, an array of bird feathers, a stockpile of glass bottles, gold teeth, and tinfoil.

And then there's Jenna Marshall.

Even by human standards, Jenna is pretty. Short and pale, her perfectly round thighs peek out from whatever cutoffs she's prancing around in that day. She's got a spray of cinnamon freckles and a sweet dimple in one cheek. A bandana usually protects her delicate scalp, spilling out waves of hair the color of pennies. The Lady of the Swamp watches her, pit-black eyes poking up out of the water like an alligator, as she cycles through man after man, hoping one will be nice to her. They never are—not for long.

Jenna treats the swamp as her own secret hideaway. No one particularly likes it there, so no one ever bothers her. It's the perfect place to bring a married boyfriend. A great love nest for a one-night stand with a stranger passing through town—especially if you don't want them to track the smell of tobacco and gasoline all over your apartment. It's a lawless land for when she's low on cash and needs to trade some favors to keep the electricity on.

The swamp swallows all of Jenna's darkest secrets, and its Lady cherishes each shame like a polished pearl. When Jenna's lovers leave her crying, the Lady of the Swamp follows them back to their cars to leave smears of muck and blood behind—and little else. When Jenna has to throw back a six-pack of beer just to make it through her trysts, the Lady of the Swamp collects the cans long after she's gone, pressing her lips to the places Jenna's mouth had rested. When Jenna thinks she's alone and mutters desperate wishes into the night air for something real—something different—the Lady of the Swamp has to clutch her palms over her chest, lest her heart beat so fast it bursts out of her chest.

A strange thing happens to her stomach whenever Jenna is around. It's not the primal fluttering of hunger. It's not the somersault of excitement she gets when a meal thinks they can outrun her. It's warm. It's gentle, which is foreign to the swamp. It is beautiful and it is aching. After all, she knows that if Jenna ever laid eyes on her, she would be horrified.

Monster. Thing. Abomination. She's heard it all plenty of times from wide-eyed men who want their last words to sting. But if Jenna said those awful words in that awful tone—if she screamed—then this loathsome creature would fall dead on the spot.

But today is different—more different than Jenna might have wished for. The air is muggy in the heat of the late afternoon, and the lanky man she leads to the swamp is twitchy. He's got a band around his left finger, but that frantic energy isn't guilt. It reeks of desperation.

The rundown little floating shack creaks and groans as they shuffle in. The Lady of the Swamp hooks her knees around one of the support posts, peering in through a fat hole in the rotted boards. As Jenna leans in for a kiss with that same sweet head tilt to the left she always does, the man with her presses a cold, black metal to her stomach.

Jenna doesn't flinch, just lets her shoulders sag on a sigh. "Fucking hell, Cam. A gun?"

"Sorry, Jenna. Really. But I need some cash real bad."

"You couldn't have robbed one of those rich bitches over in the beach houses?"

The gun shakes in Cam's grip, and his free hand jerks up to swipe through greasy, sweat-soaked hair. "No one with any real money is dumb enough to get mugged. You'll take anyone out here. You're easy."

"Thanks a ton." Jenna crosses her arms, too unbothered, given the circumstances. The Lady of the Swamp watches with sharp attention as the man's pulse jumps, jumps, jumps in his neck. He's got bloodshot, pin-prick eyes and he smells like rotten meat and vinegar, like the foul liquid drifters pass around in needles and spoons. Yet Jenna stands here like he's going to be reasonable. "I don't have any money for you, alright?"

"No. No, I know you do. You came out here with the sheriff two days ago. Everyone's been talking about it."

She presses her lips into a thin line, embarrassment coloring her cheeks a dusty pink. "I had to pay my rent."

"Don't fuck with me. You've got to have something."

"Cam—"

A loud, cracking shot pierces the air. Jenna does flinch this time, crouching low to wrap her arms around her head. The bullet flies past her arm and rips through the back wall of the shack, tearing off a large, moldy chunk. As the Lady of the Swamp watches from the safety of the opposite corner, her fury paints the world in violent shades of red. She slithers up through her peephole, inching forward on knuckles and tiptoes, light as a feather.

"You could have killed me, you dick!"

"Just give me what you have! I'll take anything."

Jenna slips a flip-flop off her foot and hurls it at his chest. "You're high off your ass, man. Maybe if you took less, we wouldn't be in this mess!"

The Lady of the Swamp lunges forward, slicing thick nails through the backs of Cam's heels. He crumples to the ground like wet paper, firing off a few wild shots in his panic. The Lady feels a burning stab of pain through her left shoulder, but it only adds fuel to the fire raging in her chest.

She crawls on top of him, slowly, to watch his eyes widen in terror. To smell the dread oozing from his skin at the slow sinking realization that this impossible creature is the last thing he's ever going to see. She bares her razor teeth, jammed tight into a mouth that shouldn't house so many. Then she snaps her head forward, locking her iron jaw around his throat and tearing away in a shower of blood.

Cam struggles against her, but every thrash rips his flesh open wider in her maw. She pins him down, densely muscled arms pressing hard enough to hear bones splinter. He gets a hand on her face to hold her at bay, but she bites three fingers clean off, swallowing them whole as she expands her throat.

He screams, coarse and grating, but it doesn't last long. Losing that much blood? Even the healthy ones go quick. This one is rancid. She plays with her food sometimes, toys with them, if she feels like they deserve it—tears limbs off at the joint, guts them and feels around inside, cuts out strips of flesh as appetizers. But he tastes too bad, like a possum carcass left in the sweltering summer sun.

The Lady of the Swamp spits out a lump of putrid meat and rises to her feet. She stands there with her skin as green as algae, stringy black hair hanging in wet curtains over her face, drenched in a cloak of blood. Her chest heaves, waiting for her world to shatter.

But Jenna doesn't scream. She just stares, mouth hanging open in a shocked little 'o.' She gestures weakly, waving a pale hand at the hole in the Lady's shoulder that's trickling out a thick, black ooze. "Are... are you okay?"

The Lady swipes away the ooze, embarrassed that something so precious has seen her ugliest parts. She clears her throat, digging around in her brain for words she barely knows how to speak—words picked up from crackling car radios and prayers to something called God. "Good."

"Good? Okay." Jenna nods. Keeps nodding, dumbfounded with shock. "I… Alright."

"Scared?"

Jenna holds her breath, eyes darting around at flaring gills and anxiously clacking claws. A peal of laughter breaks the silence, evaporating her shock. "Baby, it's Florida—what's there left to be scared of?"

The Lady of the Swamp doesn't get the joke, but she smiles anyway, red-stained teeth on full display. She takes a step forward—can't even help it, as drawn in as she is by the light in Jenna's eyes. It's one tiny step, one of a million she wants to take to get closer to her, but she stops herself. This is when it happens. It's real this time. Jenna is going to lose her smile. Jenna is going to run. Jenna is going to hate her.

Jenna does none of those things. Instead, her expression sheepishly folds in on itself. "I guess I don't have a polite way to ask it, but what are you?"

"Don't know." At the bottom of the swamp, placing things into neat, defined boxes is hardly a priority. The Lady's fascination with the ways of life on land sets her apart from most things burbling in the bog.

"But not human?"

"No."

"Are there more of you?"

The Lady of the Swamp points vaguely off toward the water. "Deeper."

"Do you have a name?"

"No."

Jenna chews on her plush bottom lip, rocking on her heels. "Do you want one?"

The strange, misshapen heart in the Lady's chest skips a beat. A name—something to be known by, from someone so beautiful? It puts her collection of stolen treasures to shame. "Yes."

Joy breaks like dawn over Jenna's face. "Okay, great! Amazing! Well… I don't want to be too on the nose. Jade seems a little obvious, you know? It'd be like calling me Peaches."

The Lady of the Swamp likes peaches.

Jenna steps closer, reaching out to jangle the tangle of shiny necklaces around the Lady's throat. "You're kind of a Magpie, aren't you? How about Maggie?"

"Maggie," she echoes. She likes the guttural sound of the hard g's, the groaning of the m. "Maggie."

"Nice to meet you, Maggie. I'm Jenna."

The Lady of the Swamp—Maggie—doesn't want to lie. From the depths of her dark waters, she's watched plenty of people lie to Jenna. She's watched them break and disappoint her again, and again, and again. Maggie only wants to do the opposite. "I know."

"What?" She blinks, more confused than uneasy. "How?"

"Watching."

Jenna's eyes crinkle at the corners, as warm and soft as the marsh rabbits Maggie likes to coo at and cuddle. "You don't say... What for?"

"Pretty." Maggie's cheeks go a strange, sickly brown at the heat of her blush. "Keep safe."

Jenna beams, smile brighter than the glare of the sun off the water. "That's awfully nice of you. Who knew I had friends in such strange places? Here, let me, uh..."

She slips her bandana from around her hair, leaning off the dock to swish it around in the water. Toeing nervously back to Maggie, she dabs the dripping cloth over her red-slick lips. Her touch is gentle—tender—as her gaze darts between Maggie's bloody mouth and her oily black eyes.

"I think you're pretty, too."

"No."

"I do," she insists.

"Monster." Beast. Freak. Devil. Mutant. *Thing*.

"Hey now, just because I don't know what you are, it doesn't mean you're something bad." She runs her bandana over Maggie's chin, follows the dribbles of blood down her neck, around her sensitive gills. She swipes away the carnage that sits at the swell of her breasts like a prized ruby necklace. "You're incredible, actually. Your skin's the color of sea glass."

"Sea glass." Maggie whispers it back in place of feelings she doesn't have human words for. If Jenna had ever brought kinder people through the swamp, Maggie might know words like, "*you're perfect.*" She might know, "*I've never felt so dizzy looking into a pair of eyes before.*" She might know, "*I love you.*"

But neither of them need words anymore. Jenna leans in, cradling Maggie's face between two trembling palms as she captures her thick bottom lip between her teeth. If Maggie had any control over her own body, she might have jerked away in pure shock. Instead, she melts against Jenna, clawed hands clutching her pale back like delicate china.

Jenna has been with plenty of men—sometimes for fun, sometimes for money, sometimes just for the sake of feeling anything at all. None of them have ever kissed her like this, like the taste of her alone could save their life. Maggie is an infinity of wild unknowns, but after one press of their lips, Jenna's pretty sure a lifetime unraveling answers would be well worth her time.

She presses Maggie against the wall of the shack, rotten wood creaking under the pressure of their combined weight. As her hands trace the swooping curves of Maggie's torso, the Lady of the Swamp rolls a clicking sound in her throat—a chitter of churning anticipation. Jenna grins into each kiss she drops across the slits of Maggie's gills.

Teasing a clever hand between Maggie's thighs, Jenna traces a familiar landscape. Like a rock skimming over the surface of a lake, Jenna uses light, petting strokes to coax a fire in Maggie. She trails bitten down nails across sensitive skin, bringing goosebumps to the surface. The tension between them is stretched so thin, Maggie could weep. She rolls her body, chasing the playful touch, desperate to guide it to her deepest desires.

Jenna grinds with intention at the point of all of Maggie's vibrant feeling, flicking quick circles that make her twitch and groan. She switches the pressure to her thumb, using her middle fingers to slip forward into fathomless warmth. Her forehead drops to rest on Maggie's collarbone, an up close look at her heaving chest and the steady patter of her racing heart.

Maggie tips her head back, throat undulating with a revving rumble like a chainsaw. Her inner-eyelids flutter across her pupils, the membrane jerking wildly.

As splashes of pleasure ripple through her body, egrets in the brush squawk and flee. Cottonmouths slither into the cover of decomposing stumps. Gators hiss and glide deeper out into the water. But Jenna only presses closer.

Dropping to her knees, Maggie shreds the denim of Jenna's shorts in a delicate swing of claws. Her mouth is far gentler as it smears a reverent path of kisses across her milky white thigh. Jenna hooks a calf around Maggie's strong shoulder, balancing haphazardly on one unsteady foot. Her fingers curl into the loops of the moldy fishing net dangling off a hook on the wall as Maggie's tongue works wicked circuits.

The sweet whines spilling from Jenna's lips are like symphony strings compared to the harsh bellows Maggie's body grants. But Jenna loves the power of Maggie—her reptilian roaring, her whipcord muscles, her serrated teeth. Maggie is a force of nature who handles Jenna with the most precious of care. She's a magnificent creature who can sever men to bits with a single flourish, yet she turns Jenna inside out with nothing less than worship.

As a holy release erupts through every nerve in Jenna's body, Maggie is overcome with the need to possess. Her keys and buttons and foil are tucked away in covert rock shelves and mud burrows, yet here Jenna is, so much more exquisite than those simple treasures. So much more than Maggie could have imagined. She wants her tucked forever in her arms.

Conceding to her most selfish impulse, Maggie sinks her razor teeth into the soft meat of Jenna's thigh. Jenna gasps, surprise rounding her eyes into wide, glittering pools. Blood floods Maggie's mouth, sweet like every atom of Jenna has been dusted with honey. Black ooze drips from Maggie's gums, trickling into the pits left by her greedy teeth.

A thread of shame ties itself around Maggie's heart. There's no going back now. Poison black lines color the map of veins beneath Jenna's porcelain skin. A glowing hue of green illuminates the morbid network, lighting her up like a star hanging happy in the sky.

The skin at the side of Jenna's throat tightens and tightens, stretching taut until it splits into two sets of fluttering gills. On instinct, Jenna's hands fly up to trace the delicate folds, but she is only more surprised to find her nails have grown and hardened into thick points.

"Yes," Jenna whispers, snipping that thread of shame in two. "Take me."

Maggie rises to her feet, lifting Jenna in her arms as if she's lighter than the summer clouds. The water is warm as it laps around her ankles, and the mud seeps between her webbed toes like a friendly "welcome home." She lives deeper in the water than any human could survive, but Jenna is more than that now. She has made Maggie something more, too. Someone more.

The Ladies of the Swamp dip beneath the murky waters in a lover's tangle. People on land will wonder where Jenna went—speculate about things beyond this world that live in their cursed swamp. They'll miss her. They'll mourn her. They might even look for her. But finders are keepers.

And the loathsome monster in the pit of the marsh will always appreciate her more, anyway.

ABOUT THE AUTHORS & ARTISTS

Hannah Birss – Fisher of Men

Knitted together by arthritic goblins and born of the swamp, the hag (she/her) spends her days sneakily eating treats in the pantry so her offspring don't hear the crinkle of the bag and descend upon her like the wild hunt.

Terry Campbell – One Last Kiss

Terry Campbell (he/his) writes and creates from The Saloon, often spurred on by the magical elixir known as Desert Door Sotol. His work has appeared in anthologies from Graveside Press, Hellbound Books, Saddlebag Dispatches, and others. His collection of short stories will be released by Rowan Prose Publishing in March 2026.

Monica Chen – Earth Song

Monica Chen (she/her) is a Belgian-Taiwanese writer inspired by the Kumano Kodo and The Legends of Tono. She weaves "natural fantasy" exploring the sacred, nameless rituals found where the trail meets the mythic.

Astra Crompton – Headless

Astra Crompton (she/they) is a queer author passionate about diverse representation in all flavours of fantasy. Their speculative fiction has been published in anthologies, magazines, comics, and TTRPG modules. By day, she's an editing and illustrations coordinator who lives in Victoria, Canada, with her queer platonic partner and three dysfunctional cats. Follow Astra's work at astracrompton.com.

Sam Crain – Devout Consummation

Sam Crain (she/her) lives in Fremont, CA. Now that she's finished her PhD in English, she's free to return to her first love, writing stories, which she does whenever she can steal her pens back from her cats.

gaast – Winch Cave

gaast (it/its/that) is a ghost currently haunting occupied Lenape land.

Arlo Z. Graves – You Go into the Woods to Die

Arlo Zven Graves (they/them) lives in a salvaged shack in the woods. Zven enjoys night hikes, ocarinas, and saying hi to dogs. They don't bite (often), so come say hi on social media @arlozgraves (especially Threads). Zven is the award winning author of *The Ice Moves for No One* and has a deep, vibrant hatred of generative AI.

Joachim Heijndermans – In the Blood

Joachim Heijndermans (he/him) is a writer, artist and filmmaker from the Netherlands. His works have been adapted to film and television. He publishes erotic SFFH through his Beautiful Beasts imprint.

LaRita JaNae – Solomon's Song

LaRita JaNae (she/her) is a Florida-based writer whose work centers horror, monstrosity, and ancestral memory. She is currently studying biochemistry and is interested in the intersections of science, black folklore, and writing.

Tonja K. Johnson – A Sigil to Bind the Night

Tonja K. Johnson (she/her) is a Black American speculative fiction writer. Her work honors the rich, diverse culture of her ancestors while also representing Blackness in all its resistance, queerness, and neurodivergence.

C. Charles Knight – Angel Beyond the Flames

C. Charles Knight (he/him) is a horror author with published short stories in magazines and anthologies, including a number of upcoming releases. He has two novellas and a collection of short stories planned to go to press soon. To find his work and updates on what he is working on, visit theknightwriter.com or on socials @ccharlesknight.

Mandy S Knight – There's Something in the Forest

Mandy S Knight (she/her) is a speculative fiction writer, primarily writing gritty fantasy romance about fearless femmes thriving through adversity and embracing who they really are. She plays too many TTRPGs, reads far past her bedtime, and never says no to an adventure.

Indigo Larkspur – Prey

Indigo (she/her) is a neurospicy queer woman from the the Midwest. She's a voracious reader across all genres and enjoys crocheting and hexing the patriarchy in her spare time.

David O Mahony – Inheritance

David O'Mahony (he/him) is an Irish horror and dark fantasy writer. He has had over 60 stories published and is author of *The Ties That Bind* and *What Gets Left Behind*.

Jeannie Marschall – A Place of No Mercy

Jeannie Marschall (she/her/any) is a European garden hag who writes queer, speculative fiction and delights fellow villagers by sticking out of hedges while foraging or bug-hunting.

Dyana McGowan – Siren
Dyana (she/her) is a digital illustrator from the US with a passion for all things paranormal and fantasy/romantasy. Throw in some gothic or witchy vibes and she is LIVING.

Evan Noren – The Kulwin Siren
Evan Noren (he/they) is a queer father who writes weird and dark fiction. His writing has appeared in various magazines, horror anthologies, and fogged bathroom mirrors.

Kelsey Christine McConnell – Swamp Pearls
Furiously writing at night, Kelsey (she/her) spends her days working as an Editor for the horror site The Lineup. She gets all of her best ideas from her sleep paralysis demon.

Nik Sylvan – Satyr
Nik (they/them) is a queer nonbinary artist specializing in linocut, pen & ink, watercolour, and digital illustration. They love to create images inspired by the natural world, mythology, folklore, and fantasy literature.

David M. Simon – Tentacle Satisfaction
David M. Simon (he/him) lives in Cleveland, Ohio, where he's an ad agency creative director by day, writer and illustrator by nights and weekends. He writes mostly horror, fantasy, and science fiction for both adults and kids. His short stories for adults have appeared in numerous anthologies, and his stories for kids have appeared in magazines such as Highlights for Children.

Jon Stubbington – For in That Sleep of Death

Jon (he/him) is a freelance illustrator and designer, specialising in book covers and book-related artwork. He has worked with self-publishing indie authors and small press publishers since 2016, creating hundreds of book cover designs for many genres, including fantasy, science fiction, and horror.

DC Valentine – Sweetheart

(she/they) Lover of cats, code, wine, dice, and life.

Celia Winter – A Rotting Crown of Birch

Celia Winter (she/her) is a Chicago-based speculative fiction writer. When not knitting, she can be found writing; when not writing, she can be found bothering her two fluffy cats.

THANK YOU FOR READING

If you have a moment, please consider posting a review, whether it's on the store you bought it from, social media, or your own blog. Word-of-mouth is the single biggest way of getting our authors seen and making the press successful so we can continue bringing you these stories!

Thank you for supporting small businesses!

Dead Fox Pub is a queer, disabled, neuro-divergent run press with a love of dark fiction and a goal of uplifting unique horror from marginalized voices. We have a strict no GenAI policy; support human creatives.

www.ingramcontent.com/pod-product-compliance
Lightning Source LLC
Chambersburg PA
CBHW071132260626
47162CB00003B/761